LIFE FOR A LIFE

Oppressed by the tensions of the hostile city, his
private and social life in disorder, Laurence Carpenter, though unaware of it, is nearing the end of his
tether. Then, one night, he rescues a man from the
river. This man, Ossie, is a gangster, who in his
gratitude offers a tempting, but to Laurence
preposterous, reward . . .

LIFE FOR A LIFE

A NOVEL BY

Anthony Bloomfield

1971

THE HOGARTH PRESS

LONDON

Published by
The Hogarth Press Ltd
40–42 William IV Street
London W.C.2

*

Clarke, Irwin and Co Ltd
Toronto

ISBN 0 7012 0347 1

Printed in Great Britain by
Ebenezer Baylis & Son Ltd The Trinity Press
Worcester, & London

Contents

Author's Note

Some readers may find the title of this book and elements of
its plot familiar. Two to three years ago, under my *nom-de-plume*
of John Westgate, I wrote a television play with the same
title and starting from the same situation, which was transmitted
in Britain in November, 1967.

In the course of writing the script, I found the theme seemed
to throw off various echoes which could not possibly be pursued
in the space of a fifty-five minute play. These echoes—intima-
tions, potentialities—were so suggestive and became so insistent
that I set to realise them in this novel.

Of course, as happens, in the process of writing, theme, plot,
characters, echoes and all gathered an impetus of their own;
so in no significant sense can the outcome be considered the
'book of the play'. And, of course, a novel is a novel and nothing
else.

A. B.

London,
January, 1970

Part One

OPENING

'Aarragh!'

The first gurgled cry for help from the dark river failed to penetrate Laurence Carpenter's consciousness.

'Aarragh!' The shout was repeated.

Laurence's relaxed stride remained unchecked. The images projected on his mind's private screen were at that moment so bright and so alluring that he was blind and deaf to his actual surroundings. The river, the tow-path, the night sky itself had the insubstantiality of a cinema auditorium.

'Aarragh!' The third cry from the black waters, like a disturbance in the stalls, bag-snatcher or pervert, disrupted the montage of his fantasies and brought Laurence back to real life. He halted at the path's edge, teetering, peering, and suddenly smelling the river's sour and chemical rankness.

The blackness was not quite absolute: the lights on the bridge upstream and on the opposite Surrey bank stippled the river's surface, and although there was no moon a sourceless metallic gleam defined masses and distances.

There came no further cry. Except for the water's lap and suck, a timeless stillness reigned. Then a darker solidification, a log or plank, or merely a figment, appeared to manifest itself a cricket-pitch distance from the bank. Laurence expelled a gust of hoarded breath.

The current was negligible, and the white-blobbed shape seemed to remain in a fixed position, though turning, white-blobbed, turning, until Laurence was left with no scope for doubt as to its form. The silence prolonged itself like an adroit falsehood.

It seemed then reasonable for Laurence to conjecture that the object, though no figment, was now beyond human aid, its movement as undirected as that of a log or plank, and he took a shuffling sideways step in token of retreat.

Then he heard another shout, weaker but more clearly articulated and, indeed, meaningful: 'Bastards!' came the water-choked cry.

Laurence looked about him, less for assistance than from a reflex of guilt. There was (except for myself) no witness of his shame, nor none to assist. The trees stood as stark as gibbets, a snatch of dance-music mocked by distance, and the speeding cars on the bridge had the remote heedlessness of objects in another dimension.

So he did what he had to, a slow-motion deliberation evincing his profound reluctance. He took off his shoes and then his jacket, folding it neatly on a dry stone, and laid the coins from his trouser-pocket egglike on top. As he tip-toed gingerly to the bank's very edge, his hands high-stretched as though seizing support from an invisible wire, an unspoken prayer rose in his gorge; but the white blob had not been dematerialized, though now a few yards further distant. Between the stirrup and the water, his stocking-ed foot poised in space, he rehearsed the role of hero.

There came a surge of panic as he sank to his calves in the clinging mud, and his mind suddenly emptied. Then he had kicked himself free and was swimming, the world reduced to an evil-tasting liquidity. One of the river's many poisons burned his eyes and he lashed out a dozen blind strokes.

His flailing hand struck a solid surface, but when he tried to grip it his fingers passed through adhesively; the pulpy carton floated downstream, as some yet nastier piece of refuse wrapped itself round his ear. Lifting his head and blinking his smarting eyes, Laurence for a moment forgot to swim, with the effect that his feet went down to no bottom. In that sinking moment he suddenly recalled how drowning men were said to fight and to choke their would-be rescuers, and, as though in the middle of a crazy drunken spree he had suddenly become stone sober, he decided to turn back to the teetotal sanity of the tow-path.

The sluggish, almost ripple-free, river roared in his head like a waterfall, and the body seemed to lift itself into his arms, white blob of face against his cheek in the parody of an embrace. There was no struggle. The drowning man emitted a grunt— acknowledgment of a courtesy.

The body was inert and deadweight. Laurence forgot all the lessons of life-saving learned years before in a green and chlorine-flavoured pool and grabbed the neck with savage hands, as though, yes, as though he were strangling instead of saving.

The bank had shifted position by forty-five degrees and the bridge had turned over and was pointing towards the moonless sky. Laurence kicked them back to their original places. Changing his grip to a knot of clothing, he hauled the body alongside him bruisingly. His legs seemed to have become heavier and yet at the same time incorporeal. There was too much flurry for further fear.

'Go on! Go on! Go on!' His mouth awash, Laurence shouted in self-encouragement.

The drowning man uttered once more: 'Bastards!' he repeated.

A sonorous, shattering howl filled the air, and the jet plane, red lights flickering, surged towards the New World. In the swathe of stillness that followed, Laurence, heaving, raised himself to a sitting position.

He felt full of the river's foulness and stench but a glow of gratification offset his discomfort and he began even then to foretaste the esteem that would be his due. The prone body, feet trailing puppet-like down the bank, made a bathpipe gurgle. Laurence scowled at it resentfully: for it to die on him now would be the ultimate ingratitude.

He pulled it up to the path, turned it over on its back. Under thick streaks of mud the face was tombstone white, water bubbled between the open lips and a mixture of water and mucus dribbled from the nostrils. The eyes were closed.

Laurence straddled him and pumped flat-handed on his chest.

This appeared to produce no effect and so he lowered his head to press the kiss of life into the slime-filled mouth.

Revulsion froze his movement; and at that instant, as startlingly as if they had been indeed the eyes of a corpse, the eyes below his opened, flickering to a vast wonder. Before Laurence could master his own less metaphysical surprise, a spasm of pain twisted the man's face and he jerked his head to one side and vomited with a great gush.

'Christ! Sweet bleeding Christ!' he uttered. He wiped his mouth ineffectually on the sodden sleeve of his jacket and then was overcome by another fit of retching.

Laurence stood up and turned his back. He found that he was shivering, from cold or damp, exhaustion or disgust. Water was still running off him and he was as mud-stained as the other. He lost his temper, seized with a sudden passionate fretfulness: he stamped his foot and howled with pain at the sharp incision of a protruding stone; thereupon he damned the rescued man to hell and cast his corpse back in the water.

'Bastards!' The man Laurence had saved still lay on his back, his chest heaving. 'Fucking bastards!' he amplified thoughtfully.

Laurence was struck with shame for the murder he had committed in his mind. He bent down over the other and saw, what he had not before noticed, a long, deep cut across the skull, from which the blood was now oozing and caking with the mud that glued his scanty hair. Little twitches and pulses gave his face a kind of subterranean life, and one particular grimace conveyed the effect of a knowing wink, so that Laurence started back as though detected in a voyeuristic intimacy.

It could have been a millionaire he'd plucked from the drowning, who in his undying gratitude would have rewarded him with a villa in Spain, blocks of ever-rising shares, an oil well, a television company, a white yacht ... It was impossible to envisage the fulfilment of this fantasy: even allowing for the highly unfavourable circumstances, the twitching form at his feet exuded the sweat of an innate cheapness.

Another aircraft, gaily twinkling, passed overhead, its passengers braced for the ordeal of earthing; a police car's bell rang out from the bridge; across the river a factory chimney suddenly shot fire—but all that was a different matter from all this. Laurence, his head thrown back in anguished frustration, groaned aloud.

He felt the open eyes watching him. 'Do you think you can stand up?' Laurence asked gently. A water-rat slid to its hole in the mud. 'If you can't, I'll go for help.'

The gaze turned up to his shone with apparent intelligence, but perhaps the cut on the skull was more serious than it looked. You never can tell with head wounds.

'My clothes. Up the path. I must get my clothes.' Laurence spoke with exaggerated distinctness as though to an infant or a foreigner. The man could, despite his familiarity with the vernacular, be a foreigner. 'You. Stay. There.' He attempted a smile of reassurance as he turned away.

'Hey!'

Laurence came back. The man had lifted his head and shoulders, propping himself on his elbows. 'You—you're not one of them bastards, are you?'

'It's all right,' said Laurence soothingly. 'Nothing to worry about now.' You never can tell with head wounds. 'Take it easy. We'll soon get you to . . .'

'Give me a hand up.' He heaved himself to a sitting position.

'Steady! Are you sure you . . .'

'Give me a hand up.'

He was a foot shorter than Laurence, stocky, heavy. Under the mud his face was now vividly mottled, giving him a painted, clownish appearance. He looked down at his own disarray, sniffed as though disgusted by the smell of himself, and then pushed his head up at Laurence. 'Call me Ossie,' he demanded.

Their faces were only inches apart.

'Ossie!'

'What's your name then?'

'My name? Er—Carpenter.' It sounded stand-offish, considering. 'Laurence. Laurence Carpenter.'

Ossie's face expanded: his mouth was a black hole. 'Friend! You saved my life, friend.'

Laurence sketched a mute modesty.

'You saved my life, I tell you.' He spoke like a man unaccustomed to contradiction. He put his fingers in his mouth. 'I've lost my bleeding teeth. The bastards!' His indignation seemed perfunctory. He clapped Laurence on the shoulder. 'Still you can't win them all, can you. You can't reckon to win them all.'

Laurence stepped back. 'That's a nasty cut on your head. Let me get my things, and then I'll call an ambulance.'

Ossie put his hand to his head, looked at the blood on his fingers, sniffed at it and tasted it.

'You never can tell with head wounds,' Laurence added.

He felt his arm gripped with surprising force. 'Not for me, friend. No ambulance for me.' He released his hold. 'I'm, like, what they call . . . resilient.'

'But surely . . .'

'Where'd you leave your clothes then?'

And it was Ossie who supported Laurence as he forced his sodden feet into his shoes and Ossie who held his jacket for him, like a barber. 'Just about done for your gear, saving my life.'

'Oh well, a good cause.'

'I'll make it up to you. I'll make it up to you, friend.'

They squelched their way along the path, towards the beckoning lights and the reassurance of the familiar.

'What happened?' Laurence ventured. 'How did you fall in? Were you in a boat?'

'A boat—me! Sailing down the bleeding river!' Ossie's throaty laugh underlined the absurdity of the question. Then he quickly apologized. 'No, I wasn't in no boat. That wasn't the way of it, that wasn't the way of it at all.'

'Well then, how . . .' Laurence began.

'Promise me something.' There was a throbbing urgency in his voice. 'Promise me something,' he repeated.

'What?' asked Laurence, with extreme wariness.

'You got to promise me.' He had halted, and his toothless mouth gaped in cajolery. 'You got to have injections.'

'What?'

'Injections.' A spray of muddy spittle showered Laurence's chin. 'All that insanitary shit in the river, you got to look after yourself. You ought to have injections else you'll get diseases.'

He turned back to the path, and they hobbled on, Laurence deep in thought.

'You mind what I say.'

'You really think it's as bad as that, the water?'

'I don't bleeding think, I bleeding know.'

'I dare say you might be right.'

'And I don't want you coming to no harm, friend, not after what you done for me.'

They had reached the steps to the road, Laurence leading, so that he was halfway up them while Ossie was still puffing along the tow-path. This was the moment, if such a moment could ever have been, for Laurence to run for it. The omnipotent author of his destiny decided otherwise.

Ossie stood by his side and spat with contempt into the river. 'Tell you what.' A late-revelling car swished by, the driver and the girl at his side obliviously conjoined. 'Tell you what, you come up to my place. Dry off. That'd be favourite. You don't want to give your good lady a fright, walking in this time of night like a drowned rat.'

Laurence suddenly felt limp and dizzy as after some long, shameful orgy. 'That might be a good idea,' he agreed.

'Just one thing. Hate to ask you. In the circumstances.' Ossie wore his embarrassment like a hat several times too small for his head. 'In the circumstances, seeing what you just done for me.'

'What is it?'

'Presumptuous like, I know that.' He braced himself. 'But they cleaned me out.'

'What?'

'Every bleeding penny, emptied my pockets. So can you pay the cab then?'

'Yes. Yes, of course.'

'That's all right then.' Ossie's relief expressed itself in a wide laugh: his black toothlessness seemed a contrivance to add hilarity to his daubed clown's face. 'Well, we couldn't hardly take a bus now, could we, even if there was one. We couldn't take a bus now—looking like two drowned rats!'

Laurence paid off a sullen and sceptical driver, over-tipping. They were in a narrow North London street of hoardings and drab shop-fronts. Among the parked cars on each side of the roadway were an equal number of car-corpses, picked to the bone. Playful stones had shattered all but one, distant, street-lamp, so that their shadows assumed a melodramatic elongation.

Ossie crossed to a peeling door beside a greengrocer's, the fruit in the pock-marked window bedded down for the night under coverlets of newsprint.

'My key's gone and all.' He heaved his shoulder against the door and then, it holding firm, started to pummel with his fists. 'Bleeding bell don't work,' he explained to Laurence, ineffec-tually hovering behind him. He stood back and raised his head to the vaulted roof of the night. 'Chrissie! Chrissie!' His bellowed cries echoed down the street like rolling dustbin-lids: 'Chrissie! Chrissie! Chrissie . . .'

A light came on above the shop, a window was pushed up, and a head appeared. There was a brief exchange of obscene epithets, during which Laurence tried his best to assume the attitude of an uncommitted bystander. This was a less blatant deception than might be assumed, for the night's events had by now begun to develop the peculiar ambiguity of one of those dreams in which the dreamer flits inconsequentially between the roles of participant and observer.

The window was slammed shut. In a moment the door was opened. Laurence feared a fresh outburst of abuse, or even physical violence, for the woman in the doorway had, save for the mammalian amplitude revealed by her sagging nightdress, both the bulk and the bearing of a professional wrestler. She flung out her arms and Ossie was folded in her grasp. Above his head she glared at Laurence in what he interpreted as a challenge to take on all-comers.

'What they do to you, boy? What they do to you?' She rocked Ossie in her arms, her voice a crooning rasp. Somehow, incredibly, he mustered the strength to push her aside.

'Come on.' He jerked his head at Laurence.

'Your head's cut, Ossie. Look at your poor head. You ought to see a doctor. You ought to see a doctor, boy.'

Laurence squeezed past with an apprehensive simper. The narrow hallway was filled with the smell of vegetables and fruit, rich and rank.

'Your poor head, Ossie. Your poor head,' her voice pursued them.

'Yeah. Yeah.' Ossie was already at the foot of the uncarpeted stairway. 'Lock the bleeding door, you old cow, and get back to bed.'

The bolt rattled home as Laurence followed Ossie up the stairs. At each step there was an ice-breaking creak; a sickly smell of mildew blended with the fruit's luxuriance. On the landing an unshaded lightbulb reproduced the melodramatic shadows of the street.

A surrealist scene-change: the room into which Laurence was led might have been transported the day before from a furniture store's display. 'Welcome, Larry—my 'umble abode!'

Laurence was in no condition to take in the details: the overall effect was of an anonymous, tasteless opulence, suggestive of a meretricious and dated film set.

'Crawling home like two bleeding drowned rats—eh?' Ossie switched on the fire and the logs hummed to life. 'Chrissie's right, you know. We got to see a doctor, both of us. I told you, we don't want no diseases.'

For the first time Laurence could see him clearly: in his own surroundings he appeared both a more human and a more profound figure, less negligible. Between the river and the room the comic element had been shed, despite his bedraggled state and the missing set of teeth. His eyes, almost lashless, were red-veined and wolfish.

'I don't want you coming to no harm, Larry.'

'You ought to get that cut seen to,' said Laurence.

Ossie turned to a long mirror. Wincing, he lifted the matted streaks of hair from his scalp. 'A bleeding jack,' he murmured.

'What was that?'

Ossie traced the ragged wound with his thumb. 'The bastards used a jack. I was out cold till they tossed me in the water.' He wiped his hand on his sleeve. 'Whisky?'

'What are you saying? You mean, someone knocked you on the head?'

'That's right, friend.' He was bending to a glittering cocktail-cabinet.

'And then they threw you in the river!' Even as Laurence heard the tone of outrage in his own voice it seemed that this was merely a conventional response, as though he had known all the time, or as though already he had entered a world in which such actions were not to be regarded as outrageous. 'So someone was trying to kill you,' he stated flatly.

'Only they bungled it.' A voice full of contempt. He straightened, waving the whisky bottle in his hand. 'The pathetic creeps bungled it, didn't they?'

'Then the police. We should go to the . . . What's the matter?'

Ossie had suddenly swayed, clutching a table to steady himself.

Laurence started forward. 'Are you all right?'

'Bending down. I shouldn't have bent down.' Pulling the stopper from the bottle, he raised it trumpet-like to his mouth and poured. While still pouring he took the necessary paces to a chair and dropped slowly. He lowered the bottle at last, a few drops of spirit running down his chin. A gigantic belch erupted, redolent of whisky and river water. 'That's better.' He raised the bottle to Laurence. 'My manners! Guests first. Get it down you, Larry. Poison some of them germs.' The cut on his head had stopped bleeding, but the long crust of blood shone with a sinister luminosity. 'Glasses—over there.' He waved his hand.

Laurence poured himself a generous measure. The spirit burned his throat and he started to cough and splutter.

Ossie laughed without malice. 'Export that is. Special stuff, straight from the docks. Too strong for you, Larry?'

'Could I have some water?'

'Over there.'

Laurence turned.

'Water! Water!' Ossie's face was purple and his whole body was shaking as though in the grip of a vibro-massage machine. 'Water!' He was convulsed by a thick bronchial cough, which ended in groans of agony. 'Water, Larry! Sweet jumping Jesus— water!' He punched both fists hard into his sagging belly. 'As if you ain't had enough water down you for one sodding night!'

He fell back. 'That's rich, eh, Larry?' His eyes were already closed. 'Water . . . water . . .'

He began immediately to snore.

So now there had arisen a second opportunity for Laurence to make his escape. The thought, the temptation, occurred to him. He put down his glass and took a few paces towards the door. No decisive consideration restrained him, only a vague curiosity, and an odd lassitude. It was as though he could not go without being released.

He took up his glass again, watered the whisky and drank. Despite his still soaked clothes, the ache of bruises, itch of the drying mud and the unpleasant smell which arose from his body,

19

he felt a strange contentment. There was a sense of freedom in being a guest accorded the intimate possession of another's domicile. He perambulated the room, sipping from his glass. The whisky slowly warmed.

There was a curtained annexe at the end of the room; Laurence put his head gingerly around the curtain, to see that it was fitted as a bedroom. He would have liked to explore further but was inhibited by a delicacy of feeling that suggested this would have been an abuse of hospitality.

Aware that he should wash, but lacking the initiative to do anything about it, he poured himself another drink. Ossie had stopped snoring as abruptly as he had begun. Glass in hand, Laurence bent over him, over the life history written on his face. It was a ravaged, battered face, morbidly colourless except for its networks of burst veins; tufts of black bristles jutted from the wide nostrils; on one cheek there was a large dun mole, and a crinkled scar skated dangerously close to the eye's verge. It was the sort of face that, looking up from your newspaper, you might suddenly see in a train . . . whereupon you begin hurriedly to read the small advertisements in order to avoid its brutal commentary on the human condition.

Yet Laurence experienced no revulsion as he peered down at the sleeping face. A shiver ran down his back, as though he were in the presence of a holy mystery, and it seemed as if the crudely delineated message of those features overlaid another communication, whose significance he could penetrate only by acquiring the key to some unknown code.

He found himself standing before the long mirror, subjecting his own face to the same detached yet passionate scrutiny. A man with hair just beginning to recede, tired eyes, pessimistic mouth, stared back at him. Those features also contained a mystery to whose solution he had not yet found the key.

The faintly complacent expression with which his image regarded him was abruptly replaced by an ugly gape of panic.

Laurence listened intently. No doubt at all: those rustlings and creakings could be nothing but footsteps . . . careful, furtive footsteps on uncarpeted boards.

They were coming nearer.

Adrenalin speeded his thoughts as it constricted his arteries. What could be more logical than that those who had failed in their first attempt to kill should come now to complete their mission? And what compunction could be expected for a solitary, defenceless witness? Indeed, the discovery of one who had — however unwittingly, however innocently — aborted their previous effort might reasonably be expected to intensify their hostility.

The footsteps had stopped. Outside the door. Laurence made a dash into the bedroom-annexe.

Ossie slept on.

What would be the sound of five desperate, violent men all holding their breath? Agonizing images, chiefly derived from scenes of film and television violence, pursued each other along the circuits of Laurence's brain. He heard the door's slow, careful opening.

There came a feral grunt, followed by quick soft steps across the thickly piled carpet. These were followed by other slithering sounds, unidentifiable.

But not, surely not, Laurence slowly apprehended, his pulse-rate falling, the sounds that would be made by five, or even fewer, desperate, violent men; not, surely not, the sounds of a killing! He put a timid head round the curtain.

A tall, grey-haired Negro, in a sailor's jersey, stood over Ossie's chair, reaching down with pink-palmed hands.

'Blanco!' Ossie was awake, instantly alert and in command. 'Blanco, it's all right, boy. I'm all right.'

The Negro stepped back and stood bowed solicitously.

'They bungled it. They cocked it up. And thanks to my good friend here, who . . . ' Ossie rose from his chair. 'Where the hell's he gone?'

Laurence emerged from behind the curtain.

'My good friend Larry here, who saved my life.'

The Negro looked at Laurence without acknowledgment, expressionlessly, except, Laurence thought, for a glint of suspicion smouldering in his milky eyes.

Ossie put his hand on Blanco's shoulder, turning him towards the door. He showed no sign of weakness nor of drunkenness; his whole appearance had altered as though he had stepped under a different light, radiating command and force. 'You get on now, boy. I'm all right, I tell you.'

The Negro backed, moving, despite his grizzled bulk, with an incredible light-footedness which had a boxer's athleticism but was even more suggestive of the casual elegance of a dancer. At the door, still facing into the room, he performed a little shuffling jig, miming his reluctance to depart.

'Go on now, Blanco,' commanded Ossie with gentle firmness. 'You don't have to worry about me. Takes,' he added cryptically, 'more than a wet fart!'

Blanco gave Laurence a last mute and suspicious glare and edged from the room.

'He's a good boy, Blanco, a good friend of mine. Works for me.' Ossie swung round menacingly. 'What was you doing behind that curtain, Larry?' He laughed in Laurence's face. 'I know what you was thinking: he was coming up to finish off the job. Blanco, you thought he was one of them bastards, didn't you?'

'I didn't know what . . .'

'No!' He spat dryly in good-humoured Cockney contempt. 'No, that's not the way they operate. They cocked it up once, didn't they. Now they'll reckon, well, he got away with it — that Ossie, he always was a lucky bleeder. They wouldn't have another go. There's rules in this game, see, Larry. Rules!' He appeared oblivious to Laurence's bewilderment. 'Now why don't you get yourself cleaned up? You want a bath?'

Unwilling to reduce himself to the vulnerability of nakedness, Laurence settled for a wash. The water gushed, bubbling, steaming. He sank down into it on his arms.

'And when you got them wet clothes off of you, I'll give you some of mine.' Ossie's voice, though he stood just by Laurence's side at the basin, seemed to come from far away, demoniacally, from out of the pipes and steam. 'Might not fit you so good, being as we're different shapes, but I got some good suits. I like to dress smart, don't I.

'Fancy you ducking behind that curtain!' His laugh rumbled through the plumbing. 'You don't think I'd have brought you up here, do you, if there was going to be trouble. Not after what you done for me. What sort of ungrateful bleeder do you think I am!

'Here, better take some clean water, that lot looks like the Paddington canal.'

Laurence immersed his head in a fresh bowl-full, the water blocking his ears.

'. . . all in the way of business, you could say, me and them. A business dispute, what might be termed a difference of opinion. I might have done the same, I been in their place, save if I had, I wouldn't have bungled it.

'Here!' A fresh, rough towel was pushed into Laurence's groping hands. 'But I've no hard feelings, not so you'd notice. Only if I should see one of them, like, getting a shave, I might just happen to jog the barber's elbow accidental. Know what I mean?'

Laurence looked up over the towel. Ossie winked. That wink seemed to unhinge Laurence's last finger-nail grasp on normality. He started to giggle without the slightest idea why.

'I know what you're thinking, Larry.' Ossie smiled with sympathetic understanding. 'You're thinking, it's your horrible luck, you dive in the river and fish out a geezer what's drowning and it has to be a geezer like me. I might have been a millionaire who'd have set you up a tax-fiddling fortune . . .'

'Not at all,' Laurence interjected guiltily, recalling his riverside fantasies.

'. . . or some burke with influence, a Lord or a Bishop or an

M. bleeding P. Or I might be running a fancy knocking shop, French girls, Jap girls, black girls flashing it all ways, and I could lumber you a free pass for life . . .' He laughed and slapped Laurence across the shoulder.

'A sort of honorary member,' Laurence suggested, surprising himself.

'Honorary . . .' Ossie reeled, roaring. 'Honorary bleeding member—that's good, that's real good that is, Larry. You got a subtle sense of humour, I like that.' He took the towel from Laurence's hands, balled it and threw it into a corner. He turned back, all mirth dissipated. 'But I want to do something for you, friend, I honestly do.'

Laurence was still smiling at the unexpected success of his pleasantry. 'I'm not bleeding joking.' The threat and anger in Ossie's sudden scowl made Laurence shiver.

'You finished in here now?' He spoke in a wheedling tone. 'Come on through then, have another drink.'

Back in the cinema-set room, Ossie held out a brimming glass. 'I want to do something for you, Larry,' he repeated.

'Really it isn't necessary.'

'Ossie, call me Ossie.'

'It's not necessary, Ossie.'

'Even if I ain't got no money, no influence, no birds not to mention.' He lowered his voice to a diffident murmur. 'But I got my talent. I got my talent, see.'

'Your talent?'

'What I said.' The diffidence was only a mask for vainglory; a dramatic complacency measured his pause. 'My talent! I'm a specialist, see. And I got a high reputation in my own field. A very high reputation, Larry.' He leaned close. 'Besides, it's not just you saved my life, I like you, Larry, I honestly do. I like you as a bruvver!'

'And what . . .' asked Laurence, to deflect this mawkishness, 'and what is your own field, Ossie?'

'You know, don't you?' He fluttered his sparse lashes with a

24

girlish coyness. 'You know really, you just don't want to say it.'

'How could I possibly know?'

'Anyone you like to name.' Gently he laid his hand on Laurence's bare shoulder. 'Anyone you like to name, and I'll look after him for you. You just tell me who, and I'll . . . make arrangements.'

Laurence lowered his arm and wriggled away from touch — but not from voice. 'Someone you want out of the way. I'm a specialist, see. I've got a talent. Not like them bastards, *I* wouldn't cock it up.'

'What . . . what on earth are you saying?'

'In the river. Or under a train.' Ossie had moved with him, so that they were facing again. 'A car smash. Or a brick might fall on his head, accidental. It'd be done professional, you wouldn't have to worry about that. It'd be a clean professional job.' He gave a little nod of encouragement. 'And you'd be all right, Larry, you'd be right in the clear.'

'In the clear,' Laurence repeated stupidly.

'That's right.'

'Well, thank you very much. Thank you very much, Ossie!' Laurence was high-stepping around the room, waving his hands. 'But as it happens, I mean it just so happens, there's no one I want looking after, not just at the moment.' He collided with the protruding leg of a tiled coffee-table. 'Goddamit! As it so happens. Not just at the present moment.'

'Don't give me that, Larry. Don't try and tell me there isn't no one.' Head lowered, he stalked him round the table. 'Don't give me that shit. Everyone's got someone, someone they want . . .' Ossie slashed his hand across his throat in elementary mime. 'Some burke who's in their way. A geezer what's done them dirt. Or there's trouble with a bird. Someone you hate in your guts, Larry.' He thrust his head kiss-close. 'Someone you want wiped off the filthy rotten face of the stinking world.'

'This must be a joke.' After what seemed a lengthy pause, Laurence heard a voice saying: 'This must be a joke.'

'No joke, Larry.' Earnestly, eagerly, he followed Laurence round. 'It's like a debt of honour.'

'Utterly ridiculous . . . insane . . .'

'A life . . .'—with a light laugh—'a life for a life, you could say.'

Laurence backed again—into the same table as before. He stooped to rub his calf.

'I know what you're thinking, that maybe you couldn't trust me. You think I ain't got the finesse, I ain't got the temerity.' He pursed his mouth, repeating his dry-spitting grimace. 'You'd be making a big mistake. Ossie's not just a pretty face, you know.'

'I never thought you . . .'

'I'm not just a pretty face, Larry.'

He laid his hand again on Laurence's shoulder, then shifted position to put his arm around his back; this time Laurence did not slip from under.

'You think about it. Take your time. Venice wasn't built in a day.' He gave Laurence a friendly squeeze, before pushing him away. 'Now you get the rest of them wet things off of you, fit yourself into my gear. You got to look after yourself. Friend!'

And to his own great surprise, with slow dreamlike reluctance but as though compelled, Laurence found himself obeying . . .

Part Two

A CHANGE OF PERSON

2

'These—what are these . . . *things?*'

Skin keen from the blade and the after-shave's smart, I, Laurence Carpenter, re-entered the bedroom to find Sarah disdainfully prodding with her foot the pile of clothing I had exhaustedly dropped before I went to bed. 'Where on earth did these come from?'

On first waking, I had thought—no, rather, I had simply accepted—that it had been just a dream, until my bleary gaze fell upon the heap of scattered and unfamiliar garments. Then, though still with a dreamlike flavour, it all came back to me. I could actually taste the vileness of the river, mixed with whisky, in my throat; and I felt the ache of new bruises. But now the memory of my adventure induced a mild exhilaration; I had, besides, my own, my very private, reasons for a certain alacrity of spirit.

'They were lent to me, actually,' I replied, walking past Sarah to the dressing-table.

'They were lent to you!'

'Though nothing was said about returning them, I assume they were intended as a loan rather than a gift.' There was no special cause for my adopting this tone of unhumorous banter; it was merely one of the several voices in which we conducted our marital dialogue.

'For any particular reason?'

'My own clothes were soaked.'

'I don't remember it raining.'

'No.'

'At least, not when *I* went to bed.'

'A rather pleasant evening, as I recall.'

I tilted the dressing-table mirror to knot my tie. Sarah was standing in the glass in her red dressing-gown. I couldn't see her face, but I had no doubt she wore an expression of exasperation, masquerading as forbearance. She sighed heavily. 'Stop playing, Laurence.'

'Playing?'

'How could you have got yourself soaked then? Or did someone throw a drink at you?'

'Now why should anyone do that?' I turned towards the door. I had been right about her expression. 'Actually ...' — my delivery was exaggeratedly nonchalent — 'actually, I dived into the river to save someone from drowning.'

'Oh, Laurence!'

'What — oh, Laurence?'

'Your romantic inventions. I know you're evading something when you make up these schoolboy stories. Even as a joke.'

'I wasn't making up anything. You shouldn't always think the worst of me, Sarah.' I tossed the last remark to her on my way to the breakfast table.

And if she had followed me then, who knows, I might very well have told her all about it, all, right up to and including the final preposterous and fantastical events in the room above the greengrocers; for, even though our marriage was now rooted in irritation and resentment, we retained a habit of mutual confidence — except, that's to say, in certain dangerous areas. But last night's adventure could not, surely could not, intrude upon that proscribed territory!

However, Sarah didn't follow me. I breakfasted alone; alone with my own thoughts, which were pleasant enough, even joyous. I allowed them to transport me elsewhere.

'Will you be late tonight?' Sarah, sweetly fresh from her bath, stood over the table in a stream of sunlight. She took up the coffee-pot and filled my empty cup, with her free hand arresting her housecoat's trailing sleeve.

'Thank you.' I smiled up pleasantly. 'Late? Hard to say. I shouldn't think so though.'

She replaced the pot on the stove, moving with the composed gliding elegance that characterized all her movements, her hem swishing on the spotless tiles. 'Unless you should happen to pass a burning school, and you climb through the flames to rescue a classful of suffocating children.'

I put down my cup carefully, wiped my lips. 'You don't believe me because you think me a coward, or because you consider me too callous, or just from your general habit of suspicion?'

Perhaps the bitterness in my tone—the gall of having one's truths disbelieved!—tended to convince her. 'Laurence, did you, did you really?' she asked.

'I've told you once.'

She studied me with narrow eyes, possibly believing me, but as though my truthfulness itself provided cause for suspicion. Then, perhaps, she regretted her wariness. 'It really happened. You did do it!'

'Thank you,' I replied, standing up.

She followed me into the living-room. 'You weren't just making up a story. You really saved someone's life.' She sounded genuinely enthusiastic, as though eager to demonstrate a warmth which, I believe, she lacked the duplicity to feign. 'Who was it? Was it a man? A child? Was it a beautiful girl? Tell me. Laurence, tell me all about it.'

I turned and waited for her, blind in the sunlight which poured into this room also, refracted in a myriad motes. 'It was a man.'

'A man,' she repeated. 'What sort of man?'

'He was . . . well, he was . . .' Ossie's wraith manifested itself in the mote-filled beam like a face in a children's puzzle-picture; the head gasping for breath on the river bank, and then—a double puzzle!—with a knowing wink and a swift hand cutting across its gullet. 'It was all very strange. Preposterous in a way . . .'

'Tell me.'

'Not so much at the time, afterwards . . .'

'Well, tell me.'

31

'A fantastic experience . . . ' I felt an inexplicable reluctance to continue, as though I were attempting to describe a dream and feared its disintegration under the weight of words.

The on-coming machine-roar rescued me: the plane rose over the river, visible through the wide, plant-captioned window, trailing vapour, alight like Icarus from the sun. Directly above us, it achieved its high-pitched acme, probing stresses, vibrating ornaments, utensils, nerves. I goldfished a few more words, confident of their inaudibility. Miming my helplessness, I pressed a swift valedictory kiss on Sarah's wincing cheek.

By the time the roar had subsided to a level of tolerance, I was by the door. I took up my briefcase from its habitual resting-place, propped against the ambiguous, multi-limbed Balinese goddess, which was and is my talisman.

'The blessed peace of the riverside!' I sneered. 'And soon they're going to get bigger, they've promised us.'

'Laurence, tell me.' Sarah pursued me, pleading.

'No time now. Dear.' I waved my watch-bearing arm. 'Behind schedule already. Traffic gets worse every day. Later, I'll tell you later.'

'It's always later, isn't it?'

'You don't choose the most convenient moments.'

'Or you couldn't explain, is that it?'

'Explain what?'

'Just why you happened to be walking home along the river.' She narrowed her eyes. 'Why weren't you driving? I thought you said you were spending the evening at . . . '

'Oh, just for a walk, just for a change. Fresh air. Or else . . . ' — I changed gear rapidly — 'or else I was picked out by Fate to be at that very spot, at that very moment in time. I must have been the chosen instrument of Destiny.'

I closed the door gently behind me, cutting off Sarah's silent scream. Along the corridor I carried with me the image of her pose, hand resting on the statuette of the goddess, her knuckles white.

I shared the lift with an overweight petfood manufacturer from the fourth floor and trod in his profound tracks across the entrance hall.

'Mr Carpenter!' I was discreetly hailed as I stepped from behind the abstract sculpture which writhed in a kind of sunken fishbowl in the centre of the hall. Frowning at my wrist-watch, I walked to the desk.

'Good morning, sir.' The clerk dropped his voice to a yet lower level of discretion. 'About your complaint, sir. Your neighbour. I've reported it to the Management Committee, sir. They're looking into the matter.'

'They don't want to look . . .'—I spoke with an indiscreet vigour—'they want to listen. And then they want to do something about it. Bloody quick.'

'I sympathize, sir.'

'Bloody quick.' I might have left it there, but perhaps the tensions set up on my departure from the flat welcomed this easy outlet. 'The man's a raving lunatic. That damned racket at all hours of the day and. Drums, I ask you! Drums! Banging away at his blasted drums. At his age! Turning the place into a bloody Bedlam. The rent I pay, am I not entitled to a little peace and quiet?'

'Sir.'

'One would suppose so.'

Puffed with righteous pomposity I strode to the doors. The porter moved smartly to throw them open, as though otherwise I might have walked right through them, leaving blood-stains that would require much wearisome labour to remove. 'Have a good day, Mr Carpenter. Sir.'

It must have rained some time after my return in the small hours. The asphalt was drying patchily with the damp showing in grotesque patterns. An electric milk-float slid noiselessly in front of me. I inhaled, filling my lungs, walking to the garage with a sense of freedom such as a space-traveller might feel, released to float outside his constrictive capsule.

My good spirits survived even the re-entry buffeting of the morning rush-hour, the vicious snarl of traffic, my fellow-drivers' doomed and anguished faces. Over the years I had cultivated the technique of enduring the inward journey in a condition of self-induced hypnosis, all thought and feeling frozen, so that when I at last parked my car, fifty minutes of living lost, I could resume existence unmortified.

With an adroit shuffle I smeared my cigarette-end under my sole and with comparable adroitness adjusted my office *persona* as I mounted the broad steps of M.C.L. House. I occupied a senior management position in the hierarchal structure of Modern Communications Limited — at a present salary of some £5,500 per annum, plus certain emoluments — and was hopeful of imminent advancement. I could not escape the charge of hypocrisy, sometimes, indeed, preferring it against myself; despising my occupation, I nevertheless sought success in it. An air of amiable and somewhat bored scepticism not only mollified my self-contempt, but also served to distinguish me from my rivals, pointing the confident effortlessness of my efficiency.

Crossing the reception hall, I nodded democratic greetings. As the lift-doors closed smoothly behind me like water over my head, I suddenly tasted again the rank water of the river and this incongruity made me smile — a smile which a diminutive, red-haired typist took unto herself, fluttering the spiked antennae of her artificial lashes.

Now, even if only as a rehearsal for a later, more significant, performance, I was eager to recount my nocturnal exploits; but I opened my office door at an unpropitious moment, for Harvey and Lydia were posed in a tableau of conflict. This was not uncommon; I disregarded it.

'Good morning! Good morning!' A separate salutation for each.

Harvey was quick to recover, slamming shut the drawer of the filing-cabinet and switching on a welcoming smile. 'Top of the morning,' he burlesqued himself.

Lydia was incapable of so swift an adjustment, and her greeting emerged acidulously squeezed between rigid lips. I didn't take it personally: I knew I was assured of Lydia's unremitting devotion and, indeed, that her shrewish hostility towards Harvey was a reflection of her loyalty to myself. She had been my personal assistant for some years before Harvey's arrival as my deputy, and she resented his authority and the diminution of her influence. If other feelings were also involved, I chose to disregard them: she lacked, poor thing, appeal to the senses.

'M.B. wants to see you this afternoon.' Lydia spoke in her recording-machine voice.

'Well, it's the privilege of office.' I bustled to my desk. The sun through the slatted blinds streaked its dun surface with shining bars of gold. I suddenly remembered an unpaid, and untimely, bill: I sighed.

'Harvey,' sniffed Lydia, 'was looking for the Blenkiron Report. I told him I hadn't seen . . .'

'Oh!—it was nothing important,' Harvey put in quickly, spluttering, as he was already munching one of the chocolates to which he was loathsomely addicted.

'The Blenkiron, I've got it here.'

'Just some figures I wanted to check.'

'I'd intended to do some homework.' I pulled a rueful face. 'But the flesh proved too weak, I fear.'

'If I could just borrow it for an hour . . .' He carried the folder back to his desk, holding it gently in both hands as though it were both fragile and precious, sanctified by its former possessor. 'You've been working on your opus?' he asked, with something of the same deference.

'Uh-huh!' I grunted non-committally.

'And how's it coming along?'

'All right.'

'It's nearly complete,' loyal Lydia endorsed.

'Well, the first draft.'

'It's a marvellous scheme, the Company will save thousands

and thousands.' Lydia directed her enthusiasm at Harvey like a death-ray. 'M.B. will be overwhelmed. After this he's bound to give Laurence the . . . '

'Now, now, let's not count chickens.'

'Well, you're very much the front-runner, anyway,' Harvey smoothly interposed.

'For what that's worth in this sort of rat-race.'

'And not before time, too, if I may say so. Old man.'

'Certainly not before time.'

'We'll see what we shall see.' I was feeling rather shame-faced, as when a good joke has been carried a bit too far. It was true that my reorganization scheme, my 'opus', was associated with hopes of promotion, but such calculation sat ill upon an image of indifference. I pulled my In-tray forward decisively. 'Well, now to immediate matters. We've got that hold-up in deliveries. Harvey, I wonder if you'd have a word with Construction about their . . . '

'Their computer problems, the poor dears. Yes, of course.' Harvey turned at the door. 'What about lunch today?'

I had my head down, busy. 'I'm afraid I can't make it today.'

'Some other time then.'

After he had shut the door, I looked up. Lydia met my blank glance. 'Do you want to answer that Ministry letter?'

'What?'

'About planning permission.'

'What?'

A sensation which seemed to have its origins in the same source as my impulse of shame had suddenly overcome me: I felt myself go hot and cold in quick succession, and beads of sweat running like minute insects in my armpits and down my thighs. The room rolled, as when a passing plane wobbles the picture on a television screen, destroying the illusion of reality.

'What's the matter?'

I shook my head. 'Nothing.'

Perhaps I was ill, perhaps I was developing a fever. *You*

ought — I heard the cracked Cockney voice — *to have injections else you'll get diseases.*

I must have laughed aloud.

'What's the joke?' asked Lydia, only partially reassured.

'What's that?'

'You were laughing.'

'Was I?'

'To yourself, out loud.'

'Oh! — just something I thought of.' But I couldn't have explained what had seemed funny; my laughter had been random, irrational.

Lydia came to sit beside me, her pencil poised over her notebook. She used a potent deodorant, whose smell I found more unpleasant than that which it was designed to nullify.

'It was something that happened last night, something fantastic, preposterous . . . ' I swivelled my chair round. The phrases I'd rehearsed re-formed themselves. 'It began as I was walking home along the river. It was a dark, moonless night. There was no one else about. Then, suddenly, out of nowhere, I heard a gurgled cry . . . '

'. . . I thought of what I'd heard about drowning men trying to strangle their would-be rescuers. But he was only barely conscious, so I was able to get a hold of him, and eventually, though not without going under a few times, dragged him to the bank. Then I . . . '

'How exciting!' she broke in. 'How marvellous! Darling, you're wonderful.'

I lifted my gaze from its modestly downcast scrutiny of the white cloth. Jackie's eyes — her lovely oyster-eyes! — were wide and shining, her lips eagerly parted — oh, that moist pink tongue-tip! — and I experienced the familiar quickening of my blood, reflex of the desperation of my desire for her, my love.

'Oh, I wasn't so heroic,' I demurred.

She put her hand on mine resting amid the gleaming cutlery. 'You shouldn't be so modest, sweet.' Her carmined nails pricked playfully into the web of skin between thumb and forefinger. 'You were very brave, you're a hero.' She squeezed my knee between her thighs. 'I'm so proud of you.'

I began to laugh, and Jackie withdrew her hand and her legs; her face closed up. For all her sexual self-confidence, she was morbidly quick to suspect a slight. 'What have I said wrong?' she demanded.

'Nothing. Nothing at all.'

'Then why are you laughing at me?'

'No, no,' I cried, frantic not to offend. 'Not at you, oh, no!' I leaned forward, as though the warmth of my breath on her face could melt her sudden chill. 'How could you ever believe that?' I laid my hand over her limp fingers. 'I was laughing at myself.'

'Don't understand.'

'Because you had said just what I wanted you to say, because I'd imagined it so many times, rehearsed it.' I rubbed her fingers gently with the ball of my thumb. 'So when you did say it, when you actually seemed . . . impressed, I felt foolish.' I leaned still closer, smelling her scent and the sweet aperitif fragrance on her breath. 'In a way, you see, I did it all for you. Even as I jumped in,' I want on truthfully, 'I was thinking of you. And all the time, as I dragged him back to the bank, the main thought in my mind was, what will Jackie think of this? Will she be moved when I tell her? That I dived from the warmth of her bed—so to speak—into the cold river to save a man's life. Will it make her proud of me?' Her fingers began to curl responsively under my thumb's friction. 'Will it make me more valuable to her? Shall I seem more worthy of her love?'

'Oh, Laurence!' Jackie murmured meltingly.

But, despite my success in mollification, despite my middle-aged knowingness, I couldn't stop. 'Because—I've told you a thousand times, you know it's true—your feelings, your thoughts, your wishes are all that matter to me. They shape and colour my entire existence.' I looked deep into her eyes, her dark oyster-eyes. 'Because I am obsessed with you.' I felt myself sweating with the earnestness of my desire. 'Obsessed. With. You. Oh—my love!'

Her leg slid between mine again. She gave a little twist of the trunk which made her breasts tremble. We swam in each other's eyes. And I was nearer far to drowning than in the waters of the murky river!

'You should get a reward.' Jackie tossed her head coquettishly in a gesture retained from drama school.

'What have you in mind?'

'I didn't mean that, silly.'

'I consider it unlikely,' I said. 'I doubt very much if I shall ever see the man again. I haven't told you half of it yet. In a way, the most extraordinary part's to come, I mean, what happened afterwards. It was quite out of this world.' I waved my free hand in delineation of the world represented by the chic and expensive restaurant in which we sat. 'Preposterous! As though the whole thing were a dream. When I woke up this morning, I really thought I had dreamed it until I saw the clothes he'd given me.

'You see, he was a gangster. He had been thrown into the river by his business associates—at least, that's what he told me.' I paused for dramatic emphasis, but this revelation produced less impression than I had anticipated. I felt discomfited.

'He wouldn't let me go to the police,' I continued. 'He took me back to his place. That was where he gave me some dry clothes. And I suppose you could say he did offer me a reward— in an odd sort of way . . .' Jackie's gaze was remote; she scarcely seemed to be listening to me at all. 'A strange kind of reward . . . What is it, darling?'

She turned her gaze on me, but without intimacy. 'You keep talking about these clothes.'

'What?'

39

'He gave you, this man whoever he.'

'Yes, that's right.'

'What did you do with them?'

'Do with them?'

'Did Sarah see them?' Her tone was remote, rather ludicrously so — another drama school echo!

'What?'

'Sarah. When you took them off to join her in bed.'

'I told you, we sleep in separate . . .'

'I suppose she was terribly impressed by her brave husband's gallantry.' Impatiently, she explained: 'I mean, if she saw the clothes, you had to tell her, didn't you, why you were wearing them. Did she "reward" you?'

'Sarah,' I said, with careful truthfulness, 'was asleep when I came home. I didn't wake her.'

She looked at me and was not deceived. 'This morning then, she saw them. You had to tell her this morning, didn't you? Didn't you?' she repeated triumphantly. 'So you told her before you told me!'

A brief pause. Then what could I say but what I did? 'Oh, Jackie!'

She was as far away from me as the position of her chair would permit. I couldn't allow this second silence to prolong itself indefinitely. 'Actually, I don't think she was very impressed. She seemed more concerned with why I was coming home that way, where I had been.'

'And you told her?'

'No, no, of course not.'

'I see.'

'She was rather . . . abrasive about it.'

'I suppose that means you'll have to stay in and comfort her tonight.'

'It might perhaps be politic.'

'You use such long words. When you talk about her you always use pompous, long words.'

'Pol-i-tic,' I counted out on my fingers, in a painful attempt at lightness. 'Only three syllables.'

'They sound long words.'

Yet another pause. Clatter of crockery and gabble of voices, reverberantly amplified. Anguish.

'I'm sorry, Jackie darling. I'm sorry.' I drew a deep breath. 'I'll come to you tonight. I'll come if I possibly can.'

'So I'm just to wait in, to see if you possibly can.'

'I'll come to you, whatever happens. Of course I will. How in the world could I possibly do otherwise?' She was young: she was entitled to be cruel; she was entitled to her perversities and wiles, to her ingenuous deceits. And who knows that I didn't secretly relish being their victim! 'Promise. Promise,' I added swiftly, passionately.

'Laurence, do you think you really ought to?' Her voice was thick with tenderness. 'I mean, I don't want to make things *difficult* for you, darling. You know that, don't you?'

'The minute I can, I will be with you. Nothing could stop me.' I was deeply moved by her consideration. '*O, my America, my new-found-land!*'

It was one of our bed-codes. Jackie's eyes and mouth – oh, that curling tongue-tip! – telegraphed rapture, and I felt a stirring in my crotch.

'Shouldn't we . . .' asked Jackie, glancing about her, 'order now? Will you pass the menu?'

I am thirty-nine years old, that is to say, nineteen years older than my spicy, firm-fleshed mistress. Many men might envy me. As the taxi which would take her from my side pulled in, panic, humiliation and a devastating sense of loss reduced me to abjection. I pressed a quick peck on her cheek, a banknote in her hand, and failed to suppress a groan as the taxi drew away. Like a schoolboy, I waited on the kerb, hoping her face would appear in the tinted window.

Perhaps, I thought, she would wave as the taxi turned the corner, but a wretched lorry cut past on the inside, obstructing my view. She would have waved. *Until tonight, sweet!* — her last words echoed in my head. A grinding bus sprayed a jet of diesel-poison at me, and I walked away from the restaurant, with a curt nod to the mocking doorman.

Age, as I not infrequently reminded myself, isn't everything, even allowing for the youth-dominated culture of our society — of which, incidentally, I theoretically approve. But, significantly or not, it was around the measurable handicap of my years that all my less precise misgivings coalesced, all those psychotic elements inseparable from a true erotic passion — the terrors, hallucinations, obsessions, fevers!

But there was also joy, of course, a joy marred and intermittent in its blossoming, but of such life-enhancing intensity, even at its weakest, as to render all the fears and miseries of love redundant. Returning to M.C.L. House, I felt as though I were wrapped in a sort of vaporous envelope which isolated me from my surroundings yet at the same time caused the greasy, miserable streets to sparkle with a transcendental brilliance.

The afternoon passed uneventfully, as had so many others. Harvey was off-stage, visiting one of the Company's subsidiaries. His absence had a soothing effect upon Lydia, so that the office — rain now softly pattering against the windows — became cosier and more intimate. I worked with concentration, by an effort of will excluding the tender, heady thoughts which nowadays constantly pressed their attentions.

Strangely enough, the previous night's adventure had passed from my mind as though expunged by my recounting it to Jackie. However, at one point I felt an insistent tickling above my temple and looked up to see Lydia regarding me wistfully.

'I can't help thinking of you diving in that dreadful river.' Her respectful smile was such as art-lovers assume before a famous painting. 'Sitting here, just the two of us all warm and snug, it's so hard to imagine.'

'Yes, I suppose it is.'

'Like something in a film or a novel. I wonder if it will be in the papers.'

'I don't expect so.'

'Then it ought to be. You ought to be famous.'

I heard a warning-bell. 'Lydia, I'd rather we didn't talk about it, eh? I mean, not spread it round the office. Keep it to ourselves.' I was not sure who or what had set off the bell, but its alarm seemed clamorous and personal. 'Harvey, for instance, let's leave him out of it.'

That pleased her. 'Oh, Harvey!' she sniffed. 'I wouldn't tell *him*. I wouldn't tell him anything.'

I returned to my papers. The recommendation I was drafting would have the effect of putting twelve men out of work and another eighteen on short time, but my motives were innocent, free of hatred; in the cosiness of my office, their harsh, labouring existence was abstract. I thought again of my unpaid bills along with my substantial overdraft. Lydia served tea and biscuits.

'It's just like you to be so modest,' she said in a fond voice, free, I knew, from all irony. 'But someone should do something about it. The man you saved, he should do something.'

'I don't suppose I shall see him again,' I said, recalling as I heard my own words that I had said this before. 'It's over and done with now.'

After I had drunk my tea, I ascended to keep my appointment with the Managing Director. M.B., although a man of shrewdness who had received an excellent education, had fashioned himself the style of a sort of un-holy fool: capitalizing on his North Country origins, he presented himself as a blunt, simple chap humbly astounded that chance—forgetting his family connections—should have so elevated him. He assumed awe of the brilliant and sophisticated young men whom he employed.

I had long since learned to adapt myself to this harlequinade

43

and was customarily rewarded by being admitted to the flattering intimacy of his indiscretions — such as, on this occasion, his suspicions, expressed with a gross schoolboy vulgarism, concerning the sexual proclivities of a senior colleague. I took these to be malicious and entirely unfounded.

'It's a foony world, Laurence,' he concluded his character-assassination. 'When you get to my age you'll know, there's nowt so strange as fooke.'

He disappeared behind a cloud of pipe-smoke. The staggering banality of his reflections inevitably aroused a suspicion of irony, but I took a calculated risk. 'Unless,' I ventured, 'unless, it be other fooke.'

When the smoke-cloud had dispersed, he was watching me beadily. I held my breath.

Then he nodded approval. 'Aye, well, you'll have to reckon with that when you move up the ladder. That's what it all comes down to in the end: the towers and palaces of commerce are built on the frail foundations of yuman-beings.' He drew sagely on his pipe. 'In other words, plain fooke.'

'I'm sure that's right.'

'You know that, a smart young chap like you, Laurence, all set for the big leap forward. And if I'm any judge, it shouldn't be long now.'

We concluded our trivial business and, duly encouraged, I returned to the office. My promotion, which would not only gratify my vanity, but also remove my small financial worries, seemed imminent; and yet my pleasure from the implied promise of M.B.'s words was infected by the virus of my self-contempt. Any success I achieved in the Company was invariably accompanied by this parallel sense of humiliation, as though I were conniving at my own corruption.

The working day was shortly done. I bade Lydia good-night.

'I was thinking,' she murmured, as I turned at the door. 'Shouldn't you see a doctor?' She flushed superfluously. 'I mean, you know what they say about the river, all the filthy things that get into it. We don't want you sickening, do we?'

'I hope, dear Lydia,' I charmed, 'that you will never find me sickening.'

The roads were greasy and dangerous. For once I allowed the horrors of the rush-hour traffic to get the better of my control, and I indulged in a prolonged duel with a battered sports-car which had encroached on my territory. After the grinning oaf had driven off with a triumphant fanfaronade, I felt ashamed of myself.

'Good evening, Mr Carpenter.' The porter came to attention in the style of a film comedy recruit. He had a face like a full moon or an uncut cheese.

'Mr. Carpenter. Sir. Excuse me.' I was halfway across the hall when the desk clerk hailed me.

'Ah, you have news! You want to tell me, the management have moved at last. They have agreed to eject my lunatic neighbour.'

'What's that, sir? Ah, no.' He simpered, as though he thought I had intended to be funny. 'Ah, no, I'm afraid there has been no development in that direction. It was another matter.'

Go on, man, for Christ sake get it out: I restrained myself from saying.

'Another matter entirely.'

Why do so many people say things twice over? There was someone else I had recently encountered who had the same aggravating habit.

'There was a . . . gentleman here asking for you, sir.'

'Oh, yes.'

'He wouldn't go away, he waited some time. Sitting over there.'

I followed the clerk's gaze over the aquatic sculpture to the unoccupied couch at the far end of the hallway. 'Well, who was it?'

'He wouldn't give his name, sir.'

'Is my wife not in?'

'I didn't think it wise.' The clerk looked reprovingly at the distant, empty couch, and lowered his voice to share a dubious secret: 'A coloured gentleman he was, sir.'

I heard the drum-beats even as I walked along the corridor. As I laid down my briefcase against my goddess, their tempo quickened and the volume increased. 'Oh, for God's sake, not again!' I cried despairingly.

'What's that?' Sarah, long legs bent elastically beneath her on the sofa, lowered her book.

'That bloody row! Never any peace.' I approached her, smiling conscientiously. 'How you can stand it!'

'Hullo.' Sarah raised her book again. The dust-jacket's entwined limbs appeared to undulate through the watery wrinkles of the plastic cover. Other books lay all around her. 'Actually, I scarcely hear it.'

'That's your fortunate insensitivity,' I remarked in a pleasant voice. 'Well, have you had a good day?' I didn't wait for a reply. 'Been to the library, I see.'

'I seem,' said Sarah, 'to be getting through quite a lot of reading at present.'

'Wish I had the time.' A thought occurred, and though Sarah had opened her mouth to speak, I hurried on: 'I suppose no one's been up here, have they?'

'Up here? In the flat? Have I perhaps been entertaining a lover, is that what you mean?'

'Just someone was asking for me at the desk, apparently. I wondered.'

'Would you object?'

'What's that?'

'If I had had a man.' She arched herself back on the cushions. 'A man up here, bouncing on top of me.'

The drumming stopped. I took up the book which Sarah had allowed to fall on to her lap. 'What erotic fantasy have you been reading?'

'Or would you have welcomed it? Convenient.'

'Looks pretty hot stuff. No wonder! Now isn't she that woman who always writes about . . .'

'Would you?'

'. . . multiple orgasms? But then most of them do nowadays, don't they? So it seems.' I replaced the book gently on her stomach, keeping her place. 'Listen! It's stopped. Those bloody drums! Listen! Thank God for that.'

'Someone to keep me occupied and happy, someone civilized, not too demanding . . .' She swung her legs to the floor, and the book bounced, the pages fluttering. 'While you pursue your own squalid little affair. Whoever she might be. Whatever little tart this time.'

Some women, I suppose, would have been crying. I have always admired Sarah's dignity. She was not even breathing hard. Her cheeks were perhaps faintly and, rather attractively, flushed. She picked up the fallen novel and put it in a tidy pile along with the other books. 'I notice you don't bother to deny it.'

I had backed, creating as much space for myself as possible, although there was no neutral corner. 'What would be the use?' I had composed my features into a formulation of careful concern, but to no point for Sarah was not looking at me.

She put the pile of books on the coffee-table and then, deciding that there they cluttered the room, removed them to the window-ledge. She looked out of the window. I cleared my throat, though I really had nothing at all I wished to say.

'I suppose you're going out again tonight.' She still wasn't looking at me.

'Well, actually, I had thought . . . was going to tell you, but . . .'

'What about our meal?'

The simplicity of this question, or some nuance of unintended sadness in her voice, touched me – damnation! – momentarily overcoming my temperamental distaste for a scene of this nature. 'Oh, Sarah . . .' I began, starting forward. 'I'm sorry. I'm so sorry that . . .' I didn't know how to go on.

'I'll prepare you something first, if you wish.'

'Sarah . . .'

She was past me and going through the door to the kitchen. I took a step in pursuit but then halted. The glow of my tenderness and melancholy was not entirely quenched, but it was dimmed by a sudden bright vision of the future. Now all, or almost all, was out in the open, I thought, I could bring to Jackie a love less furtive and harassed. My whole life would become simpler, more innocent, more truly loving.

'*Licence my roaving hands, and let them go, Before, behind, between, above, below. O, my America, my new-found-land . . .* What's the next line?'

'*My Kingdome, safeliest when with one man man'd*'. I tied the laces of my second shoe and straightened unsteadily.

'That's nice, I like it when you say it to me.'

I faced a wall of photographs: Picasso, Robert Graves, Cassius Clay, the late Robert Kennedy and the Earl of Harewood were prominent among various film and stage actors, pop singers, bullfighters and poets; there were also a number of private photographs, bearing affectionate inscriptions in hands of varying maturity; and some picture postcards, mostly verging on the obscene.

'You haven't given me your photo yet. You promised you would.'

'Did I?' I turned to the bed, in which Jackie lay snug, the sheets pulled up to her chin. 'Then I think I've changed my mind.'

'Oh!' she pouted. 'You promised.'

'I don't want to be in your damned pin-ups.'

'Oh, Laurence!'

She lay with her head cradled on her bare arms, her hair a

black stream across the pillows. I observed a red-tipped pimple in the shaven mat of her left armpit. She put out her tongue at me, slowly.

I shuddered and pulled down the bed-clothes. Each time I saw her body naked it was as though I were seeing it for the first time, as though I were seeing the body of a naked woman for the first time. She lay with her legs slightly apart . . . pollinated. By pulling back the clothes I had released the piscatorial smells of our love-making. I threw my fully-clad body on to the bed.

'Between . . . above . . . below . . .' Jackie murmured, lying quiescent under my hands.

Groaning, I pressed my mouth into the curve of her arm, feeling a hot little swelling under my tongue.

'Haven't you had enough yet?' Jackie enquired in a gentle, self-pleased tone.

'No. No. No. Never,' — my voice muffled. 'Never enough!'

'Then you'd better take off your clothes and come back to bed. You'd better stay all the night.' She moved away from me and pulled up the sheets. 'It's nice in the morning,' she added reflectively. 'It's different then, sort of all warm and cuddly, when you're still half-asleep. I think I like it in the mornings best of all. I always have done.'

I was on my knees by the bedside. 'Oh, my love, sweet Jackie, I can't. You know I can't, however much I want . . .'

'Anyone can say that. Any old middle-aged married man!'

'Oh, please!'

She kissed me swiftly. 'You're not to leave me. I order you to stay. You know you have to obey, Fido, when I order you.'

Creakingly I rose to my feet. 'Some day. I promise you some day. Soon! You know there is nothing in the world I want more.'

Jackie yawned. 'A cigarette,' she demanded.

I lit it for her and put it between her bruised lips. 'I love you,'

I said very earnestly. 'I want you . . . more than life. I will do anything, anything . . .'

'Go home, Laurence.' She was smiling. 'You know you must go home.'

She adjusted the blankets, stretched out her arm and turned on the record-player which stood on the bedside table – along with our used glasses, the cluttered ashtray, crumpled tissues, stained handkerchief, etc., all sacred objects. An adenoidal, but strangely haunting, voice, accompanied off-beat by what sounded like a toyshop harmonica, began to intone a heroin-inspired lyric of lost love. Jackie hummed behind a blue undulating curtain of smoke.

'It was wonderful, sweet. Again. As always.' I stood limply in the middle of the room, waiting for a response, but her smile was distant and impersonal. I dragged myself round.

'Laurence.' With my hand on the door-knob, I turned hopefully. 'Laurence, don't go in the river again tonight, darling. It can't be good for you, swallowing all that water.'

I trod softly down the stairs. While I no longer exercised the same furtiveness as when, six weeks before, my visits had begun, I still felt embarrassed if I encountered any of the house's other occupants. They all seemed to be under twenty-five – and a pretty freakish lot too, whose idiosyncracies of adornment made Jackie appear by comparison almost primly conformist. Their eyes I found derisive.

The house itself was a decaying Victorian terraced building, converted into single-room apartments; its mouldering ugliness and disreputability seemed sanctified in the same way as the combings and dottles of her bedside table.

Closing the front door gently – no one encountered – I stepped into the empty roadway and looked up at the pink glow of Jackie's window, although she never appeared there to wave me on my way. When I had gone did she put on a nightdress to sleep in? Or did she always sleep naked? Did she sleep naked only on the nights of my visits, on other occasions garbed?

Funny thing, I'd wondered about this every night I'd stood in the roadway saluting her empty pink window, and every night I'd made a mental note to enquire. And never remembered. Turning away, I attempted with a youthful leap to click my heels in mid-air. Unsuccessfully.

I was trilling the harmonica-tune as I strode along the river-bank. A boisterous wind, the devil's wind, had sprung up: the lights in the water shimmered like chorus-girls, and from the waving trees black dancers high-kicked across the tow-path.

My exhilaration, the sense of adolescent fervour regained which always inspired me at these moments, was mixed with, perhaps enhanced by, the underlying tension. born of my fears and the anguishes of duplicity. But tonight was subtly different: now that Sarah knew of this particular *affaire*, although there would be further bitter and racking scenes, the time of duplicity was past and I had moved significantly closer to the condition of freedom to which I aspired. I felt it, this promise of freedom, throbbing within me like some transplanted organ.

A sheet of paper, blown by the wind, wrapped itself round my shins. Why had I not told Jackie of the scene with Sarah? Because it would have upset her, would have made her fearful, the sweet darling, that she might lose me. Besides, it might have put her in the wrong mood at the wrong moment: all I'd wanted the instant after I'd been admitted to the aphrodisiac intimacy of her disordered room had been to tear off my clothes and get her into bed, to hear her little animal yelps of delight, to feel her nails drawn down my groin, to part her manfully and to enter her. I no longer wondered, as I had at the beginning: where had one so young learned so well?

But afterwards? Surely then, when we lay together as one body, without secrets or shame, surely then was the time for me to have unburdened myself. Those moments of fragile, mystical harmony were, however, so precious that I could not bear the intrusion of any spectre that might de-consecrate them.

I could, of course, have told her at the end, but then she

would have urged me even more strongly to stay. If Sarah already knew, what difference would it make if I were to return after the milk? There was an answer to that one, there had to be, but I could have found no explanation that would not have hurt Jackie's sensitive feelings, even perhaps have made her to doubt my constancy. She wanted me so much, she did, she did!

This was the exact spot at which last night I had been startled by the cry from the river. I stopped. If it had been tonight, I wouldn't even have heard it. The air was filled with the roar of the wind, the slapping water, the creaking and rustling of the trees. There was the sense everywhere of restless, erratic movement, the shadows bucking and leaping. As I turned from the river to continue, one kicking dancer jumped the other way, into the concealment of the thicket.

It was a favourite place for Peeping Toms, and the river–bank always harboured a quantum of morose madmen, but somehow that quick movement, in synchronization with mine, suggested a rational, purposeful quality. It might, of course, be an oppor-tunist footpad, but my suspicions, not unnaturally considering my situation, took a different cast.

I walked straight on, and when I came to the spot where the shadow had disappeared nonchalantly paused to light a cigarette. I could see no one. But as I proceeded I had an eerie conviction that my steps were being dogged, a spy's sharp eyes were pinned to my back. I resisted the temptation to turn. I would make it easy for him until we reached the road, then I'd show the bastard, I'd show Sarah, the sort of man they were dealing with. Knock his ill–fitting dentures down his scraggy throat: let him put that in his report, item for his expense account.

I climbed the steps two at a time and, ducking beneath the level of the wall, backed into the bus shelter. A mild blow took me in the kidneys. I gave a cry of alarm. In the darkness it was impossible to distinguish the collocation of the tangled bodies on the bench, nor even their sex or numbers, but the urgency of their protests left no doubt as to the untimeliness of my intrusion.

Even as I gabbled apology I was aware in one segment of my mind of footsteps passing, and when I emerged there was a figure some twenty yards ahead, walking with rapid unconcern.

I broke into a trot but, without running, the figure seemed to keep exactly the same distance ahead of me, a disembodied shadow. Eventually, my frustration exploded in an angry shout, upon which, with one quick glance over his shoulder, the figure crossed the road to the fields on the other side; and disappeared.

I took half-a-dozen steps in pursuit, then changed my mind. Steady, I told myself, steady. Don't let them get at you. Don't let them drive you mad. By 'them', I didn't mean merely Sarah and her private detective, I meant all of them. You know what it's like at certain moments. They've all ganged up on you, everyone you've ever met since your ejection from the womb. For Christ sake!—you must know. I can't be the only one.

Resolutely I refused to look back, all the way home. The light from the entrance hall, in which as I approached I could see the porter sprawled asleep in his chair, spread over the empty courtyard as though for a festival. A tom-cat miaowled, but otherwise there was no sound save for my own ringing steps. I marched up to the door, silently humming the harmonica-tune. To push the door open I had naturally to turn. And turning, I glimpsed a tall figure gliding along the wall at the light's periphery; it moved with a nimble, feline ease, with the casual elegance of a black dancer.

The porter remained asleep, mouth gaping. I stood over him and coughed and had the satisfaction of seeing his dreaming content replaced by a twitch of panic. I coughed again, more loudly, but before he'd woken fully to the mean servility of his existence I was entering the lift.

In the bathroom, where I undressed, I saw myself in the mirror and was agreeably surprised; I bore no scars. I crept barefoot into the bedroom and into my single bed, as I had done the night before and, come to that, a good few other nights besides. But my precautions turned out to be superfluous, for after a little while I became aware that the room was empty. Apart from myself, that is. Apart from myself.

3

'Oh, for God's sake, what now?'

The Works Director's secretary, who had pursued me along the corridor, bridled. My peevishness was a personal affront. 'You're wanted on the telephone,' she tartly informed me.

She tip-tapped back, leaving me to follow—a tall, tubular girl, with an indignant spine. To hell with her! I was in no mood for propitiation: it had been a bad morning.

Starting with Sarah. No, she hadn't gone, merely removed herself to the spare bedroom.

Starting with Sarah, even at breakfast, by custom a time of truce. I made no reference to her transfer from the bedroom. I chose not to challenge her about the detective she had hired to follow me; and not only because in the clear light of the morning I had begun to doubt his shadowy existence; because breakfast was by custom a time of truce.

She spoke in curt monosyllables, crashing plates. Our differences were not of such rare occurrence; this form of behaviour seemed excessive, and was out of character, and so I was disturbed. I ventured a pained remonstrance, and she had turned on me with sharp abuse, like a fishwife.

'Like a fishwife,' I had mildly protested.

She had a cup in her hands; she raised it above her head and dashed it to the floor. A choking cry escaped from her throat and she rushed from the room, the dignity with which I had accredited her the day before discarded, and leaving me with an increased and growing sense of unease.

That was when my headache had begun. Then, as in the corridor I waited for the lift—my hands still shaking and my stomach boiling—a bony finger was prodded into my back. I turned to see my neighbour, in dressing-gown and slippers, hair fuzzed, eyes sticky, and smelling of unlaundered sheets.

Apart from his drum–beating mania, he was an odd little man: a house–trained eccentric, with the face of a wrinkled baby, and a woman's high voice. He pushed his head aggressively towards my breast–bone. 'I've been told you're making complaints about me,' he squeaked.

'Complaints,' I repeated stupidly. 'Complaints, yes, I should bloody well think . . .'

'Behind my back.' He wagged his finger at my eyes. 'There's such a thing as slander, you know. There's such a thing as slander.'

'Slander! I'll give you sl . . .'

'That's all I have to say. For the present.'

'Here, wait a minute,' I called after his retreating back. I took a step in pursuit, and then became aware that the lift-doors had opened and that three pairs of eager eyes were staring at me from faces set in rigid impassivity. With a sickly grimace I entered the lift, all my un–uttered protests fermenting in my bowels like sharp and indigestible spices.

The traffic was no worse than usual, but on a crossing, in a moment of abstraction, I almost killed a child.

As if all that weren't enough, on my arrival – what with one thing and another, a few insignificant minutes late – I found M.B. awaiting me, in my own chair, regaling Lydia and Harvey with some apocryphal account of his besting of a Government Minister. He had ignored my entry, but on the conclusion of his lying anecdote he turned and, with a fierce jab of his pipe-stem, despatched me promptly on a mission to The Fridge.

This might have been his original intention, but, on the other hand, he sometimes demonstrated a cunning perception in matters of malice, and so it could have been a punishment. The Fridge – one propitiates demons, as children know, by the adoption of homely nicknames – was a technological prodigiosity, fully computerized, remotely controlled, with lustrous avenues of glass, aseptic surfaces, and the air perpetually vibrating with a queasy atonal hum. Although I acknowledge the inevitability of progress, The Fridge for some reason always aroused in my nerve-ends a sensation of eerie, itching discomfort; a spiritual blight would afflict me, as in those terrible presentient dreams of nothingness.

Consequently, I conducted my dealings there with an uncharacteristic anxiety and inefficiency. That morning's business had gone badly, storing no doubt all manner of vexatious problems for the future. No matter, so long as now I could escape.

Retracing my steps, I followed the tall, tubular girl into the glass–walled office and lifted the telephone. Two minutes later and I would have been clean away; I feared M.B. had devised some diabolic scheme to keep me here for the rest of the day.

'Oh, Laurence, there you are! At last.' Despite the petulance of her tone, I felt myself blushing with delight. 'Such a job getting hold of you. Why didn't you tell me you wouldn't be in your office? Some bitch of a woman gave me this number, I had to drag it out of her, and I've been holding on for ages. For simply ages!'

'I'm sorry.' I turned my back on the secretary. 'Been rather busy.'

'And now you don't even sound pleased to speak to me. Aren't you? Aren't you pleased?'

'Of course I am.'

'You don't sound it.'

'It's rather difficult,' I muttered. How can one hide in a room of glass walls?

'Of course, if you're just sticking it up a typist! Are you? Is that what you're doing?'

'No. No. Naturally not.'

'I wouldn't want to interrupt anything like that. It was just I had this marvellous idea, I thought it would make you happy, as it's such a wonderful day, isn't it?'

I looked out through the wall. The sky was cloudless, the

vista drenched in colour, a meandering stream was transmuted into glittering tinfoil; in the landscaped gardens below, girls in summer dresses threw crumbs to the sparrows. It must have been like this all morning, I realized with surprise, as though I had only just woken up. 'What? What did you say?'

'. . . so when this wretched man put off the audition—can't you hear me properly, is the line bad?—I thought we could have lunch and then we could go out somewhere. On the river, or in the country, or somewhere. I thought you'd like that.'

'Oh, I would have done. Very much.'

'Now it's too late for lunch. But we can still go somewhere this afternoon. We could go to the Zoo. You've always been trying to get me to go to the Zoo with you.'

'But I'm working.' I heard the secretary impatiently slam a drawer. 'I can't just walk out, however much I . . .'

'Oh!' A tragic lamentation. 'I thought it would make you happy, darling.'

'Right then,' I decided in a sharp business-like voice. I flashed my wrist-watch. 'I'll pick you up at two-thirty, if that will be convenient.'

Cutting short Jackie's delight, I replaced the receiver. Out of courtesy, I asked the secretary's permission before I called the office. She grudgingly assented.

Lydia had already left for lunch, so I was obliged to tell Harvey.

'Of course, I'll mind the shop. Got lumbered there, have you?'

'Something like that.'

'I'll know where to find you if anything special upcrops?'

'Er, well, no,' I said.

Harvey laughed pleasantly. 'Must be very nice in the country a day like this. Got your clubs in the boot?' He laughed again. 'Don't worry. Not a word to Auntie. You can rely on me, old man.'

It might have been an altogether different road, a different day, as I drove back to London. The countryside, to which I had been blind in the morning, was bathed in a benign radiance revealing dream-like felicities, the more enjoyable for my truancy.

Jackie kissed me when we met—jumping from the bed she lay on. She was wearing a fluffy, black half-sleeved jersey and thin tight jeans; she looked very young. 'Well, where are we going?'

'Don't want to go anywhere,' I growled, reaching after her.

'Down, Rufus, down!' She evaded me with ease. 'But that's the whole point, to get out in this lovely sunshine.' She turned off the record-player. 'We can fuck,' she said in the sudden silence, 'any old day. Where's my handbag?'

She seemed to have forgotten her suggestion of the Zoo and proposed a drive into the country or to the sea. When I demurred, she gave way with a kind of grumbling sweetness.

'You and your old Zoo! But just because I want to please you.' She snuggled up close to me in the car seat. 'You should want to please me too.'

'Of course. Anything.'

'But you won't, I know you, you're so greedy, you'll just want to rush me back into bed'. I smiled fatuously. 'I'd like to go out for a really nice dinner tonight, and then to that new club. I'd like to go there tonight, will you?'

'Well, I don't know that . . .'

'Of course, you'd have to take me home first and you'd have to come in and wait while I change.' She gave my thigh a gentle nip. 'You will, sweet, won't you?'

'I suppose . . .'

'Sweet, you are good to me.'

That settled, sealed with a final promissory nip, she slid away from me. Opening her handbag, she made a considerable display of concealment while rummaging in its disorder for her cigarettes, so that I was compelled to enquire what it was that she was keeping hidden.

She mimed a delightful annoyance at my perception. 'It's a surprise. You'll see later, if you're a good boy.'

She was full of surprises that afternoon: she told me how twice that morning her telephone had rung, and when she had answered it there had been no voice at the other end: just breathing. 'Twice,' she repeated. 'It must have been someone who fancies me. Some disgusting old pervert.' It was a thought she evidently found not displeasing.

I pondered. 'You could tell it was a man – that breathing? You're sure?'

'Of course, darling.' She giggled. 'You don't think it was some old dike after me, do you? What a nasty mind you've got!'

No, such an obscene thought had never entered my head. 'I wondered, just wondered that's all, not seriously, if it could have been . . .'

'Sarah! But how could it? I mean, she doesn't know me. She doesn't know I exist.' She turned accusingly. 'You haven't told her about me, have you?'

'No. No, of course not.'

'I mean, I don't want a jealous wife chasing after me. I couldn't stand that. That would be the end.'

'Oh, Sarah's not like that,' I said, with conviction. 'She's far too dignified and civilized.' I was just parking the car. As we walked towards the Zoo entrance, I told her at last my little marital upsets. 'But,' I reassured her, 'Sarah's no idea who you are, your name, where you live, anything about you at all. You're safely anonymous.'

Jackie was silent.

'So that's all right, isn't it, darling?'

'I don't like being "anonymous".' Lack of consistency was, I had already judged, forgivable in one so young. 'I'm me,' she said. 'I'm not ashamed.'

'Of course you're not. But you did say that . . .'

'I know what I said, but . . .' But? 'But she's got to know

some time.' I said my darling was full of surprises. 'When you tell her you're going to leave her, when you tell her you're going to live with me.' I stuttered in my stride. 'Come on, come on.' Jackie was pulling at my arm. 'Let's see this old Zoo of yours.'

We passed through the turnstile—with a brave and merry quip from me that she might use the children's entrance.

'Ugh—the smell!' She put on her dark glasses, as though they would protect her sensitive nose. 'Why are you so mad on this old Zoo, anyway?'

It was not often she gave me the opportunity to talk about myself. Her lack of curiosity about my life before we had met— while I was frantic to consume each raw morsel of her biography —was a source of galling disappointment to me. So I tried to explain to her. How, first, as a child, I had been brought here by my father three or four times in the last summer before he went away. Then, in the following years, I had come often by myself, without informing my mother, in the hope that I might encounter my father again, though I knew this to be impossible, as I was aware that he had taken his new wife to a distant country. I told her all this; and how, by the time I had arrived at adolescence a kind of habit had been formed, a habit I'd since retained, so that the Zoo was the place to which I came at times of despair or spiritual weariness, in search of something to atone for my sense of loss.

I spoke swiftly, disjointedly; I had never before had the opportunity to reveal so intimate an aspect of myself. 'Do you understand, darling?'

'But you're not missing anything now,' she said. 'Are you? You've got me.'

'Yes, of course.' I wanted desperately to make her understand. 'It's rather like a man who once held a religious faith and, though he's lost it long since, still goes to church when he . . . when he's feeling low. Hasn't everyone got some place like that? Haven't you?'

'When I'm feeling low,' said Jackie, 'I know what *I* want.' She giggled and indicated.

'Anyway,' I said, overcoming my disappointment, 'it seems somehow to work, it always has done. It . . . eases me, it soothes me, it takes me outside myself.'

'Me, too!' laughed Jackie.

We argued about the ethics of keeping animals in zoos. 'They can't like being put in cages,' she said. 'It's unnatural. Everyone, every creature wants to be free – to live their own lives.'

'Even if it's only to fight and to kill or to be killed?'

'Well, it's natural,' she said. 'Isn't it? How would you like to be locked up in a cage?'

My love, she made considerable efforts to please me, though I must admit the afternoon was less rewarding than I had hoped for. Jackie's interests were fleeting. When I halted before my favourites – the primeval reptiles, the solitary, savage birds of prey – she was impatient to move on to more striking attractions. She enjoyed the colour and chatter of the parrot-house; the buttock–rolling cats seemed to strike a sexual chord; and she was childishly entertained by the grosser antics of the monkeys. 'Did you do it like that when you were a little boy?'

I dallied before the gorilla's cage, fascinated as always by his awesome power and mournful dignity. Jackie had left my side; but then I heard her call my name and turned to see her click the shutter of a camera.

'Got you! Got you!' she cried, as though she had potted me with a concealed pistol. 'That was my surprise,' she explained. 'That was what I was hiding. I borrowed it from Adrian.' The most obnoxious of her fellow-tenants. 'Now I've got a picture of you to put in my pin-ups.'

I feigned displeasure but was secretly touched. It was one of those cameras which produce the print immediately. The picture showed me alongside the gorilla; by a freak of perspective, we stood in the cage together.

'You're just like a gorilla, anyway – hairy brute, with your great thing dangling!' She didn't seem to care who overheard her; I took her shamelessness for her generation's candour.

We made some more photographs; but shortly Jackie lost interest and complained that she felt tired. She didn't want to go straight home though, she needed a drink. Two.

'I smell all animal,' she said, lifting the neck of her jersey and sniffing, when eventually we returned to her room. 'You and your stinking old Zoo!'

She was naked in a moment but wouldn't let me touch her. To go to the bathroom, which was along the corridor, she put on a brief, flimsy wrap which would conceal nothing from the casual amoral eyes of, say, Adrian or any other young lecher she might encounter. I washed in her hand–basin while she was gone, and waited turgidly.

She returned pink and bare and shiny, like a schoolgirl from the tub, and suffered me to fold her still bath–warm body in my clothed embrace. 'My gorilla!' she whispered.

But then she had slipped away from me – 'Down, Rufus. Down!' – and was already opening disordered drawers in search of her underclothes. I groaned my desire.

'Be a good boy, please. We're going out. Remember, you promised.'

She seated herself before the dressing-table, busy with bottles and jars and tubes. 'Put on the record-player, darling. Don't just sit there staring at me. You know I loathe being stared at when I'm putting on my face.'

'Madam's wish is my . . .'

'And pass me my handbag while you're up.'

To find whatever she sought in the dustbin of her handbag, she up–ended its contents on the already over–flowing dressing-table. Some of the photographs we had taken fluttered to the floor. I picked them up and, shouting above the record–player, asked if I could keep one or two of her. One, she graciously assented. To make my selection I spread them on the bed as for an invalid's game of patience. Jackie's form beguiled me in half-a-dozen different poses; and I suddenly recalled, as a fragment of memory unveiled itself, a plaited schoolgirl against a tennis-net whose photograph had slowly grown more cracked and dog-eared as the hot summer passed through which I bore it in my blazer-pocket. What was her name? Linda ... Laura ...

'Christ Almighty!' I suddenly forgot the dusty courts of that faraway summer. I picked up one of the photographs. Jackie stood beside a tiger's cage. It was the only picture which I had succeeded in taking, seeking to avoid her self-conscious poses, without her knowledge. I had obtained a lively impression of her young-animal grace, although her movement had blurred the image.

There was, however, no blurring of the ice-cream kiosk behind her, at which stood a cluster of children and adults. One a head taller than any of the rest. A woman. She turned with her ice-cornet into the camera's lens, and thus now into my startled gaze. I recognized her with just the same quality of shock as that with which one reacts on seeing in life a face which one has only previously seen in dream. But she was no creature of dream; she had loomed, rather larger than life, in an ill-lit and dubious doorway, accompanied by a smell of rotting fruit. What had he called her? Cathy ... Carrie ... Chrissie!

'Christ!' I repeated, as though in explanation of the miraculous.

'You don't want that.' The picture was taken from my hands. 'It's all fuzzy.' Jackie dropped it on the bed and picked up another. 'Take this one. I meant this for you.'

After all, coincidences happen every day, millions of them; it's just, like the millions of birds that must die each day, one doesn't often come across them, so that a single example encountered, a ball of bloody feathers, will prompt an unreasonable disquiet. A dead bird never hurt anyone, I told myself, in an effort to inter my unreasonable apprehension.

I took the picture Jackie handed to me. I had snapped it with her standing by the gorilla's cage; she wore a mischievous expression, and held her hands apart like an angler measuring a prize catch. I asked if I might have a more conventional study, but she refused.

'This one. I did this one for you specially. I want to write on it . . .'

So I passed it to her, but she thrust it back at me impatiently, saying, 'Not now. Later. Let's go now.' She pirouetted in front of me. 'Well, tell me I look sexy,' she winsomely demanded.

She was wearing a flame-coloured dress in some heavy, shiny material which looped to her neck, leaving her shoulders bare. In the restaurant, when she leaned over her plate, I could see her pendant breasts to the mauve penumbra of her nipples.

'You've got to have good ones.' She received my compliment complacently. 'Some girls, if they're floppy, look revolting without a bra.'

In the restaurant, I was pleased and proud to be on display with her. It was an extremely expensive, modishly fitted establishment, but the food was tolerable. Jackie's greedy delight compensated for my own indifferent appetite, the more so as she playfully translated the act of eating into a provocative sexual mime. Her eyes, elaborately decorated, glittered from the wine and the drinks we had had before. Our reflections were glamorized with flattering artistry in the walls of mirrors. I observed that there were a number of attractive young women at other tables, though none so desirable as Jackie; and it also gave me satisfaction to note that their escorts appeared older and grosser than myself.

It was a different story in the club to which she took me. Here, as soon as my pupils had adjusted themselves to the crepuscular light in the bar, I became aware of the predominant youthfulness, the half-naked nymphets, the casually elegant boys, and I felt as though I had wandered, uninvited, into a children's party.

I welcomed Jackie's suggestion that we should dance, hopeful that when I held her in my arms the precipitous chasm that had suddenly opened between us would be bridged; but I didn't know the steps, the music was outlandish, and in the press of pubescent bodies, raked by psychotic shafts of light, I felt more than ever alienated.

'This is my sort of place,' said Jackie happily, as we settled at a bouncing table. 'Everyone comes here now, you know.' She pointed out three celebrities of whom I had never heard.

In her delight might lie my consolation: as she was evidently oblivious to the yawning years between us, so my apprehensions were phantoms; and if she seemed a trifle remote, well, she was understandably distracted, and, anyway, conversation was next to impossible in all this bloody racket. My headache, which had slipped away unnoticed on the return drive to London, quietly resumed its place.

Of course, I was not the only middle-aged interloper. Looking about—Jackie had excused herself—I could see a few men of my own age or more. And how absurd or seedy they appeared —scavengers feeding on youthful flesh! And how beautiful was that youthful flesh, I thought achingly—that child dancing there, for instance, her thighs bare under a swirling skirt, the exact colour of Jackie's!

'Who was your partner?' I enquired, trying to sound casual, when she returned glowing from the dance.

'How on earth should I know? Just a boy.'

She had some acquaintances. They stopped briefly by our table, exchanging slangy badinage, dotted with references to people unknown to me. She didn't introduce me—no insult intended, it was all part of the informality—and after one level, unastonished glance they would ignore me entirely so that I felt as though I were taking part in someone else's dream.

Jackie seemed content not to dance again, not to mingle: just to sit and be seen and to listen, foot tapping to that cacophonous music. But I had ceased to find consolation in her rapture: she ought, my love, to sense the disgruntlement I was, naturally, too considerate to express. 'I've got a bit of a headache coming on,' I ventured.

'Oh, you poor sweet!' She put a hot hand on my brow. 'It must have been that awful Zoo.'

I drooped into silence. A kind of dysphoria beset me: I could not cast off the sensation, ridiculous though it was, that I was being secretly observed, and scorned, and derided; and that I was on the threshold of some peril. When an over-energetic dancer lurched against our table, sloshing the drinks, I detected an act of malevolence, and sprang to my feet poised for violent retaliation. 'Darling,' Jackie reproached, 'it was only an accident.'

It came to an end at last. She stretched herself daintily, yawning, and enquired with consideration if I would be willing to depart.

Conscious of the amount of alcohol I had drunk, I drove slowly through the eerily empty streets, Jackie curled against my side, her eyes closed, her head resting trustingly on my shoulder. I drew up gently and turned off the engine.

'Are we here already?' She brushed her lips against my cheek. 'Lovely evening, sweet. Thank you.'

I removed the car keys.

'Oh, no, darling, not tonight.' She slid away from my hand. 'It's so late and I'm too tired.'

'Please! Please!'

'And I've got this T.V. audition in the morning, I told you. Be a good boy.'

'Just to come up . . . for a little while. If you're too tired, we don't have to . . .'

'But we would, I know you.' She reached. 'See—already! No, darling,' she said firmly.

For a few moments she limply accepted my despairing embraces, moaning, as though reproving her own indulgence. Then a car, though with the whole street empty to it, drew up just a little way behind, its headlights flooding us, and she wriggled free.

No, I couldn't bear to let her go. Darkness would blind me, nothingness swallow me up. As a child at bedtime seeking a last respite, I clutched blindly and came up with an inspiration to detain her for one more precious moment.

Shaking with exasperation, she took the photograph from me. 'Quick then! Give me your pen.'

Standing in the roadway, she inscribed the picture against the roof of the car; then she threw it, with the pen, on the empty seat beside me, and ran up the path, key already in her hand, heels dagger-sharp.

I slammed shut the door and switched on the ignition; but I couldn't go. I sat gripping the steering-wheel as though on a mountain switchback, shivering uncontrollably. The car that had parked behind came slowly forward, and I had an impression of the driver, at a lefthand wheel, peering in curiously at me as he passed. The agony of my sexual longing was like a wound that's painless but irrevocably mortal. And in the end one's left with nothing but self-contempt for one's weakness in succumbing.

As no light appeared at her window, an insane jealousy propelled her, snickering with anticipant lust, through another door—Adrian's?—evidently left by pre-arrangement on the latch.

The light came on in a moment. Some perversity made me vow not to look, and when seconds later I lifted my head, her upraised arms were closing the curtains with symbolic finality.

I crashed home the gears. My groin was tender, my reflexes deranged, and the ache in my forehead was now a sharply thrusting probe. I drove with mindless abandon. Couldn't be bothered to garage the car and left it slewed across the courtyard like an accident.

I picked up the photograph. At any other time the playful lewdness of her inscription with its accompanying ideograph would, doubtless, have provoked a tender merriment; but I was still beside myself, still, I suppose, for all practical purposes out of my mind. I tore her picture across, as I did so experiencing such a sharp satisfaction that it sobered me; that it frightened me. Even empty gestures of violence were foreign to my sensibility.

The porter must have heard the slam of the car-door — which probably made its way as thunder or gunshot into a number of flat-dwelling dreams — for he was unusually wide-awake, and stood to attention even as, with the two halves of the photograph screwed in my hand, I mounted the steps.

'Oh, Mr. Carpenter! Mr. Carpenter, you're here!'

What the hell was wrong with the man? One madman was enough! He stood facing me, waving dolphin-flappers, moon-face voicelessly opening and closing.

I followed his gesticulations over the spiky protrudences of the water-sculpture to the couch, dream-distant at the end of the silent, deserted lobby. And Ossie rose to greet me.

The carpet was a bank of dry sand, dragging and precarious. It took me an inordinate time to cross it.

'Hullo, Larry boy.' His proffered handshake unaccepted, Ossie converted the movement into a comradely slap on the shoulder.

An elongated shadow at his master's side, Blanco hovered, poised to spring on command.

Be still, my heart, be still. 'What the hell do you want?' I demanded, pleased at the levelness of my voice. 'What are you doing here? This time of night!' My voice rose. 'It's intolerable. How long have you been hanging about?'

Though retaining his welcoming smile, Ossie looked reproachful. 'We only just got here, Larry, only just before you. That right, Blanco?' He didn't look towards his companion and didn't wait for confirmation. 'We sort of reckoned you wouldn't be long, Larry.' His gaze fell to my hand which I held clenched against the side of my chest. 'Is that her photo you got there?'

Despite myself, I opened my fingers and looked. 'What do you mean?' I said. 'What do you mean—"her photo"?'

'What's that, Larry?' He appeared surprised. 'You must have misheard me. A photo, I said. That's all I said: is that a photo you got there? That right, Blanco, you heard me? Well, anyone could see.' He peered down at the two scraps in my open hand. 'Why, you've gone and torn it, Larry. You've had an accident.'

Choler replaced my trepidation. The alarm I had felt at first on entering and seeing him had been merely an irrational fur-raising reflex, as a cat to a dog, or to the suspected presence of a spirit. 'And what's he doing here?' I demanded, prodding my finger at the tall, unsmiling Negro. 'He was here yesterday, too, wasn't he? And ...' Parts slotted into place. 'And he's been following me. And this afternoon, that woman ...' I broke off: the parts had slotted into place to make a construction I found incomprehensible.

Ossie turned to Blanco for the first time, murmured something in his ear which I couldn't catch and sent him away with a gentle push. 'Just the two of us now, eh Larry!' He smiled placatingly. 'That better?'

I dropped the scraps of the photograph in my pocket. 'Do you know what the time is?' I said weakly. 'You've got a bloody nerve pestering me this time of night.'

'Not night, Larry, morning.' Ossie smiled more broadly, revealing what was, presumably, a brand new mouth of teeth.

'You're a hard man to get hold of, see. Lead a busy social life, or so they tell me.'

'And what the hell's that got to do with you?'

'Now, Larry.' There was hurt in his lupine eyes. 'You don't have to be touchy. Not with me, you don't.'

I looked away – and was just in time to witness the pantomime being played out at the door, as Blanco, staring balefully, hovered above the porter until, with surly reluctance, he rose from his chair and held the door open. My temper a trifle improved, I asked my visitor again, calmly, what he wanted. 'If you've come for your suit . . .'

'My suit!' Ossie chuckled. 'I've got a million!' He squared his shoulders complacently. He was wearing, over an immaculate white silk shirt, a midnight-blue suit of heavy, downy material, with wide lapels, artfully cut to camouflage his paunch and giving him a broad, box-like appearance. He was freshly barbered, with a strip of pink sticking plaster lying along a shaved path across his scalp. 'My suit,' he repeated. 'Tell you what, you keep it as a souvenir, Larry. I just come to see you was all right. You had them injections yet?'

'What?'

'Injections, like I told you. All that shit in the river, you got to look after yourself.' With a movement which I remembered, he thrust his head close as though in threat. 'No one else will, Larry, no one will do it for you. Not in this rotten, stinking world, they won't.' He paused and shifted away. 'That's a funny creation, ain't it?' he opined, nodding in the direction of the sculpture. 'Just like a bleeding octopus.'

Dumbly, I followed his gaze; and then I felt myself suddenly rolling. I had that impotent, insubstantial sensation I had experienced in the nightclub – that I had become merely a figment in another's dream-world.

'Eh! You all right, boy?' Ossie took me by the arm and drew me down on to the couch. 'You should have had them injections. Or maybe you've been living it up a bit, eh?'

Seated, I felt a little better. I shook my head to clear it, and concentrated on re-establishing my familiar identity.

'Know who I am, don't you?' I heard a solicitous voice. 'I'm the geezer what was pulled out of the drink. And you—you're the geezer what did it, Larry.'

'Well,' I said wearily, conscious again of the stabbing pains behind my eyes, 'if you would tell me what I can do for you . . .'

A wave of curry-breath sprayed me as my companion snorted indignantly. 'Not *you* do for *me*, Larry. I'm the one what's obligated, ain't I? That's why I'm here now, isn't it, and to hell with the bleeding time! The question is: what can *I* do for *you*, Larry?'

There was a pause. Perhaps, after all, it was a dream of my own, merely cast and staged differently from the usual run of my dreams. In that case, of course, it would be my companion who was the abstraction. 'How did you know?' I asked, with cunning. 'How did you know me?'

'I reckon that's irreverent.'

'I beg your pardon. Oh, I see. No, I think it is relevant. I want to know, how did you find me?' I remembered the black dancer in the shadows and the face above the ice-cream cone. 'I'm aware you've been having me followed, but in the first place, how did you know . . .' The question seemed not merely relevant, but of supreme importance. 'How did you know who I am?'

'You don't remember, Larry?' I shook my head. 'Right at the start, there on the bank, you told me, Larry. Carpenter, you said, Laurence Carpenter.'

'Yes,' I said, 'but . . .'

'And then back at my place, you spelled it out: name and abode and occupation. You don't remember? All about yourself?'

It was difficult to doubt his assurance. I must have done what he said I had done. But, yet, I could not quite recall . . .

'You remember now, Larry.' His relief had a childlike

72

freshness. But, assuming I had, that posed another question: the why and the wherefore. 'That's the why and wherefore of it, Larry. Seeing as you told me so particular, spelling it out.' He spoke eagerly. 'That's why I reckoned a geezer like you, respectable, boorjuice—no offence!—you wouldn't be wanting a rough bastard like me for a friend, social like. So I reckoned, as you told me so particular . . .' He lowered his voice to a hoarse whisper. 'It had to be because you wanted me.'

'Because . . . I wanted you!' I repeated.

'And because you needed me.' He pressed close to my side. 'My offer. Because of my offer. You haven't forgotten that, have you? Friend!'

I shook my head again, and felt the probe skidding agonizingly deep into my cranium. 'For God's sake! For God's sake, you can't imagine I took that bloody nonsense seriously. You can't imagine that.'

I was unaware that I had shouted until Ossie nodded conspiratorially in the direction of the door, and I met the porter's open-mouthed gaze. The porter looked away with fatuous innocence.

Ossie clapped me on the shoulder. 'Larry boy, I know, I know, you're proud. You don't like admitting nothing, you don't like asking no favours, do you. I respect that, sincerely I do. And tell you why, because I'm like that myself, ain't I. I don't like asking no favours, neither. I got my pride, too. And that's why I don't like being obligated. Now I'm obligated to you, ain't I, 'cause you saved my life, and I'm grateful, don't let no one tell you different.' It was a swift, hypnotic street-trader's patter, calculated to lull. 'But just supposing, some day in the way of business, I might have to carve you up. Or I might fancy charvering your lovely wife. Well, I'd like the slate to be clean then, wouldn't I, I wouldn't want to be owing you no reciprocal favours.' He evidently misinterpreted my incredulity. 'That's just a joke, Larry, no offence. I know you got a sense of humour—one of the reasons why I like you. Fact is, it's not only because

73

you hauled me out of the water. I want to do something for you because I like you—honest to God!'

He put his mouth very close. 'Who'd you want it to be, Larry? Just tell me. Just tell me the name.'

Still, heart, still! I drew on all my resources. 'There is *nothing* you can do for me. Nothing at all. How many times have I got to tell you? I . . .' There was a patronizing knowingness in my companion's smile which destroyed my determination to remain calm. 'Absolute fucking nonsense!' I exploded. 'For God's sake, get it into your thick, ugly head, I don't want you to . . . there's no one in the world I want . . .' My voice died on me.

Ossie drew back, but not out of offence; he spoke in a tone thick with gentleness and consideration. 'All right, Larry, I know, I know. I'm perceptive, like I told you. Geezers like you, well brought up, what you might call civilized, sometimes you're a bit in'ibited. You don't like coming out with it, do you? You keep it all buried inside.' He stood up and regarded me with speculation. 'You don't want to be like that though, Larry. It goes rotten in your guts, like a load of sour apples. It goes rancid on you.' He appeared to be contemplating adding to this, but then, with a comradely nod of the head, turned about. 'Be seeing you,' he said. 'Look after yourself, friend. Mind how you go.' He walked away.

I was alone. Perhaps, if I closed my eyes for an instant—like this—I would find that it had never been otherwise, and the preceding dialogue had all taken place inside my head.

But when I opened my eyes this comforting illusion was dispelled. Ossie had halted beside the artificial pond and stood regarding the sculpture with the same speculation as he had just accorded myself. 'Like a bleeding octopus!' he murmured. He was amused, and at the same time absolutely confident of the accuracy of his assessment.

4

In plays and films and, usually, novels, it's different. A character undergoes a remarkable experience, and his existence is so concentrated that that experience dominates all his subsequent actions, excluding all the petty business of his day-to-day routine. He can give up going to work, there are no bills outstanding, acquaintances unconnected with his crucial situation just fade away . . .

That's in an artificial world. Unless it is—and these were the thoughts I had as I drove homeward—that it's the life we've made for ourselves which is artificial, cluttered with so much meaningless garbage it's impossible to get at, to fix one's attention on, the really significant happenings. Occupied as I had been throughout the day, I had scarcely given a thought to the encounter of the previous night, which at the time had seemed so extraordinary; nor, for that matter, to the spectres of my own imagining which had then assumed such prominence.

Were they all unreal? Or was this—the growling, crawling by-pass, the cardboard factory façades, the tin creature I occupied, heaving to my toe or hand?

I should say that I not infrequently indulged in such quasi-metaphysical reflections on my homeward journey. It was only this time, as I was garaging the car, that it occurred to me that these skatings around the periphery of things might also be a form of avoidance.

'Oh!—Mr. Carpenter. Excuse me.' With uncharacteristic eagerness, the clerk ran from his desk to intercept me in the middle of the hall.

For no discernible reason, there was a frantic busy-ness, with people rushing to and fro as at a railway station; and a schoolgirls' secret society was holding a coven beside the pond.

'I've heard from the Management Committee, sir.' He radiated cheerfulness. 'Reference your complaint.'

The porter emerged from a doorway I'd never known existed and started towards the lifts but amended his route.

The clerk gave a chuckle of pure happiness. 'And I'm afraid, sir, that while they naturally regret any disturbance to which you might have been subjected, they cannot accept that the music constitutes a nuisance, under the terms of the lease.'

'Music!' I said. 'Lease!' I said, wondering how it was that I'd previously never noticed that this insolent little runt was a pederast of the most blatant type. 'Did you say music?'

'Not under the terms of the lease,' the clerk repeated.

Mind you, not that I've anything against pederasts as such, but. 'Not a nuisance! Those bloody drums, day and night, driving me out of my head. Not a nuisance!'

Rubbing his hands on his filthy apron, the porter now stood beside us, mouth ajar.

'So I'm afraid the Committee feel, sir, they can take no action in the matter.'

'They don't, eh?'

'I fear not, sir.'

'Explain to me, if you would,' — I spoke urbanely — 'what makes you look so deliriously happy?'

'Sir?'

'You blatant lit ... Oh, never mind!' I swung about; and swung about again. 'And you can tell your precious committee that if they don't take any action, I damned well shall. If I have to take the law in my own hands!' And swung about yet again ...

Two-thirds of the schoolgirls' sabbath followed me into the lift, and there was a lively disputation around the control-panel. Shrill cries accompanied the lift's inadvertent descent to the basement. I shouldered my way to the panel and was half-aware that something in my expression muted the girls' gay chatter, and, as the lift rose again, placed me in the centre of an uneasy, nudging conspiracy. I was relieved to escape and to return to the sanctuary of home.

'My gorilla!' A drawled and saccharine throatiness made

Sarah's voice unrecognizable. Holding the two pieces of the photograph together, she pretended to read the inscription. 'For my greedy gorilla, with his great thing . . . Ugh!' She made a sound of deep disgust.

To my intense chagrin, I felt a slow shamed blush flooding my face.

'She sounds,' said Sarah, in her own voice again, 'a jolly girl, your little Miss Jackie, whoever she may be.'

'So you've taken to snooping now, have you!' Humiliation added to my belligerence; it was intolerable, intolerable that I should be made ashamed of Jackie and her sweet playfulness. 'I hope you're proud of yourself.'

'And I hope,' said Sarah inevitably, 'that you are proud of *yourself*.' She allowed the pieces of the picture, too disgusting to hold any longer, to flutter to the carpet. 'I wasn't, incidentally, snooping, as you call it. You left it where I was bound to see. Careless of you, I would say.' The pieces of the photograph lay face upwards, ignored by us both, but not disregarded. 'Unless that's what you intended. Or unless it was some form of Freudian lapse – perhaps a confession.'

I said nothing.

'Or a challenge to me.'

This proposition I ignored.

'I wonder why you tore the picture. Surely you weren't ashamed of it?'

I still said nothing.

'Who is she, anyway, your latest? I mean, I know her Christian name – unless it's just the name she uses, professionally that is. And I know that her draughtsmanship doesn't match the dirtiness of her mind. And I know that she dresses like . . .'

'Sarah, please!'

'. . . an over-sexed, delinquent schoolgirl. And has the general appearance of a cheap . . .'

'Sarah!'

77

'. . . ignorant, mean-spirited little . . .' Whichever of the two or three possible words she had been about to utter was held back. She opened her eyes very wide. 'And I know that you think you're in love with her, don't you, Laurence?'

'I don't very much wish to discuss my feelings.'

'This past month, six weeks—is that right? Like a silly schoolboy. You've been going round in a sort of crazy dream, and do you suppose I hadn't noticed?'

'It's immaterial to me whether . . .'

'Oh, poor Laurence!' Sarah made an odd, irrelevant sort of gesture, tapping her forehead with all five fingers of her spread hand as though dabbing on powder. 'To find yourself . . . obsessed. At your age. Obsessed—that's a better word than love, because you're not really capable of love. Poor Laurence, at your age, to fall for, evidently, such a cold and selfish little bitch! Who'll probably castrate you, who'll eat you up. Poor Laurence —you've had your little adventures before without getting involved, and now . . .'

'Do I have to remind you?' I interrupted dangerously.

'. . . and now to find yourself, at your age, infatuated with . . .'

'As you must remember, the first little adventure, in your happy phrase, was not mine.'

Sarah blinked. 'Yes, you were bound to bring that up, weren't you?'

'That it wasn't I who first betrayed.'

'You always do, as though it excused everything. As though . . .'—she whispered—'because I once hurt your pride, you have the right, the obligation, to go on hurting me for ever.'

'Just,' I said, without looking at her, 'so long as you remember.'

'Oh yes, I remember. You don't ever let me forget it.' This was the point at which she began to lose control of herself. 'And why I did it. Once. One man. And the way you'd behaved that made me. The way you . . .'

It was a wearisomely familiar lament. I closed my eyes as

though by that I could close my ears. There are times when life seems only an unending downpour of shame and pain; and that the very best one can possibly hope for is a momentary diminution of their intensity. Sarah's voice rose. She paced the room, her cheeks flushed. From beyond the wall began the monotonous, hysterical beat of the bongo-drums.

'Stop it. Stop it,' I cried at length. I tried to catch hold of Sarah but, with a flashing ugly grin, she evaded me, putting a table between us.

'So my one infidelity, which you not only condoned but even instigated, provided the excuse for you to wallow in a succession of squalid little affairs. And now at last—I can't help laughing— you're caught yourself. Because you're frightened you're getting old and past it—I can't help laughing—you've let yourself become obsessed by . . .'

'I said, stop it.'

'. . . a girl who's young enough to be your daughter. After all your years of using women, abusing them, and now you find yourself—I can't help laughing—blushing and sweating for some . . . Vicious. Delinquent. Little. Slut.'

'Stop it! Stop it!' Fists raised, I rushed across the room. When my blows produced no effect, I seized the statuette of the Balinese goddess and, careless of the damage to the paper, hammered it against my neighbour's wall.

The drumming ceased. I turned about with an air of triumph. But, meanwhile, Sarah had departed, locking herself in the spare bedroom.

Slowly I stooped to pick up the pieces of the photograph. My heart was still beating poundingly. I regretted the direction our quarrel had taken. Sarah's infidelity, to which I had so tactlessly referred, had occurred some years before, at a gloomy alcoholic party. This escapade—her partner an inoffensive Australian dentist we knew only as Wal—had taken place on a bed bumpy with the guests' coats, and afforded her, I believe, but slight physical gratification. Subsequently, it's true, I sometimes excused my own adventures with mild apology and laughing reference to Cobber Wal. But these were decorous, transient affairs, and we never discussed separation or divorce. Speaking for myself, I was satisfied with the convenience of our situation, and was in truth greatly surprised when one night Sarah told me how she carried in her heart, as after a bereavement, an impossible dream of re-creating that which once had been. She stayed, she said, with me, she said, not in content, but because of the tyranny of habit, from guilt, her fear of uselessness; and then, in a small voice curdled by self-loathing, confessed how sometimes when we slept together she thought of the girl I had, perhaps, just come from or was, perhaps, just going to, and derived excitement from her own humiliation. After that conversation, I abstained from references to Cobber Wal and exercised discretion about my own exploits.

Now, I supposed—I juggled the two halves of Jackie's picture together on my spread palms—it was Sarah's intuition of my present passionate involvement, rendering her abasement intolerable, which had driven her finally away from my bed.

I put the pieces of the photograph in my pocket. From the spare bedroom came the sounds of drawers and cupboards being opened and closed—though not of course, Sarah being who she was, slammed.

Pouring myself a drink, I lay down, aching, on the couch, and let my thoughts, without conscious direction, continue their exploration of the stony inclosure of our marriage. Call it weakness or not, but I found myself luxuriating in a wash of regret. Shame and tender memories of what had been between us threatened to submerge me. Most particularly, and inopportunely, I regretted, to the edge of sudden tears, our childlessness, feeling a profound lack; and I had a sentimental vision of myself in the role of father. However, it was too late now . . .

But, no, it wasn't. My thoughts abruptly changed direction: the tide of regret retreated, leaving only a trail of rubbishy, useless recollections. It wasn't too late, not . . . not if I were to make a new start. Elsewhere.

It was then, I think, as I lay supine on the couch, that the notion of liberty, of attaining my freedom, first assumed a definite shape. I believe that there was a spectacular sunset over the river, which filled the room with a red glow, and I remember clearly a nearby radio relaying the oom-pah-pah oom-pah-pah of martial music. From the spare bedroom there came no further sound.

5

With that quarrel, the relationship between Sarah and myself entered a different stage. I was, naturally, altered by my new ambitions, though I kept them private, and I dare say that, if I'd paid sufficient attention, I would have observed that her attitudes had undergone a comparable change.

However, in the succeeding days we mostly went to some pains to avoid each other. When this became impossible, the space between us had a cold ice-like fragility which caused us to move with unnatural caution, for fear of the sudden crack which might open under our feet. There were also sullen, rancorous silences.

Then, Sarah announced that she had arranged to go away on holiday: she would stay with an old college friend and her husband who owned a cottage in Brittany. Strangely, when she told me this, I experienced a momentary qualm of dismay; but this was quickly succeeded by relief and pleasurable calculations for the exploitation of my temporary freedom.

'I'll get everything in order before I go. I'll stock you up with food. One of the porters will clean the flat for you, if you tip him. I take it,' she added with brisk formality, 'that you have no objection.'

'Of course not. Of course not. You're absolutely free to do whatever you like.' Even old Cobber Wal himself: I didn't say that, naturally.

'Or perhaps,' Sarah suggested, 'you might prefer to go away yourself. You have some leave still due, haven't you?'

I was ahead of her, already lying on a pearly beach with Jackie's oiled body glistening beside me. Or sitting, knees pressing, in some shadowed pavement-café – say, in Paris. No, better not Paris; too close. Copenhagen? Amsterdam?

'It's a possibility,' I replied cautiously. 'I might be able to get a few days off.'

There was no doubt in my mind. I was, indeed, projecting

more ambitious plans. M.B., however, raised unforeseen objections. One, specified, week was the most that he would allow me, and that only after I had fabricated a story about a dying aunt of Sarah's.

Still, a week, a whole week, offered prospects of an indulgence, a permissive bliss hitherto unexperienced. Amsterdam, I had decided: a setting sophisticated enough to satisfy Jackie's tastes, yet not too exotic seriously to distract from the matter in hand. I rushed to tell her.

She was rushing to tell me. 'I've got that T.V. part, after all. The other girl dropped out. My agent 'phoned this morning.' Her eyes shone under longer-than-usual lashes. 'Of course the producer wanted me all the time. It was just that the other girl was cheaper.'

That afternoon all her gestures were over-size; throughout lunch she talked about 'the Stage' and associate matters in a voice which carried to surrounding tables. She was contemptuous of the play in which she had been cast, although it was a consolation that her part, if not the longest, was, actually, the best thing in it. Actually.

She chattered on: 'Only two weeks for rehearsals. I know it's just a wretched little telly thing but. Only two weeks for a fifty-minute production! Two weeks,' she trilled, 'darling, I ask you, what sort of shambles do they expect?'

'And which two weeks,' I dolefully asked, certain I already knew the answer, 'which two weeks will these be?'

I was right. But then I was very wrong.

'You mean, I should give up the part.' Incredulity stretched her voice to a squeak. 'Just so you can screw me in some dreary Dutch hotel. I don't think you take my career seriously, do you? I don't think you really want me to succeed, or you'd never have suggested.'

'Of course I do. Of course I do. I wasn't thinking. I didn't really mean.'

'That's what it sounded like.'

'I know how dedicated you are,' I affirmed. 'Like all good actresses, like all true artists.'

Jackie allowed herself to be mollified. 'But I don't see the difficulty, sweet, anyway. I mean, after the recording Sarah will still be away, you said. You'll just have to alter your leave a week.'

'Ye-es.'

'Well, can't you?'

'Yes. Though it might be a little . . .'

'But why it matters whether your wife's away or not, I can't understand. You're a grown man, aren't you?'

To which there was no satisfactory answer. 'I'll fix it, you'll see,' I promised, and cast around for the waiter.

Champagne was the only drink appropriate to her actress-y mood and matching the holiday spirit which had already overtaken me. The bubbles rose like good deeds in our glasses. I toasted her dramatic success; and she with a pretty grace, smiling over the rim of her glass, whispered throatily: 'To our sexy week, darling. To Amsterdam!'

'Hull . . . Halifax . . . Aberystwyth . . . or Khatmandu – I don't care . . .' – M.B. thrust forward a chapped and tuberous lower lip – 'where you've made plans to go to. I call it damned cheek. You're not going next month and that's flat.'

'But I . . .'

'No buts. You take your leave when I say you can take it, when the company can spare you, and if you don't like it . . .' M.B. leaned back. 'Anyway, what's Amsterdam to do with your wife's aunt?'

'What?' His bluster had confused me; he had never spoken to me like that before. 'Oh, the Dutch side of her family.'

'Well, I'm sorry to disappoint your good lady. She'll just have to make the trip alone.'

I turned away.

'Laurence.' He waited until I faced him again. 'Your own fault; you shouldn't have presumed.'

I thought I knew for the first time the actual taste of bile: I swallowed.

'A grand girl, Sarah, I'm very fond of her. But she'll understand when you tell her, she knows business is business, where the salary cheques come from.' He paused to see if his more benign tone had worked a reciprocal mollification. It hadn't. He again pushed forward his lip. 'You can't just go off during the audit. Then straight after that, as you know, there's the overseas salesmen's conference . . .'

My attention was turned off. The loss of 'our' week, of Amsterdam, ached like a torn internal membrane. Perhaps in order to distract myself, I conjured up tableaux of self-assertion. I pick up that ashtray of nauseous pipe-dottles and hurl it in liberation through the window. I curtly resign, dropping some symbol of servitude contemptuously on the leather-bound blotter. The inner censor withheld his licence for these productions. But then I thought of another, more practical, way to bring the senile charlatan to heel: I would nonchalantly disclose the existence of my 'opus'. True, there were still details to be worked out; true, I had been conserving it to impress when the Board vacancy arose . . . but the temptation was almost irresistible – to shut off that spurious short-vowelled rasp, to hear his shamed recantation.

'Laurence?' A sharp interrogation in the inflection captured my attention. 'Laurence, I said, what's the matter with you these days?'

'The matter?' Nothing that your extinction wouldn't put right. 'Nothing that I know of.'

M.B. took up his pipe. 'Sit down again, lad. I've a few more things I want to say.' He took his time lighting the pipe. 'Seems to me you've lost a bit of your edge.' A cloud of rich, blue smoke gusted over me. 'This past month or two, not so . . .' — he sought for a word in the smoke — 'dy-nam-ic. What do you say?'

'I don't think so.' I had never considered myself dynamic.

'*I* think so.' He leaned into the smoke like a Guy on the bonfire. 'You've done passing well here, lad. Your own way of getting things dun, your own . . . style, if you like. It's not my style, but then I'm an old fogey. You think I'm an old fogey, don't you, I know.' He allowed no time for my lying disavowal. 'Still, that's the proper way of things, the keen young dogs snapping at the heels of the old . . .' He sought again for a word, failed to find it. I suddenly felt, with a great weariness, that the whole world of industry and commerce was a giant playroom constructed solely to permit grown men to re-enact their nursery games. 'Lost your edge, lost your keenness . . .'

Those old alarm bells started to ring: the same bells that, heavily sweating, a schoolboy had heard outside the head-master's study; and the conscript frozen at attention before the Adjutant; and the drink-oozing motorist when the police car . . . A sudden tremendous consuming fury, compounded partly of apprehension but more of resentment, rose in my throat chokingly. I felt myself begin to rise from the chair. One cleaving blow — with the telephone, with that befouled ashtray — could obliterate the headmaster's unctuous frown, split the captain's skull down to his painted moustache, transform the policeman's enormous face into a crimson mash of bone. An elbow nudged me confidentially, and a hoarse voice whispered in my ear: *Who'd you want it to be, Larry? Just tell me the name.*

Still, heart, still! I fought to keep contact with reality.

'Sit down. I haven't finished yet.'

My bottom was again tight upon the cushions. I felt the nails of my right hand repeatedly jabbing into my palm. I looked at my hand with curiosity, and then laid it flat on my tense thigh.

'I may be an old fogey, but I keep my eyes open, I know what's going on. Like these long lunches you've taken to indulging in lately.'

'It's never been the policy, as I understand it, for executives to punch a time-clock.' I heard my words with some surprise; their lack of discretion troubled me. 'Sir,' I added.

'Happen so, happen so.' The old man looked suddenly bored and vague; and sad, so that one less provident might have been tempted to expend pity on him. He laid his cold pipe in the ashtray's dust.

'If that's all, sir . . .' I rose.

He allowed me to get as far as the door. 'And another thing . . .'

'And another thing . . .' I said. I had reduced Lydia to a quivering, rustling speechlessness, and even the silverplate coating of Harvey's self-complacency was showing signs of tarnish. I enjoyed particularly the pulsing of a fine but agitated tic under his left eye. Nursery games! 'And another thing, the work of this department is confidential. I'm talking about security. Too much chattering . . .' — I glanced at Lydia — 'before the mirrors of the ladies' lavatory. Too much chattering — over saloon bar gin and tonics.' Harvey's left eye gave a most satisfying twitch. 'It's not just a matter of security. There's such a thing as loyalty. And trust.'

In my pause, Lydia gave a little hiccup of dismay.

Harvey cleared his throat. 'If there's anything specific, Laurence . . .'

'And the way in which we organize ourselves is no-one's concern but our own. That other day, when I went down to The Fridge, for instance . . .'

'The Fridge?' squeaked Lydia.

'The Works.' You stupid cow! 'I don't expect to be asked to account for my movements like an office-boy.'

That was a mistake. Harvey cleared his throat relaxedly. 'Has M.B. been getting on at you about that?'

'No. No. Not exactly,' I quickly lied. 'There was just something he said which . . .'

'His secretary came through asking for you,' said Harvey. 'I covered, of course. Naturally.' He gave a little laugh, all his cockiness recovered. 'Not a word about the golf-clubs.'

'Golf-clubs?' Lydia found her normal voice. 'You don't play golf.'

'But I told you,' said Harvey, 'the next morning. I remember quite distinctly. Told you, I was happy to oblige. After all, might want you to do the same for me some day.' He looked at me curiously. 'Don't you remember I told you?'

I nodded vaguely. It was strange how in a moment I seemed to have lost all my advantage: my seniority and the strength of my superior intellectual and moral capacity counted for nothing.

'Glad you remember,' said Harvey. 'I wouldn't want you to think . . . But of course you know me better than that, old man.'

As though I had delivered in inadvertence some shameful, ineradicable confession, the flavour of guilt lingered on my palate.

'What is all this?' Lydia whined. 'What is all this about golf-clubs?'

'And I'm sure Lydia wouldn't have let anything slip,' said generous Harvey, casually rising. 'Even by accident.' Bad nursery games! 'Have a choccy.' He opened a florid box under my nose. 'Liqueur centres. Anything could have happened, of course: M.B. might have been speaking to the Works himself. Or *vice-versa*. You never know, do you?'

At my desk, the taste of chocolate, though not unpleasant, failed to dispel the guilty acridity. I felt a weight of imponder-

ables piling up. It was a sensation I had experienced two or
three times before, on occasions of incipient disaster. Shapeless,
insoluble problems, self-multiplying, formed a honeycomb
construction whose waxy cells imprisoned me. There was some
peculiarly subversive malignancy in operation: I could feel
it burrowing away, even here at my desk, where, confident in
my skills and surrounded by loyal friends, I was accustomed
to feeling most secure. I thought, with a welcome, if bitter,
irrigation of humour, that I could do with a holiday.

Checking some returns, I was incensed when I uncovered an
instance of Harvey's carelessness, and realized that I had—at
least temporarily—surrendered the authority to admonish
him.

'What was all that about golf-clubs?' asked Lydia again,
after Harvey had departed—a presumptive ten minutes early.

Even she, out of some strange female resentment or jealousy,
might have deliberately betrayed me. I made an effort to dis-
miss my suspicions, and explained.

She gushed solicitude. 'But still,' she brightly consoled.
'you've your holiday to look forward to, haven't you? I do so
envy you. This time of year, it must be lovely in Amsterdam.'

It was with considerable apprehension, and the palliative of
the gift of a quite expensive cameo brooch, that I informed
Jackie that Amsterdam was off—or, rather, would have to
await a more accommodating future.

Naturally, I was pleased that she should take the disappointment so well, for to pain her—so young, so sensitive—was more
hurtful to me than my own regret. After my first relief I was
even a trifle piqued that she should not have been more
upset, but she was, of course, distracted by her television part;

which also accounted for her relative lack of appreciation of the brooch.

My visits to her room were for a time taken up by helping her to learn her lines, instead of our usual activities. Reading the other parts, I began to feel myself like an actor, or several actors and actresses in one, with a consequent dislocation of the personality, which left me strangely indeterminate. It added to my growing intuition that I was starting to leave my ordinary life, my accustomed self, behind.

One day she permitted me to call at the dingy hall where the rehearsals were taking place. I watched as the director—a chain-smoking woman, with scurfy hair—repeated a bedroom scene many times over.

The lines I knew by heart sounded quite different. Jackie in the oddly cast role of a naive and virtuous young wife was required to resist the importunate attentions of her husband's best friend, a part played by a hirsute young man for whom I felt a certain dislike.

They scuffled in horseplay which took them to the bed—for rehearsal purposes a battered couch with the stuffing leaking—whereupon Jackie, presumably detecting some un-actable development, cried suddenly: 'Jimmy, what are you doing? What are you doing to me, Jimmy?' Then promptly collapsed, feebly repeating: 'Stop it. Stop it,' with 'Jimmy' on top of her. At this point the—imaginary—door opened, and in came husband and husband's Calvinistic employer. Cut.

At the start a certain ribaldry attended the proceedings, but this gave way to a detached professionalism, and I found myself touched by Jackie's docile surrender to the demands of her art. It was as though, through some proleptic magic, I were seeing her at some distant point in time-past before our life-paths had converged, or I were being vouchsafed a glimpse of her existence in another incarnation. Or as if, flushed with paternal pride, I were watching my child engrossed in classroom play. Standing, as unobtrusively as possible, at the back of the dusty, echoing hall, seeing Jackie repeat her stylized movements, hearing her utter her banal lines, I felt a sandy prickling under my eyelids and had to blow my nose – which, to my embarrassment, drew an officious 'Shush' from one of the young men assisting.

I also felt my suspicions of 'Jimmy' mounting. Was it really necessary that he should fall on her so weightily?

It was the placing of the bodies on the couch that seemed most to concern the director. She took considerable pains in arranging Jackie's pliant limbs, pointing out, in language which surprised me, that her dress for the recording would reveal intimacies her present tights concealed. The ash dropping unregarded from her cigarette, she leaned over adjusting Jackie's buttocks. Jackie giggled: 'What are you doing to me, Jimmy?'

When she came up to me at the end, I babbled my praises. They were utterly sincere. I thought, at that moment, she should be a great star.

We accompanied some of the other members of the cast for a drink. The feeling I had had in the hall of being a detached outsider persisted in a less pleasant form, as they chatted among themselves about theatre matters in a shorthand which I could scarcely transcribe. As in the nightclub, I experienced the bleak sensation that Jackie and I inhabited divided hemispheres.

After initial introductions, she practically ignored me. I found myself talking with 'Jimmy', and it was, I suppose, in a childish effort to make an impression that I began to give an account of my river adventure. In order to extract the full value from the story, I described Ossie's version of how he had come to be in the river, and started to recount my subsequent dealings with him. As sometimes happens, although I had begun speaking to only one listener, I found that by the end I was holding the floor with several around me, and I started to grow confused, as though instead of retailing fact I was trying to tell a fictitious story I only half-remembered and whose conclusion

I had never learned. They were polite enough when at last I stuttered to a halt to make appropriate noises of interest, but they were quite unconvinced of the truth of my tale – as unconvinced as I now was myself.

It was 'Jimmy' who saved the situation. 'Ossie, did you say he called himself? I heard that name somewhere . . . in that sort of world . . . ' He screwed his eyes in recollection. 'A pretty rough club I was taken to, a hell-hole . . . A fellow was pointed out to me, someone warned me: they said he was the very last person in London I should ever cross, a real killer. I think he was called Ossie.'

'Jimmy's' intervention drew sundry comments and, happily, the attention away from myself. He and I went on to talk about cricket, in which we had discovered we had a mutual interest. At one point, however, he broke off to mutter: 'Ossie, yes, I'm near as dammit certain that was the name . . . Ossie!'

My gratitude to 'Jimmy' for his social consideration did not prevent me, when Jackie and I were alone together again, from mentioning my suspicions concerning the impersonality of his rehearsal embraces.

Jackie looked at me in innocent amazement. 'But you know – everyone knows – he's got this big thing going with . . . ' And she named a renowned theatrical knight. 'If you're so concerned about my virtue,' she added brutally, 'you ought to look sideways: any excuse and that old butch of a director's feeling me up.'

'You don't mean that she . . . ' I choked.

'Lovely hands she's got, strong and soft at the same time. I wonder,' reflected Jackie dreamily, 'what it would be like with . . . ' Her eyes focused on a remote vista. 'You idiot!' then she snapped, seeing my darkening face: 'I was only joking.'

So, with such light inconsequence, another false spectre was added to my daymare-terrors, which were perhaps the more potent and insinuating at that time for Jackie's refusal, on the plea of preserving her strength for her arduous art, to make love with me at all.

Instead of a murmured 'licence my roaving hands' or — with that madly aphrodisiac breathiness — 'my gorilla!', it became, playfully but firmly: 'Stop it, Jimmy. Stop it.'

6

Midway through Jackie's rehearsals, Sarah departed on her holiday. Our relationship now again correct, though colder, I drove her to the airport. Small, playful clouds chased across the sky on a bright, bustling morning. The traffic was heavy: in the space of a couple of miles we passed three accidents, at the last of which they were sprinkling sand, and a chalk-faced body wrapped in blankets lay at the roadside, under a garish hoarding.

I said: 'Isn't it funny—you can drive for weeks without seeing an accident, then suddenly you can't get away from them.'

Sarah didn't reply.

Just before we turned into the airport we came upon another collision, but this was only a minor affair, with the two drivers exchanging the customary threats and abuse. 'What was I telling you?'

It was also very busy at the airport, with an atmosphere of cheerful excitement as holiday-makers prepared for departure, bidding animated goodbyes, and occasionally stilling to listen, heads cocked, to the loudspeaker voices. 'K.L.M. announces the departure of its Flight 123 for Amsterdam.' I gritted my teeth.

Despite the road conditions, we had arrived with plenty of time in hand. I took Sarah for a drink. Having been unnaturally silent on the journey, she now became loquacious. We were sitting on stools side-by-side, not turning to each other, but facing ourselves in the mirror above the bar. Dressed smartly for her journey, her hair done in a new style, Sarah appeared an elegant, exotic stranger.

Then I realized that she, that both of us, had been silent for a few moments. Sarah was staring hard at our reflections. 'I feel in a false position,' she said suddenly. 'I am not me at all, and you are not you. We are just, if you like, casual acquaintances: I am a visitor to London, say, a visitor into your life, and now

94

you are courteously seeing me off. Seeing me out of your life. We don't know when or where or whether we shall meet again. Or even if we care to very much.'

I wanted to say something, but the first remark that occurred to me, to the effect that I had been thinking much the same, sounded vindictive, so I sought for more sympathetic words. I was looking straight in front of me, and I suddenly saw a third head in the glass, in suspension just between our shoulders. It disappeared as if twitched by a string, and I had to force myself not to turn about, for I had for a moment imagined that it had been the face of Blanco.

It was too late for me to reply to Sarah. She was saying: '. . . as much as the fridge will hold. Eat the fresh food before you open the tins . . . the milkman will expect to be paid . . . water my plants . . . the windows . . . the air-conditioning . . . And don't forget the laundry comes on Thursdays.'

She turned to me and took hold of my arm. 'One thing I would ask you, please.' Her fingers dug into my arm. 'Please, Laurence, don't ever bring that girl into our flat. Please.' She looked at her watch. 'I think it's time I should be going through.'

We left our stools. Plenty of coloured men were walking through the hall. There were three or four who moved with Blanco's dancer's casual elegance. I thought of the accidents — you could go weeks without seeing one, then . . .

'Please, Laurence,' said Sarah. 'Will you promise me? Please!'

I promised.

'Take care of yourself,' she said, reaching for the bag I had been carrying for her.

I stood watching as she went off among all the others hurrying to their holiday aeroplanes. Just for an instant, a matter of seconds, I didn't want her to go. In those seconds I was unable to move, and I had the strange sensation, as though I had lost a limb, of making an attempt at movement while at the same time being aware of its impossibility.

Sarah disappeared in the press of travellers at the gate, releasing me. I walked slowly away. In all this bustling throng, I thought tritely, there was no one who knew who I was, no one to care at all, with whatever ambivalence or even animosity. And I was acutely aware of the seemingly uncountable hordes of children—children coming, children going, children merely there—and mourned that none was mine. For the first time for ages, I found myself recalling the tender emotions I had experienced at the, remote, time of Sarah's pregnancy; and I raged again with the same bitterness at the bloody mischance which had put an end to our enthusiastic plans. In the months and years that followed, the project had ceased to be desirable or valid, but my lack of fatherhood seemed now a sorry deprivation—another form of limblessness.

I went back to the bar for what I intended to be a quick reviving drink, but I found myself lingering over it sluggishly, in fractured consciousness, the echoing diaphonics of the building reduced to a faint distant buzzing, so that I might have had wax in my ears.

By contrast, when I at last went outside, the roar of the aircraft taking off was exceptionally loud and even the slamming of car doors and the grind of changing gears seemed to rattle inside my head. At the car-park the smell of petrol in the sun broke over me in sickening waves.

I drove fast and badly, in a spirit of reckless immunity as though detached from the consequences of my actions. I had the sense of having been excavated. What made my emptiness so intolerable was that I had been anticipating Sarah's departure as an inspiration of freedom.

The car I was overtaking gradually gathered pace, so that I found myself slowly, as it seemed slowly, but then with increasing irresistible speed, heading towards the oncoming lorry, with no space for evasion. Quite distinctly, but without alarm, I saw the chalk-white blanketed figure under the garish hoarding, as at the last moment the car on my inside started to brake, allowing me room; and the lorry clattered past, its driver, with distorted face, shouting inaudibly. Safe: the sweat ran down my face and the back of my neck.

After that, I drove with excessive slowness, so that I was the object of protesting hoots from following vehicles. At a traffic-light, before I started to move away, the car behind sounded its horn in a playful carillon. A gangster's battered, black Cadillac drew out, and I seemed to remember somewhere, not so long ago, having been slowly passed before by a car that had been not dissimilar. This time the driver at the left-side wheel and his passenger, face black as the car itself, turned and waved. I braked and swore. And two stork-legged beauties in tight mini-skirt strut giggled and returned the salutes they had assumed for themselves. And the Cadillac roared off with a farewell tantara . . .

And when I arrived home what should I see in the forecourt, leeringly conspicuous among the unscratched saloons and the sleek sports-cars, but a battered, black Cadillac with a lefthand-drive? I averted my attention from it, as from a clumsy practical joke that had fallen sickeningly flat. Of course it was not the same car, and even if it had been it had no connection with myself. Yet omens without validity or relevance may still seem ominous.

When I opened the door of the flat I thought I heard a clattering noise from within—as though Sarah were busy about her kitchen chores. I almost called out to her, and in the succeeding silence railed at my unsteady nerves. My heart was set on having a shower—to feel the piercing, scourging needles against my tender skin. I tossed my jacket down and made for the bathroom, as from the kitchen emerged the moon-faced porter, carrying a blue bucket. He passed me with a silent nod.

I found my voice. 'What the bloody hell do you think you're doing?'

He had reached the front door. He turned slowly, gaping, and tilted sideways, borne down by the enormous weight of the empty plastic bucket. He is looking at me as though I am mad, as though I have no right to be here. Is this my flat?

The porter became indignantly voluble. Mrs Carpenter had told him . . . doing of a favour like – on top of all the other . . . And if Mr Carpenter wanted him to come regular he'd want some payment in advance, sort of . . . I picked up my jacket and opened my wallet.

Through the splash of the shower the telephone sounded distant. For a moment I made no move to answer it, letting the water continue to beat on my upturned face and channel into my arid mouth. Then I thought it might, it could, be Jackie. Nearly blind, I dripped a wet trail through the living-room.

For the joke's full flavour I should have been permitted to stretch my hand to the vibrating telephone before it went dead, but the timing was slightly premature and I was still half-a-dozen paces away when it mocked my nakedness with a truncated tinkle.

The impish joker hadn't finished with me yet; or, supposing there to be no malignant extra-mundane influence, I was still conjuring up my own demons. Dressed only in my underclothes and flapping shirt, I had a sudden impulse to ring Jackie, although she had told me she would be at the hairdresser's. As lovers do, I indulged the notion that the very conception of the thought was evidence that she was awaiting my call, had perhaps even demanded it telepathically.

When, after only three or four rings, the receiver was lifted, my heart leapt at love's omnipotence. 'Hoo Flung's Chinese Laundry,' said a sepulchral male voice.

I made noises.

'Hoo Flung's Chinese Laundry,' the voice repeated. 'Drop your drawers and get undressed.'

'What? I didn't quite catch . . .'

'I said, suits and trousers sponged and pressed.'

'Er!'

'Grab hold of this and give it a bite.'

'Is this some kind of a . . .'

'Double-bleaching overnight. Special cleansing removes all the muck . . .'

How long this might have continued I couldn't say. For one thing, an aeroplane roaring overhead—yet, yet again—obliterated the voice; for another, because my hands were sweating so profusely the telephone receiver had turned rubbery and I had difficulty in holding it to my ear.

I managed to straighten it and bawled out my questions.

'Adrian,' said the voice, in a different register. 'I'm Adrian, cock.'

'Where's Jackie? Let me speak to Jackie.'

' 'fraid that's not possible, sweetie. She's . . .' The same aircraft, presumably, now overhead at his end rendered the rest of the answer inaudible.

'What did you say?'

'Oh, let's not start all that again, shall we?'

I was suddenly surprised by the furnishings about me becoming nebulous and the walls blowing like curtains. These were the trick effects of a nightmare. But there were, it seemed, two nightmares proceeding simultaneously, one outside, one in.

'. . . you see,' Adrian was saying, 'when I heard the tinkle, and knowing our little darling was having it off, I mean her hair, the thought occurred I might catch him with the laundry. It would all come clean in the wash, so to speak. Rumpelstiltskin would . . .'

'What in sweet God's name are you talking about?'

'Old Rumpelstiltskin. The Bogeyman. Little Puffing Billy.' He sighed heavily—in such a way as to lead one to imagine his shaking his head with resigned forbearance. 'You know these calls the little pet's been getting. I'm talking about The Breather. And come to think of it, you're blowing pretty hard yourself, love. I suppose, after all, you're not him, are you, sweetheart— you're not The Breather?'

At this point, bemusedly returning to a world in which physical objects obey the natural laws, I lightly replaced the receiver. I had ceased to sweat; the walls were immobile; I blinked and the furnishings remained solid and defined. My hallucinations, coming with the apparent causelessness of summer lightning, though possibly presaging distant storms, had left behind a curious stillness. I had the feeling that I had made a descent into a whirlpool and what was terrifying about it was not the turmoil but the calm and emptiness at its centre.

Strain. Over-doing it. Or I'd got some kind of a bug—hadn't I somewhere been warned ... Perhaps, after all, I should have had those recommended injections. Absurd! That was days, weeks, ago—or was it months or years? Absurd, that business was all over.

The telephone rang again. I—still clownishly in my shirt-tails, remember—took a deep breath and, prepared for anything, announced myself firmly.

'Hullo, Larry. How're you keeping, friend? You had them injections yet?'

Prepared for almost anything—not quite that patness to my thoughts, as though a voice inside my head! 'What do you want?'—with effort I achieved.

'Rang a little while back,' Ossie carried on, regardless. 'But you wasn't answering. In the bath or shower or something, was you?'

'As a matter of fact, I was ...'

'Doesn't matter. Me, I've all the time in the world far as you're concerned, Larry. Just thought, seeing you're on your own like, we might arrange a get-together.'

'I'm afraid it's not poss ...' I swallowed. 'How did you know I was on my own?'

'Me, I like to keep apprised. Not one of your fair-weather friends, Larry, am I? I want to help you, I have to know your troubles, don't I.'

'I am not in any trouble. I do not require any help from you,'

I began with a weary sense of inevitability. 'I've told you before, I...'

'Still, only gone off for a holiday, hasn't she, your good lady. She'll be coming back, let's see, when is it?'

'Now look here, it's no business of yours when...'

'Oh, Larry! Larry!' cried Ossie with every sound of emotion. 'Larry, don't you go on trying to offend me. You know, your business is my business, manner of speaking.' He said it again: 'Your business, my business, Larry. Like you was my own twin-bruvver. Like you was myself.'

He paused, as if in anticipation of a reciprocal sentiment. Next door, just behind the thin plaster-board, against which I weakly leaned, soft hands began to caress the skin of the drums, with the implied muscularity of an orchestra tuning up.

'Dare say,' Ossie briskly continued, 'you got a date tonight, I wouldn't be surprised. Taking full advantage. I wouldn't want to put myself between a man and his 'ot dinner. Next week then.'

I moved away from the wall, stretching the telephone to the full length of its flex.

'Wednesday.'

'No.'

'Thursday.'

'No, I can't.'

'Friday then, it's a good night Fridays.'

'Not Friday. Not at all,' I thought I said. The drummer had now settled into his rhythm, still tapping lightly, but in a fast, frenetic tempo.

'And she'll be tied up Friday, your 'ot dinner, at them Studios then, that right?'

I made no answer, and in the silence I heard his bronchial breathing.

'That right, Larry, ain't it?'

'Hoo Flung's Chinese Laundry,' I said, my own words less audible than his because of the drums.

'What's that, Larry? Didn't catch.'

'Old Rumpelstiltskin.' The drums drumming, I giggling. 'You're Rumpelstiltskin, aren't you, Ossie?' I was delighted for once to have surprised him; my giggles nearly choked me. 'I know who you are: you're The Breather.'

The drumming rose to a crescendo. I banged on the already scarred wall with the telephone receiver. This had no effect. I let the receiver fall, crashing to the floor, and as it lay there I heard faint squeaks emerging from it as mice-squeaks from their hole.

Eventually I squatted and picked it up, putting it to my ear as I slumped my trunk against the wall. At that point the drumming suddenly stopped.

'. . . well that's fixed then, I pick you up your place . . .'

Holding the receiver away from my head I looked curiously at the punctured ear-piece. Punctured, yet still articulate. '. . . just this one occasion, Larry, you won't mind.'

The three small holes resembled crack-shots in the target's bull's-eye. 'Time's come you and me, Larry, time's come, it's in our stars, we got to know each other better.' There was a pause. 'Hey, Larry, you still there? Larry! Larry . . .'

The receiver clicked. I wondered what I was doing, sitting on the floor in my shirt-tails, holding a dead telephone. I wondered how long I had been sitting there, how long I had been holding it. I wondered.

7

'My 'ot dinner ... Are you my 'ot dinner, darling?' I lay beside her, my face against her side. Her heart was still beating thunderously.

'What ... What you say?'

'Doesn't matter.' I drew in my breath deeply, taking her moisture into my mouth.

Surprising myself, a coward become hero, I had practically raped her to overcome her abstinent devotion to her art. My fervour had contained such a hungry desperation, it might have been the last time I would ever enter a woman. Jackie was stirred to a grateful reciprocation and then at last delirium — despite her concern for her just attended hair. Now, lazily licking her armpit — that little spot was remarkably slow to heal — I would have been willing to die, like a drone-bee after its single, fatal ecstasy. I probably slept for a few minutes.

'What was that horrible expression — hot dinner? Where does that come from?'

'Did I say that?'

'Where on earth did you pick it up? Doesn't sound like you at all.'

'Someone,' I said, 'I must have heard someone.' I raised myself, feeling now less drone-like. 'Unless it was my other self,' I added with careless inconsequence.

'Don't look at me,' Jackie murmured, closing her eyes as I knelt above her. 'I must look dreadful. And my hair! You've ruined my hair, you ... ' She shuddered and let her body open. 'You gorilla! What are you doing now?'

The taste of her in my mouth seemed the taste of her essence, containing both her youthfulness and her mortality. In the pungent liquidity flowed the inner distinctive quality of her being and by absorbing it into myself I was merging our two spirits into an unalterable symbiosis. Jackie let out a shrill, piping cry . . .

'We must have made an awful noise. The whole house will have heard us.' She was passing, smeared and naked, by the foot of the bed, totally candid as though she had walked with precisely the same abandonment—shoulders slumped, belly forward, one hand scratching at the inside of her thigh—through all my fantasies since puberty. A greedy glint entered her eyes and she picked up the remains of a chocolate-bar and began to munch. 'You don't want any, do you? There's only two bits left.'

Chewing, she looked at me and snickered. 'Awful, I scarcely recognized you. I would never have thought you . . .' I flattered myself there was a look of wonder on her face. 'You really frightened me. Gorilla!'

She turned and pointed at my photograph with chocolate-crumbed fingers. Already beginning to curl at the edges, it occupied a central position among her pin-ups—like a currently favourite gramophone record on top of the pile. Then, bending over me—inert on the utterly disordered sheets—she, in fact, selected a record and put it on the turntable; and, although the song was different, I recognized the smoky voice as though it too had always occupied my dreams; while, wriggling her shoulders in time, Jackie crossed again by the foot of the bed and again, catching sight of herself in the dressing-table glass, cried: 'Oh, my hair! You've ruined my hair!'

She went up close to the glass, filling it with her lemon-white nakedness.

'Do you sleep,' I asked from a long way away, 'when I've gone, do you sleep in a nightdress?'

'And he'd done it so well. It looked so nice. Now it's ruined.' She seated herself, bare buttocks splayed, and began to brush her hair with vigorous crackling strokes, the strokes punctuated by little cries of frustration which seemed to counterpoint the rhythms of the record.

The man lying on the bed, salt in his mouth, his skin sticky and in places raw, closed his eyes and dreamed a delicious abstract dream. When I woke from it, after seconds, I had the sensation that I had just experienced unsullied content for the very last time in my life . . .

She had left the bathroom awash, the bath itself ringed with a communal grime, and I had only her soaked towel with which to dry myself. While, jigging on one foot and still very damp, I was attempting to dress, a man came up and tried the door, shouting and repeatedly rattling the handle as though finding it incomprehensible that the door should be locked.

'He probably thought it was me in there,' laughed Jackie to my complaint. 'Why didn't you answer him?' She laughed again. 'All that noise we made—you were trumpeting like an elephant—then we go and have baths, everyone certainly knows now just what we were at, the things you were doing to me.' She put out her tongue. 'I shall blush when I see them.'

But she didn't mean it; she was, I realized with a sudden insane fury, delighted; her candour no longer denoted an innocent animality, but a vile and perverse corruption. 'It's like a slum or a sty, this filthy house, the way you all live heaped together. A pigsty! A brothel!' I don't know what had come over me: all hatred is—it's dazzlingly obvious—a form of self-hatred. My explosion of outrage was unforced, and yet there was also something factitious in it, as though I had been merely seeking a pretext; but the great wave of bitterness, long dammed, which had burst within carried me onwards irresistibly.

As surprised as I was myself, she listened to my furious ragings without remonstrance, as if she found difficulty in taking them, in taking me, seriously. Only when I cited, as additional evidence of disgusting moral standards, Adrian's casual entry into her room to answer my telephone call, did she feebly protest: 'But you knew I was out, you knew I was at the hairdresser's, I told you.'

'That's scarcely the point. The way he walked in here, as though he had the right. Your room! Unless he was in here already. Even perhaps lying in the bed!'

Jackie began to laugh nastily.

'So bloody promiscuous and squalid. No respect! And then the way he spoke to me, sneering, a lot of damned nonsense. No respect, no dignity, no decency ... Stop laughing.' I gripped her by the arms. Still, heart, still! 'Stop laughing, will you. You filthy little slut!'

At that point I was seized with a sudden elation; whatever it was that, by chance, I had accomplished had fulfilled some deep unrecognized inner need, so that I was now closer to the free man I wanted to become. An electric charge flowed from the tips of my fingers biting deep in Jackie's bare arms. Where had that light come from, that pink light turning the whole room bloody?

'You're hurting me,' she whined.

And that metronomic thudding, like the bongo drums?

'Christ, you're hurting me!' she cried again.

Then suddenly the current through my fingers was cut off, so that my hands fell. When I opened my eyes the room was de-rubified. Time, which had been in suspense, made a skip forward—during which my heart-beats slowed to normal.

Jackie was rubbing her arms. She was staring up at me in a curious fashion, her eyes huge. There was a look on her face like a dark shadow. I lurched away and dropped down on to the bed, lowering my head.

Her arm appeared close before my face: in the redness where she had been rubbing were the imprints of my fingers, already darkening. 'I'll be all bruised,' she murmured. 'You really did hurt me, terribly.'

I was too ashamed to look up. I felt her hand on the back of my neck. 'It hurt like hell, you cruel sod, you!'

I looked up. Now her eyes had narrowed and her un-lip-sticked mouth hung open. Whatever she says to me, whatever censures, I deserve; whatever penance she demands, I shall fulfil with grateful humility.

'That's your little way, is it?' There came a tug of my hair, which in different circumstances I might have taken for flirtatiousness. 'You want to play games. Your secret desire, you want to hurt . . . you want to hurt poor Jackie.' I became aware of her biscuity odour under the soap's freshness.

'We'll have to see then, shan't we.' She moved jauntily away. 'Some day perhaps. But not now—not till after my play, anyway.' She turned her head towards me, drawing her tongue over her upper lip with a slow tantalizing lewdness which I swear was uncalculated, not—I'd go to the stake on it—not one of her tricky drama school devices. 'But perhaps . . . perhaps when I feel like it . . .' Her tongue curled upwards as though testing a cold-sore. 'Some day perhaps, when you've been a particularly good little boy . . .'

And what, apparently, being a good little boy implied at this present juncture was that in Sarah's absence I should admit Jackie into the flat. She had evidently set her heart on this. Up to a point I could understand it, and was even moved by her fancy: that she should wish to penetrate more deeply, more intimately, into her lover's life. But her insistence began to seem unreasonable: during the next few days, apart from brief stories of the production's ups and downs, she seemed scarcely to speak of anything else.

'To bring you closer to me, darling, so that when we're apart, I shall be able to imagine you better. I want to feel I really belong in your life, sharing everything.'

I offered various substitute treats, but to no avail. The trouble was, I had no convincing objections to pit against her pleas: I wanted it too, sharing everything. My scruples lacked all logic. So how could I explain them to her when I myself was at a loss?

It was not that I was unduly sensitive to Sarah's wishes; nevertheless, her quiet injunction at the airport seemed to have assumed something of the nature of a malediction, the flouting of which would summon unknown demons. Or it was as if— begging the Court's patience—some vestigial sense of propriety inhered, like the last good suit of a gentleman on his uppers, who knows that when that's gone it's downhill all the way. Ending in the gutter. Moreover, the accused had an obscure intimation that by admitting his mistress to the conjugal home, by, to speak frankly, enjoying carnal knowledge of her in the conjugal bed, or even more esoteric practices which had been augured, he would ... Very well, as Your Honour pleases. One doesn't want to explain, for God's sake! It's the defendant's privilege to keep his trap shut. Why don't I just stop the car and push her out?

'But it's your own flat, isn't it? I don't understand. I should have thought you'd have been happy for me to come, to have me in your own home, as though we belonged together.'

'We do, darling, we do!'

'Then what's the matter? What's the matter with me? Aren't I good enough? Are you ashamed of me? Do you think I'll contaminate it? Do I smell perhaps?'

'Oh, darling!'

'Don't touch me.'

There was the sound of breaking glass, and from a greasy alley ran two dark shadows, almost under the wheels of the car. A hundred yards further on, outside a public-house, one man was holding another by his lapels and shaking him backwards and forwards. Before we spoke again—before I spoke—I had seen a young girl vomiting in the gutter, and sprawled by the dustbins in a brilliant shop doorway the body of an old man with what looked like, but of course it couldn't have been, the haft of a knife protruding from the rags which swaddled his chest.

'I'm sorry, darling,' I said. 'Please forgive me. Yes, please come. I want you to so much.'

After that, it was all right. Naturally, she needed persuading —I mean, who wouldn't in the circumstances? She had her pride, too. But in the end she graciously, even tenderly, accepted. My pressing invitation. Not until the play had been recorded of course. I'd have to restrain. My boyish impetuosity until.

But everything was all right. I went home happy, happy.

Across the Atlantic, a wave of racial riots, the first of the bad summer, swept across the land; in other places, wars and tyrannies and famines continued; an assassin's bullets had struck down a young man who had represented the brave hopes of a generation which, however confusedly, wished the situation altered. All of these happenings were depicted on the television screen before which, in the empty flat, a bottle of whisky to my hand, I fell asleep, cachectic. I had a dream in which the cause and cure of the world's troubles—yes, one of those old things! —were revealed to me in a single conclusive apophthegm; and when I awoke from my waxen sleep, before the now dimmed screen, I heard myself saying: the gatling's jammed and the Colonel's dead.

Suppose the un-ticking electric clock—which hung in the kitchen, where I ran the water for my parched throat—suppose the clock were twelve hours fast, or twelve hours slow, how in one's solitude could one ever tell?

We are moved by random forces. Random and null. I knew I wanted to destroy.

8

There came a long letter from Sarah, the first she had written since she had gone away. To begin with, she described in cool detail her journey and how she had passed the early days of her holiday; but then—the difference in content marked by a difference in her handwriting: it grew jagged, the lines downcast, and towards the end was barely legible—in the succeeding pages she anatomized the structure of our marriage and the state of her present feelings. The tone of her analysis maintained the cool objectivity of the earlier pages, but the effect of this reserve, contrasting with the emotion revealed in her handwriting, was strangely foreboding, like a glittering sheet of ice under a fiery sun. Not that she accused or threatened; such blame as there was arose reluctantly, with reiterated apology, from her dispassion, and was equally distributed—even to the point of a self-derisive reference to Cobber Wal. What most disturbed me —reading conscientiously word by word, slowly because of its deteriorating cipherability—was the letter's gravity: it produced a sense of matters having reached rock-bottom.

Perhaps in self-defence, I applied the detachment with which one customarily reads a novel, so that I was impressed by its coherence and its insights, moved in an abstract way by the emotion it, restrainedly, 'reflected, and even found myself smiling inwardly at what might be termed its aesthetic qualities; yet the more expressive its style the greater the distance created between myself and the words—running away on their downcast lines from our involvement.

There was a P.S., comprising small domestic advices, and concluding: *I ask you again to remember your promise.*

I tore the letter into fragments and dropped them into the sink, turning on the tap and the waste-disposal apparatus to chop them up and flush them away, into the city's unimaginable sewers.

A few of the phrases and images from the letter still bubbled on the surface of my mind but I was determined quickly to forget them, while at the same time uncomfortably aware that — as with a tatty paperback left behind on the train seat at the end of a journey — some fragmentary elements would survive, perpetuated within myself, for I was no longer exactly the same man I had been before reading the letter.

I poked the last scrap of paper away with an eggy knife. Knocked a cup into the sink. Handle broken. Like a question mark. The last remaining thread gave way, and my cuff-button rolled under the bed.

It was not that the flat was excessively dirty or untidy, but everything seemed to be covered with a kind of invisible dust, producing an effect of abandonment and lovelessness. Before Jackie comes, I must get the porter to give it a special cleaning. And flowers. There must be flowers — for joy!

The porter was not at his post, and I had to wait for the clerk to conclude a lengthy telephone conversation, impatience throbbing in my rib-cage, an impending stroke.

'Yes, sir, I'll certainly tell him for you, but . . .'

'But, what?'

'Of course, I can't promise.'

Promise! What was a promise worth, for God's sake!

'As it's explicitly laid down that staff may only undertake private tasks if and when their normal duties permit.' Once, dare say, there was a time when service was willingly accorded, without grudge or servility. 'But I expect it will be all right, sir,' thinly smiled the clerk, picking up the notes I laid on the counter. 'And what kind of flowers would you have in mind?'

A long traffic jam delayed me still further. When at last the line of smoking cars moved forward, I came upon the minor collision which had caused the hold-up. One of the drivers, crimson-faced, was still dancing with rage in the roadway, his arms beating the poisoned air. What would he have done if he'd had his prick torn off instead of his bumper? Some day soon, I idly fantasized, some day soon that was how it would start: first, two at each other's throats, then all the drivers would leap as one from their stalled cars, falling on each other wordlessly, or else they might force their way through, their vehicles tanks bouncing in a crash of metal, and scything a path along the crowded pavements, until stopped at last by the steering-column rammed through the breast-bone, or when the mutilated survivors tore them from their seats and stamped them, before they in their turn would fall beneath the crushing wheels, or were consumed in the flames already swiftly spreading.

Had there also once been a time when the world was so empty that the existence of others was not an involuntary threat or an affront to one's manhood?

Harvey had perpetrated a blunder so egregious that I at first reproved him more in astonishment than wrath. It was only his indifferent, sulky shrug that roused my temper, and even then, I considered, I controlled myself, limiting my spleen to sarcasm.

He suddenly hissed at me, and in his eyes there was a strange look. He muttered something which I didn't catch, and went out, closing the door with an altogether unnatural lightness.

'Did I pitch it too strong?' I asked Lydia in surprise. It was unusual for me to plead for her reassurance; a warm flush signified her pleasure. She agreed that Harvey's conduct had been intolerable.

'Intolerable,' I echoed.

'But ...'

'But, what?'

Lydia shook her head.

'Go on.'

She moistened her lips. 'But I don't think you should make an enemy of him.'

'I don't understand you.'

'He could make trouble,' she muttered. 'You remember when you took that afternoon off ...'

'What afternoon?'

'When you . . .'

I remembered. 'Don't tell me it was Harvey . . .'

'. . . who went and told M.B. He might have done,' said Lydia. 'He could have. Else who?'

'But that's absurd. Absurd! Harvey! Harvey's too . . .' — too negligible was what I thought, but that was not the sort of word one could use— '. . . too decent. Besides, he's a friend of mine. And all I've done for him!'

Lydia, as was her familiar way, had begun busying herself, a sheaf of paper in her hands, shuffling it on the desk to align the edges. I suddenly saw again, as an hallucination, the naked look that had yellowed Harvey's eyes, like a jaguar's.

'I just think, that's all.'

Regarding Lydia, I felt I understood what led tyrants to execute those messengers who bore them unwelcome tidings. 'Think what, for God's sake! Clarify yourself.'

'Harvey,' she said, at the same time slapping down on a stapling-device with a sharp crack, which made all the pins and papers and oddments on the desk-top rattle. Then she looked me bravely in the eye and amazed me: 'You don't understand. Because you're such a kind man yourself. Yes, yes, you are,' she went on vehemently, as though I had denied it. 'You're good. You never want to hurt anyone.'

She blushed unprettily and ran from the room.

Well, it wasn't how Sarah had assessed me, and though flattered, truth to tell, it was not quite as I saw myself, however certainly I knew that in my heart I strove for goodness. As to that, the opposing forces were too numerous and too powerful. Alone in the office—there was no one left for *me* to close a door on—I felt a grey melancholy: a Zoo melancholy, yearning for that which I knew I would never find.

But—over the years one acquires techniques—I swiftly threw it off. This of all days was no day for wistful repining; and when I went outside, surprised by the mild limpidity of the light, my head was filled with visions of the night before me. Whatever my former, fatuous, reservations, the prospect of Jackie coming to my own home now produced intense excitement. There were no more taboos. I recalled precisely the drawling tone of voice in which she had murmured, 'if you're a good boy', and the sly suggestiveness of her upturned tongue. It was as though at last all my most unconstrained dreams were going to be fulfilled in a shameless reality.

With Jackie at the Studios, I had no desire for lunch. I thought I remembered a pleasant pub I had been to once, some-where in the maze of ancient alleys at the back of M.C.L. House. Walking with, as it were, my visions lewdly dancing around me, I was only marginally conscious of my surroundings, until I found myself in a street that had no right to be there. The tall, white glass-glittering buildings reared upwards as unexpectedly as a film-set in open fields. There were no familiar landmarks. The rows of dingy, crumbling shops and houses which I could now by a determined effort of memory recall had been entirely *consumed*. The effect was oddly disquieting, comparable to what one feels when people one has always seen in a particular form reveal themselves in an entirely different aspect. They have no right!

Literally lost, and craving for things to be as they had been, I turned about, and found myself on the edge of a desolate wasteland where the old buildings had been razed but no new construction had yet taken place. Most of the rubble had been cleared and there was a scarred and pitted surface of naked foundations and cracked paving, broken only by mounds of debris and collapsing workmen's shacks. The static expanse was veiled by, presumably, a cloud of low dust—or else, why, with the sky above still an unblemished cornflower blue, were there no shadows?

Having nowhere else to go, I advanced a few uneven paces. Within the wrapping of the city's unceasing hum there was a fragile package of silence; also an effect of motionlessness, which was emphasized, rather than repudiated, by the sudden appearance of a lean ginger cat scuttling across the foreground, devil or imagined mongrel at its heels.

The cat disappeared; the haze of dust—within which glittered mica, shards of glass, wrapper-less tin cans—re-formed and settled like still water. Distantly came the doo-da doo-da doo-da of an ambulance's alarm; and from close by me, almost under my feet, as the klaxon died, there arose—yes, literally arose—a thin piping of invisible song.

The voice was sexless and the words and melody unrecognizable, in the hushed seconds of 'real time' before, instinctively turning, I stumbled and clattered against some rusting kitchen junk, and the song ceased, leaving behind it in the still complete vacancy an echoless impression of a distant island greenness.

I re-balanced myself; a few more seconds of 'real time' passed, and then there singly emerged from the levelled ground—yes, yes, all right, a hole I hadn't seen, not five yards distant—a troop of creatures, men and women barely separable, hair as pelt, their clothing vivid for all its tatters, who, with grotesquely clumsy birdlike hops and in silence, ringed me.

Despite their poses of hostility and the dangerous bottles in their hands, I wasn't frightened of them, rather, relieved by their explicitness. I could almost taste the sweet and nauseous odour of the spirit emanating from their black mouths. Backing—no one made a move to check me—I attempted to mime apology for my intrusion. One of the men threw his bottle—not in my direction, over his shoulder, dissolving in a tinkle of fine rain. One of the women danced a little lurching jig, birdlike again, an irate crow stamping the ground.

'Ah well, then, if you will be so good as to excuse me, I'll be on my way, wishing you the best of fortune.' I didn't say that, of course, but attempted to express it with fluttering hands as I retreated.

Someone, sexless as the singing, swore at my back, and when I had taken only a couple of insouciant paces another bottle was thrown: no thin rain this time; a sharp shower of glass spattered my calves. Instead of running, as I would have done in a dream, I turned around into the barrage of their cat-calls and their mocking laughter. My gaze, level, slowly stilled and silenced. Unarmed subaltern cowing the dhoti-ed rabble. I mean you no harm. Go back to your homes. Raised arms were lowered. A bottle held in menace was uncorked and its bearded possessor put it to his mouth. Spitting – but not at me – a young crone grumbled and withdrew. Just a few seconds longer, I coolly estimated, and their nerve would be broken. Not dangerous if you let them see you're the master. Like children really. I tapped my swagger-stick against my leathered shin.

'Mister! Mister!' The man who hobbled forward had a smooth, white hairless face, distorted in a rictus of ingratiation. 'You looking for something, Mister, was you? Was you?' Perhaps from his thick Irish accent, I identified him retrospectively as the singer under my feet.

I winced at his breath as, pawing my lapel, he grinned toothlessly into my face. His eyes were an astonishing light blue in a deeply pink inclosure. 'Was you, Mister? Was you searching?'

The others, though I hadn't seen them move, all seemed to be a little nearer. The black-nailed hand was lifted from my jacket and hovered by my cheek in contemplation of an embrace. I stepped back.

'You won't find it here, Mister, though. It's too late. It's all gone, you see. They've all gone away, all the people, all the good people. There's only,' he went on wildly, 'the soughing of the wind, the cats on heat, and the lonely curlew's song. It's a hero of dead graveyards, that's what it is – dead graveyards.'

As though hearing that something had gone wrong with his last words, he gave a little click of exasperation, and his eyes became sorrowful. I turned, but he followed me around and came at me again. 'Mister, Mister, I tell you, it's too late.' He held me back without touching me, with the force of our complicity. 'Mister,' he again apostrophized in his thick, choked, poisoned-bog croak, 'Mister, the Colonel's jammed and the gatling's dead.'

Gentlemen of the jury, I . . .

I spotted a passage-way between the shored-up buildings and ran, unbelieving sole survivor escaping over the shell-holes and the rubble of the blitzed defences. Supporting myself against the chipped wall, I looked back, blinking. Funny how merely by screwing your eyes you can make the solid external world blow like smoke in a draught! The entire, and boringly ordinary, expanse of urban landscape was quite empty.

Back in the office, Harvey behaved as if nothing in the slightest untoward had passed between us that morning. His manner was unruffled—a little short on deference perhaps, but had I not always encouraged a democratic informality? 'Have a choccy.' Hard to convince myself, in the face of his bland friendliness, that our clash had not taken place in my own mind alone. Gentlemen of the jury, Herr Doktor: what must a man do in times like these to keep a fingerhold on sanity?

Skip the homeward journey, which I endured in a torment of impatience. Come to the collision alone in the lift between myself and my drum-beating neighbour: not a physical collision, not a touching, but an encounter which generated during our smooth and wordless ascent an animosity which made my scalp tingle, my penis stiffen.

There we stood, each facing the closed doors, each sightlessly observing the panel of lighted numbers, neither acknowledging the existence of the other, neither lifting a finger: a space of some thirty inches between. And boiling both with a silent, deadly loathing. Supposing the lift, instead of being sealed, had one wall open above the forty . . . fifty . . . sixty foot drop: just a nudge needed. Any understanding jury would return a verdict of *involuntary* homicide.

The lift stopped, the doors hissed apart. My erection subsiding, I preceded my neighbour, good neighbour, along the corridor. At the moment of inserting my key in the lock I looked back, to see that he, with his hand to the lock of his door, had turned his head to look at me.

Inside, I found myself waiting for the drumming to start, so that I could hurl myself, fists flailing, against the battered wall. Nothing happened. Was I relieved? On the contrary: by his abstention the cunning devil had left me suspended ...

But still, as best I could, I turned my thoughts to, call it, love. 'Will you let me do this?' I would say to her. 'And will you do that to me?'

After all, the flowers had been delivered: two large bunches I couldn't put a name to, dropped carelessly on the draining-board, still wrapped. I took a long while to arrange them to my satisfaction, for I found my fingers clumsy.

After all, the porter had cleaned the flat, but indifferently of course, so I had to follow in his steps, straightening cushions, wiping down a glass-ringed table, etc. etc. —all under the threat of the drums. If he starts up while we're ... 'I swear I'll kill him,' I concluded aloud.

Meanwhile, time, which was bringing her nearer, was slipping away. They must have finished the recording by now, though I understood, naturally, that she couldn't just rush off, however eager her desire. Lay out the food, wine on ice, find the right records, clean sheets, and —'Oh, God, hell!' —I'd forgotten to disinfect the lavatory.

It all got done at last. I showered and changed; I poured myself a drink and sat down to wait. Found myself facing a smiling wedding photograph and jumped up to conceal it in a drawer. I looked at my watch, held it to my ear: she was surely due —if the watch wasn't twelve hours fast or slow —at any moment.

The day at its close had turned heavy and thunder-laden. I opened a window. The clouds were brassy and swollen into bulbous shapes whose unceasing mobility seemed strange with the air so still. On the lawn far below some children were jumping on a trampolin, their cries shrill and distinct. A cabin-cruiser glided along the river in a haze of jazz. Out of sight a dog began to bark frantically.

I took another drink and looked at my watch again, possessed by an uncontrollable itch. How odd that after my first reluctance my eagerness now should be so agonizing! Even if I had been laying a long dry siege to her virtue and this was the night when my persistance was to have been at last rewarded, I couldn't have endured a more raging anticipation. Matter of fact, her virtue had been surrendered at the end of our first evening together when, following my exploratory good-night kiss, 'Wouldn't it,' she'd briskly proposed, 'be easier in the back seat?' We hadn't made love in the car since.

We haven't made love in the car since, I thought, again consulting my watch, and this time unable to arrest a little howl of pain.

Ten minutes passed. Anything might have happened to her, illness, an accident. I tested the telephone. Or—hadn't I always known it?—some day she was bound to tire of me, seduced by a younger, stiffer ... 'Jimmy' perhaps, his alleged peculiarity a cover or evidence only of indiscrimination? What about, even, that chain-smoking ogress with the insidious hands? But why had it to be tonight of all nights, when I stood on the very brink of such unutterable joy? Didn't she know—howling again—didn't she care, how much she was making me suffer? O, my-sweet-Jackie! Bitch. Slut. Cow. Whore ...

In a little while, my forehead pressed against the coolness of the bathroom mirror, I was telling myself I was glad she wasn't coming, glad it was done, that now—all right, allow a day or two to overcome it—I could resume a decent, orderly, un-obsessed existence. I believe the bell had been ringing for some few seconds before I identified it.

At any rate, 'Took your time, didn't you?' she grumbled, pushing past me. She was wearing a distinctly grubby shirt over wrinkled slacks. I caught a faint smell of alcohol and dried sweat.

'Give me a drink. It took me hours to find a bloody taxi.' I
still hadn't uttered a word, incapable. 'I haven't brought
anything.' She addressed me with a sort of sullen belligerence.
'A nightie or toothbrush or anything. And don't ask me about
the fucking play, it was a disaster.'

None of my loving preparations, the flowers, the champagne,
impressed her, nor the spacious elegance, compared with her
own squalid boxroom, of the flat. She stood by the window,
clutching a whisky glass and furiously smoking.

I came to her side, slipping a hand on to the bare, and somehow stale to the touch, skin under her shirt. But after a moment
she moved away. The children had disappeared, but I believed
that I could still see the shape of the trampolin in the gathering
dusk. A distant rumble might have been thunder or a train.
'Don't you want to look round the old homestead? You said . . .'

Whatever she had said previously concerning her curiosity
about the way I lived, she displayed no interest in my possessions
nor in the general purtenances of the flat, slouching through the
rooms like a sulking child in a museum. It was a somewhat
different story, however, when we came to the bedroom, for
there she straightaway opened the cupboards containing Sarah's
clothes and examined them with prolonged and silent calculation.
Afterwards, she sat on the stool in front of Sarah's dressing-
table and took up Sarah's brush and with long, lazy, thoughtful
strokes, like a woman alone in a window, began to brush her hair.

Seeing this aroused in me a very complicated sensation: there
was something distasteful buried deep, but it was also both
touching and cerebrally exciting. It could be, I found myself
imagining, my daughter, our daughter, sitting there innocent
before the secret glass, arm crocked, eyes sleepy, mouth drooping
. . . and I, like a monster, lurking with the knowledge that
before the night was out I would have ravished her. I slipped
quietly from the room.

When the tour of inspection, for what it was worth, was over, I
opened a bottle of champagne. Jackie accepted her glass without

enthusiasm. While drinking she grudgingly disclosed the causes of her dissatisfaction: among other things, the play had over-run, and they had cut entirely what she considered her best scene—the scene in the bedroom with 'Jimmy'. I sympathized with heated indignation.

'Laurence, do you think I'm after you for what I can get, just for your money?' Jackie interrupted me abruptly. 'All this!' She didn't even bother to make the gesture that would embrace my possessions. She spoke as to herself then: 'It's not easy being a girl like me. I'm not much good, I know I'm not much good at anything. I think,' she went on with a quiet weariness, 'life's lousy, awful. The world's a . . . *shitty* place. I wish I could just . . .' She didn't complete the sentence, for, profoundly moved by the desperate ring of honesty in her voice—possibly because of its unfamiliarity—I had hurled myself on my knees at her feet, burying my head in her thighs and babbling of my love.

After a moment, she patted me and said in a soft voice: 'Down, Rufus, down!' I didn't move, so she gently pushed me away. I saw that for the first time since she had arrived she was faintly smiling, and in her eyes there was what I took, with happy heart, for a gleam of tenderness.

Shortly, however, she resumed the off-handed, distant manner which seemed to have settled on her like a blight. It made me desperately anxious. Nothing I did could please. The gramophone records I'd chosen with some care were sneered at. When I opened the second bottle of champagne, she asked for a glass of orange-juice instead. My increasingly nervous attempts to fill the silences met only with an apathetic chill, which once or twice flared into outright hostility.

'Perhaps you'd like to have a shower before we eat?'

'Why?' she brusquely snapped.

'No reason, I just thought . . .'

'If you don't like the way I smell, say so!'

She didn't want to eat at all, and especially not those exotic delicacies I had carefully selected. My appetite, of course, was poisoned also. We had to eat something, I insisted with a manufactured leer, to keep our strength up. My jocularity sank like a stone in a bottomless well. Forcing down the food— whatever it was—I'd finally set out was chewing sawdust. The champagne I drank as water.

She yawned with unshielded mouth; I, though straining to suppress it, emulated. There was another, not so distant, menacing rumble, which was this time unmistakably thunder. She stubbed out her cigarette in the debris on her plate, leaving an acrid smell of burning meat.

'Well,' said I, breaking the silence, 'if you've finished, darling, I'll clear away. No, you sit still.' Though she hadn't moved. 'Would you care for some coffee?'

She gave no sign of even having heard.

'Oh, my darling! Sweet Jackie!' I burst out in a voice which I doubt I would have recognized for my own. 'What's the matter? What's the matter? I thought it was all going to be so wonderful . . . having you here . . . the two of us. And now, and now . . .'

'Nothing's the matter,' she answered me in a dead voice.

'I had such high hopes, such visions. Sweet . . . sweet . . . my darling . . .' I scarcely knew what I was saying. I reached for her with hands over which I had but partial control.

With face averted, she suffered me at first. Then she let out a little cry and drew back, wincing. She pulled up the sleeve of her shirt and displayed her arm to me: on the sallow flesh there was a cluster of grape-purple bruises.

'That's what you did, you. The last time, when you . . .' She caressed the marks softly with the tips of her fingers. 'You hurt me then, hurt Jackie . . .' Her tongue slowly curled.

Quite beside myself and groaning, I reached for her again, but she was off the chair in a flash and swerved past my arms with extraordinary agility. I took a few paces in pursuit, but she was out of the room.

After a long minute, I called her name, tentatively. And then again.

I walked heavily into the bedroom, where she was sitting, small and huddled, in her grubby shirt, on the edge of the bed. She was staring blankly at the wall. Frightened—of what I didn't know—I halted beyond reach, and whispered her name again.

Slowly, she turned her head and looked at me, at first without apparent recognition. Then she drew a quick breath, and her face became alive and familiar. She raised her eyebrows and mischievously smiled—as if to say: what now?

The thunder roared and exploded close at hand, and the lightning coruscated, searing ghastly flash-light pictures. After a while there came torrents, hissing and lashing. But not for hours did the storms finally spend themselves.

At some time, presuming I had slept for a few moments, I carefully disentangled my tender limbs. When done in the bathroom, I felt a reluctance to return, as though all the night's murdered victims were awaiting me in the bed; and I went wandering, naked, through rooms which had once been familiar.

At the window, shivering convulsively, I was amazed by the dawn. The quiet and the emptiness belonged to another order of existence which had previously been kept concealed from me. In the nacreous sky the moon resembled a street-lamp left on in spendthrift error.

9

I stand at the window again. The children are gathered round the sagging trampolin below; in the afternoon there must have been a light shower, for the paths are still damp, disclosing the tracks of bicycles and pedal-cars; elsewhere, the concrete is drying patchily, making patterns from which an observer above may create whatever pictures his imagination selects.

I turned away from the pictures on the concrete, but they persisted invisibly, like psychic wounds—scars from the enormities I had committed and had had committed upon me. From darkness we had dredged our fantasies to actualize them in light as stark as in an operating-theatre, and now they were burned—as though by lightning—on my retina. To put it another way, I drooled over a collection of obscene photographs, already dog-eared and sticky with thumb-marks, which I found myself unable to discard despite my revulsion.

How long had she stayed? The clock, twelve hours fast or slow, had become redundant, behind closed curtains day and night merging. Sleeping, like animals, whenever, where, we fell. Familiar furnishings metamorphosed in childhood make-believe. Hallucinations and hysteria. Coffee and cornflakes. Alcohol. Out of cigarettes, so that I called down to the desk to order, which was when she had opened the door wide to the porter, wearing her nakedness like a bridal gown—or had that been merely one of our more innocent fantasies? For, like the night and the day, like the hitherto distinctive genders, reality and figment had merged into one. The cigarettes had been real enough, anyway—as these burn-blisters evidenced. Talking of wounds, the comical inappropriateness of her insistence, even in frenzy, that I should not mark where it would show, welt or blood. Fair enough!—I, too, even in frenzy, had jibbed at certain sharp-edged implements. Though when we fought bare-handed, bare-skinned and slippery, no holds—'licence my roaving hands . . .' —no holds were barred. And no holds barred, no veils of modesty, no shames at all, when ultimately, jaded and seated distantly, we had sought ingeniously to do it all again in a cold coupling of words and images and gesture . . .

She had departed mysteriously, so that on my awakening she might for the briefest instant never have been; and then I had thought that she was staging a new diversion of hunt and capture, and—as in a dream, a dream of underwater, silent and murky, my movements languid as a diver's—I'd searched the disordered rooms, until in the wrecked treasure-ship of the bathroom I saw the cheerful, valedictory obscenity scrawled in lipstick on the mirror.

Diligently I had restored the flat to order. Except for one puzzling stain on the wall above the bed—for which I had already prepared the explanation of an exploding can of beer— no visible traces remained. Yet the rooms, the furnishings, the ornaments, all the things I had lived with—along with Sarah— for eight years, had subtly altered, and, though I felt no awareness of guilt, seemed to regard me with reproach. In the bedroom—which I still couldn't help regarding as our bedroom, despite Sarah's withdrawal—ghostly presences, accompanied by a faint, characteristic odour, re-enacted various unusual congresses. One phantom, almost *tangible*, was more persistent than the others: she sits on the bedroom stool, ankle crossed over her knee, her hands clasped resting on her stomach's mound, demure but utterly artless and exposed . . . a slight smile on bloodless lips, savouring the effect of the outrageous words she calmly murmurs, murmurs . . . I fancy that she will go on sitting on that stool for ever.

Since, in the flesh, she had gone, I had tried, unsuccessfully, three or four times to telephone, but this had been from courtesy or habit rather than a desperate desire to speak with her. I was not any the less enchanted, you must understand, but for the time being felt akin to a hermit for whom all life's passions are mere shadows on the screen of his solitary imagination. My skin was acutely sensitized, so that any touch would aggravate the nerve-ends; at the same time I felt light, disembodied. Curiously, I was less aware of noise, even the drums and the low-flying jets didn't annoy me. I needed to drink large quantities of water.

I had telephoned the office. Despite the croakiness I injected into my voice, Lydia had sounded uncharacteristically dubious of my excuses. This had concerned me no more than had the odd unease displayed by callers at the door: the postman, the porter—whom I smartly dismissed—and two prim, glassy youths, carrying pamphlets and Bibles.

Yet there was nothing unnatural in my behaviour; I simply felt a great reluctance to resume everyday life. I found myself frequently thinking of the creatures at the Zoo, their morbid, enviable loneliness . . .

Bills piled up, unopened. I suffered from constipation. Something in the fridge had gone off, filling the kitchen with the smell of decay.

Now, I am standing at the window again. A flight of starlings passes heavily across the river. Birds, I had somewhere heard, fly more strongly against the wind. I test this statement against my own observation, and begin to laugh. My laughter bounces off the walls, as in a completely unfurnished, carpetless house. When I stop laughing, all is silent.

All was silent until the doorbell rang.

His bulk made the hallway seem suddenly as narrow as in a doll's house. And then, sniffing suspiciously, though maintaining a sort of bouncy cordiality, he filled the living-room, disrupting the dimensions, like an intruder into a space-reduced dream. He glittered from his brilliantined hair to the pointed tips of his mirror-bright shoes. A powerful smell of lavender and lemons surrounded him.

'Well, tonight's the night,' he said. 'Tonight's the night,' he repeated. 'Don't tell me you'd forgotten, Larry. Don't tell me you'd forgotten our date.'

He clapped his hands noisily, dispersing the room's stagnant shallows. 'Better get some clothes on then, hadn't you.'

Looking down automatically, I wouldn't really have been surprised to discover myself naked. As I went obediently to change from the old house-clothes which, in fact, covered me, Ossie's voice followed in resounding companionship. 'Still, I suppose if you had forgotten, I was lucky to catch you, considering the busy social life you lead, Larry. Reckon it might do you good to have a night out.

'You don't have to dress fancy,' the voice from the other room continued, with eerie percipience, as I hesitated over the choices of my wardrobe. 'You don't want to put on your best gear. The going might get heavy, see. Know what I mean, don't you?'

Hanging in the wardrobe, now cleaned, was the suit I had been given on that first night of our ... acquaintanceship: bright, bold blue, like the one my guest was wearing now. Laughing suddenly, as I had when looking out of the window at the striving flight of birds, I had the fancy to put that on, so that I would emerge—yes, there was a snow-white shirt—the double of my guest, and we would appear as twins; or, allowing for the difference in physiques, the fat man and thin, comic and stooge in a music-hall duo.

'Bloody music-hall act it was getting up here,' the companionable voice broke in as, rejecting temptation, I selected some nondescript clothing. 'First I had trouble with the porter, then that little nance of a clerk said he had to ring up, see if you was home ...'

The phantom that had inhabited the bedroom had been dispelled by Ossie's unghostly presence. Pulling on my trousers, I looked at the stool on which Jackie had sat so blatantly exposed; it was stool alone.

'You might have had a bird up here, sitting in her birthday

suit, the bleeding fuss he made.' The voice seemed to come from a less distant source, as though Ossie had approached the bedroom door but, from modesty, refrained from entering. 'I told him, Mr. Carpenter's expecting me. I told him to get stuffed. Get knotted, mate, I said.'

Knotting my tie, I tried carefully to control the direction and vocabulary of my thoughts in order to avoid being forced to suspect the presence of sorcery. I recalled my obligations as host, and invited my guest to help himself to a drink. The very act of speaking reduced the aura of unreality. So much that seems ominous exists only in one's own imagination; jangled nerves are known to reach out for coincidence.

'What's that thing down there?' Ossie, glass in hand, turned from the window as I re-entered the living-room. 'The kids are jumping on.'

'You mean the trampolin.'

'Tram-po-lin,' Ossie repeated thoughtfully. 'I like to learn new words, improve my vocabulary. Trampolin,' he said again. 'Reckon you could jump up to the pearly gates of 'eaven on one of them things.'

What an extraordinary remark, I didn't say.

'That's an extraordinary thing for me to say, ain't it?' Ossie turned, beaming. 'You wanted to ask me something?'

'No, I don't think . . .' I broke off, and sniffed.

'It's my new after-shave—lavender. Better than stinking of that muck in the river, eh Larry?' He took a swig from his glass and belched. 'Pardon! So you not been at work then?'

'How did you . . .?' I began uselessly.

'How did I know? That was what you were going to ask me, Larry.'

'It doesn't matter,' I replied. 'Shall we go now?'

I thought I had said it clearly enough, I heard my own voice; but my guest stood there with that meaningless smile on his face that people assume when an awkward silence befalls. In a moment, to fill the gap, he started to stride about the room extolling the qualities of the flat and its appointments. 'Yes, indeed, a very nice place you've got here, Larry,' he concluded, putting down his glass. 'Shall we go now?' he politely suggested.

'If you're sure you're ready,' I assented, not without irony.

The drumming started before we reached the door. I felt all my old fury return but, except perhaps for the merest flicker of annoyance, concealed it. Ossie halted, blocking the doorway. He wasn't looking towards the source of the sound but into my face, his eyes — not only his eyes, somehow all his features — had suddenly become sharp, the slightly alcoholic geniality replaced by a formidable acuity.

'The bastard, eh Larry?' he whispered, so close that I felt his breath on my eyeballs. 'The lousy rotten bastard! Nice place like this you've got, and you have to endure that sodding row. No wonder you 'ate his guts.' His venom exactly matched the intensity of my own. 'It's a diabolical liberty, Larry. Something got to be done about it. Something drastic!'

Like a workman assessing a job, he measured the dents in the wall, evidence of my past assaults. His eyes flickered and he smiled, showing his gleaming, nerveless teeth 'We put his name on our list, eh Larry?'

10

It was, after all that had passed, without any surprise at all that when we had descended, crossed the hallway—'tchk-tchk' clicked Ossie reproachfully at sight of the sculpture—and emerged into an evening smelling of water and mown grass, with a low-angled light gilding the lawns and asphalt, I found myself led to a black, battered Cadillac.

Other considerations aside, the car fitted Ossie, and he it, with an aptness transcending common reality, approaching the perfection of art or myth. One hand and forearm laxly encircling the wheel, he drove with a screen gangster's assured contempt. After the third or fourth turn—remember, the world outside was strange to me—I had lost all sense of direction. Passive in the part to which I had been assigned, I saw the streets and buildings and the other vehicles as blurred images on a back-projection screen.

The air had become a dusty mauve; at certain intersections where we moved out of shadow, the setting sun would explode in the driving-mirror or a shopfront with a stroboscopic flash, which for a moment turned black to light, light to black, like a photographic negative.

'Know where we are then now, do you?' enquired my companion, after we had been driving for five or fifty minutes.

The road looked just like ten thousand others in London, or for that matter almost anywhere in the western world: chain-stores and dustbins, a forest of indecipherable traffic signs. Making a sharp, unsignalled, turn—needless to say, the car had a left-hand drive—we entered a narrower street. 'Course, it would have looked a bit different then, in the dark.' Ossie chuckled reminiscently. 'Like two bleeding drowned rats we was,' he affectionately recalled.

I could not with conviction have asserted that I had ever been here before. Or that I had not.

There was a conspicuous gap, like a missing incisor, in the line of cars parked head to tail. 'Know better than to park here, they do,' Ossie vaunted, neatly filling the gap. 'Mind you, it's been tried, but it didn't do their motors no good, not bloody much it didn't.'

'Why have you brought me here?' I asked, with a sort of unfrightened fearfulness, as I saw the greengrocer's shop.

No sense taking the car, it was reasonably explained, not with the fucking breathalyser. Asking for trouble. Asking for trouble he didn't believe in. We stood in the now sullen purple dusk and the sweet smell of the sleeping fruit. Ossie waved a key. 'Don't have to hammer up the old bag this time.'

But she, the old bag, appeared of her own volition as we climbed the creaking stairs. Sheathed in a shiny black dress, cut low, the broad whiteness of her chest and her ham-like arms shone in the near-darkness phosphorescently. Ossie slapped her across the buttocks. 'You had your 'air done, Chrissie, you look gorgeous.'

Chrissie disregarded both the blow and the compliment, regarding me with heavy impassivity.

'Remember Chrissie, don't you? Course you do.' He began to pull me past her. 'Best landlady in London, even if she is a retired 'oore. That right, darling?'

I shook my arm free. 'Were you . . .' I began. 'I saw you at the Zoo.'

'The Zoo!' cried Ossie with amazement.

'I took a photograph . . .'

'A photograph!' Laughing blithely, he grabbed hold of my arm again. 'You ever had your picture took with a n'ape, Chrissie? In the old days, I mean, when you went in for that sort of lark.' He slapped her again and held out a limp hand in pretended agony. 'Christ! What you keep in there?'

Somehow, we had left her behind. 'No bloody ape would have had the strength, I tell you,' he confided, opening the door.

I thought I recognized the room: that's to say, no trickery: I had been there before, and any impression of strangeness was attributable, perfectly naturally, to the difference in the circumstances. I looked about me with some curiosity; but Ossie, bustling, gave little time for reflection. A glass was in my hands.

'Water with it, I seem to remember.' He winked. 'Now get it down you, Larry. Seem to remember saying that, too—that night. That night, eh Larry! That night when it all began.'

Since—how many days ago?—waking in sudden hazed solitude, I had abstained from alcohol. Strange its taste and sensation: not pleasant, but, but . . . The word escaped me. I watched a column of ants scurrying along the edge of the carpet by the blocked-in fireplace.

'Never did see that doctor, did you, like I told you?' Ossie, re-entering, shouted above the roar of the cistern. 'Come on, Larry, let's get going. What you staring at?'

Curious how the ants all stopped moving at the sound of his voice. I emptied my glass. They remained quite motionless— like a line of black carpet-tacks against the white paint of the wainscot. Doubtless, there is a perfectly natural explanation of all apparent hallucinations.

Silently a dinner-jacketed comedian grinned and grimaced, grimaced and grinned. He gave way to a kaleidoscope of commercials, and they, in their turn, to a juvenile pop group, also mute. All this time, Ossie, his gaze mostly concentrated on the television screen above the bar, had been keeping the conversation going with cheerful banalities. What in God's name am I doing in this dreary little pub?—I asked myself. What has happened to my will, that I am incapable of turning around and quietly walking out?

'Just one more here, eh? Then we'll move on somewhere a bit more lively.' Ossie tapped his glass on the counter. 'And one for yourself, guv'nor.'

A girl fed the juke-box, and on the screen the singers went on mouthing their contrary song.

'Not my favourite sort of boozer this,' Ossie murmured in

the privacy of the music. 'But you live in the neighbourhood and you're well-known like what I am, you got to be friendly. Friendship's important.' He nodded to a departing drinker. 'So, you made up your mind yet, Larry: who's it to be?'

An open-topped car speeded along a mountain pass, between on one side soaring pines, on the other a fall to a glittering ravine, the girl's hair streaming in the rush of wind. Cut to close-up driver, cheroot in mouth. Superimpose product slogan. 'Suppose,' I said, 'I told you I had.' Top-shot car into sunset. I removed my stare from the screen. 'Here and now, I give you a name. A life for a life, as you promised.' Ossie's eyes softly swept my face, as a caress, from brow to lips. 'That would be calling your bluff, wouldn't it?'

'You don't believe that, Larry.' The loving quality of his gaze remained unaltered. 'Not really you don't, not in the secret places of your 'eart.' He sighed, and smiled with forbearance. 'So many names, eh? So many names to choose from, that the trouble? Well, take your time, friend. Take as much time as you like. Within reason,' he added, lifting his glass. 'Within reason, of course.'

'What did you mean?' I asked, when Ossie returned to our table from wherever he had been in this larger, far noisier, and barn-like pub in which we were now sitting at a table awash. 'What did you mean—so many names?'

His face was white, with an oily sheen, but otherwise he showed no sign of his drinks. For my part, whatever my appearance — and I had the impression that my eyes were reddening and my hair was disordered—I knew I was at the point of maximum lucidity. A couple more, and I might become confused, but at the moment my mind was a formidable sharp-edged instrument capable of extraordinary incisions.

'So many names, you said. We were talking about . . .' One had to bawl to hear one's own voice above the howl of the organ and the youth sobbing into the microphone. 'In that other bar, when you asked me to tell you . . . when you wanted to know who . . . a name . . .' I was aware that I was expressing myself haltingly, but this was because of the difficulty of competing with the microphone. 'You said, so many names . . .'

'I said — what?'

'Did you mean — so many names, so many people, I want you to . . .' Loud applause at the end of the song drowned the last monosyllable.

Ossie was leaning across the table, a faint frown on his face. He shook his head regretfully. 'Don't recollect,' he said.

'You did,' I cried; and as the organ hadn't re-started this caused several people at nearby tables to turn their heads. 'You did,' I said again, more quietly, but with less conviction.

'Oh, Larry!' Ossie's hand stretched across to lay gently on my arm. 'Larry, what's it matter? What's it matter whether I said it, or whether you just thought I said it?' He gave my arm a consolatory pat. 'In vino veritable, as the saying goes. So long as you know it's true.'

'It's not true,' I replied weakly. The clear beam of my perception had been refracted into a myriad shimmering flashes. 'It's not . . .'

'Want me to name them for you?'

'No,' I said. 'Yes.'

'Well then,' said Ossie, 'there's . . .'

There came a crashing chord from the organ, during which Ossie's lips shaped sounds. The chord gave way to a spattering of applause. Ossie's mouth was closed; then opened again. 'Lovely voice she's got, this girl,' he observed, turning towards the bandstand. 'And similar tits.'

Following his gaze, I saw a pair of identical and identically attired twins both take hold of the microphone with a single hand.

'Best soloist we got . . .' I heard Ossie begin; but I was no longer there.

Here or there, it made no difference. If it wasn't the same pub — the same over-flowing table, the same organ, the same singer, with similar tits—it was as alike as its mirror image. Consider: I am recollecting in—for want of a better word— tranquillity. You will appreciate, those who have passed similar evenings, that one's memories become shuffled haphazardly, amnesia abstracts, time telescopes; moreover, one can't always distinguish with certainty between that which was in reality said and done and the, equally opaque, extravagances of the imagination.

Ossie knew them all: the rouged abortionist; a weeper; crone procuress with a chicken's cackle; face with a hole where the nose should have been; Detective-Constable What's-it, in plain clothes; Ossie knew them all: child prostitute; transvestite; the razor-scarred twins ... the faces repeated themselves, as on a frieze.

'Not your kind of world, eh Larry, not the company to which you're accustomed, this load of rotten slags.' Our aboriginal companions of the moment chuckled good-naturedly. 'But we're all the same under the skin, eh Larry—the Colonel's lady and Judy O'Grady, even you and me, Larry—the same under the skin.'

Did I then protest, or was it elsewhere, later? He put his arm around my neck, his face to mine. 'You know what your trouble is, Larry.' His breath was urgent in my ear. 'You keep it all bottled up. It's like there's another man inside of you, kicking and squawking and effing and blinding, only you choose to pretend he ain't there.' He turned my head with soft fingers, so that we were looking eye to eye. 'Well, I'm like that man inside of you, Larry. I'm the geezer who'll do your kicking and squawking for you. Seeing as you're so respectable, so bleeding fastidious. Stop me if I'm offending you.'

In the cramped urinal someone had written on the wall, in precise, painstaking capitals: IT IS LATER THAN YOU THINK.

And in another, where the entire surface was decorated with drawings and verbal obscenities, near the top, by the rusting tank, I read, in the same immaculate hand: THE GAT-LING'S JAMMED AND THE COLONEL'S DEAD. I felt a hot breath on my neck.

'Don't shake it off, mate,' exhorted an impatient voice behind me. 'Never know, you might need it.'

So I decided that I would simply walk away, as one can often walk out of a dream in which one has created an environment that is inimical.

I saw a man similar to myself, wearing familiar clothes, lifting his glass to his mouth with a white hand, a man surrounded by indifferent drinkers, and he lowered his glass at the same moment as I did; it was disconcerting to find him obliterated by the shirt-sleeved barman's sudden emergence before the mirror, while I went on standing there, holding steady to the bar rail.

'Larry, I thought I lost you. You come back to the wrong bar, friend . . .'

You arrive at a point where the senses are jangled: you hear colour, smell sound, touch smell, taste touch. If I tripped, I remember thinking, I wouldn't fall but float.

'You're not going to trip, Larry.' A clap on the shoulders sent me lurching over the cobbles. 'Just getting your second wind. Besides, I'd hold you up. What are friends for?'

I bounce from alley-walls of maze-like complexity, flit, immune as a shadow, between the roaring juggernauts of the glaring motor-track. Am surprised by an illuminated clock which affirmed that it was later, later than I thought.

Down an ancient flight of steps, and ahead of us a narrow street where men are dancing. As we near, I see they are not dancing, they are fighting. The fight has, however, the ritualistic quality of a dance, the grappling a sexual embrace, the quick and savage blows in rhythm with the chants of the choir which forms the circle.

We pass through unimpeded, and, shoulder to shoulder, we raise our glasses in a green and muted cellar, where ragged peons suck tequila and an iguana slides across the baked earth.

My second wind must have arrived: I knew there were no peons; the iguana was a low-bellied mongrel — now cocking its leg against a lady's fallen reticule. And ordered two more.

With queasy surprise that for so long I had forgotten, I suddenly remembered Jackie. Her loveliness contrasting with my abasement made me weep dry tears. In penance for my neglect, I turned to my companion and told him.

'Sounds,' he flatteringly observed, 'you got a good one there, Larry — a right hot, sweet little number. You ought to be a proud and happy fellow.' And he ordered two more.

'Yes, of course,' I said, as though there had been no pause. 'What's more, you know, you might find it hard to credit, she reciprocals my . . . I mean, she feels the same.'

'Sure she does, Larry,' he encouraged. 'Sure she does. It's as plain as the nose on your face.' And he prodded my nose with a spatulate finger.

'But, all the same,' I persisted, 'all the same, it isn't easy. We have our ups and downs. We . . .'

'Like that thing in your garden, eh — that tram-po-lin.'

'. . . have our difficulties. Life isn't easy, in times like these.' I paused to consider how the times rendered love difficult. 'In times like these,' I began again, 'when life isn't easy, you know what I mean.'

'Sure, Larry,' he concurred. 'Times like these — when the gatling's jammed and the Colonel's . . . Here, steady!'

I imagine I must, somehow, have startled him, turning on him as though he were a vision of my own private madness.

'That's what you said, Larry, before. You said that already.'

One would have expected to have remembered what one had said before. One was perfectly in command of all one's faculties. One was not to be surprised by perfectly explicable phenomena. But where in any imaginable world had all these people come from? Jostling and bawling, they swarmed over the pavements and the roadway like a football crowd, bouncing us — for he held my arm in a firm grip — backwards and forwards from one tumbling collision to another. A screaming girl threw her arms around my neck and kissed me on the mouth with steamy breath which tasted of alcohol and tobacco.

I remember sitting in a taxi; and I remember the smell of the seats: smoke, ashes, brimstone. 'You don't have to shout at me, Larry,' he said, his arm around my neck. 'I can hear you. I'll always hear you, even if you only whisper. However far you was away, I'd still hear you when you called me, if you was in Timbuktu, or even Amsterdam. Turn left at the next,' he called to the driver.

I remember that I was sick—easily, painlessly, as though under anaesthetic. I threw my soggy handkerchief over a high fence, and knew with absolute certainty that it would fall in unseen water. 'Feel better now then,' offered Ossie solicitously. 'What you need's another drink, set you up.'

The stars were very bright and cold and distant. The last streetlight was as remote as the stars. We walked into a spongy darkness, at the very end of which, and emphasizing the insubstantiality of the space between, mysterious fires were hotly burning and there came, clear on the night air, the nostalgic clanking of chains and the ring of wheels and hammers.

Following, I could hear, or sense, his steps. Man must have cat's eyes to guide him, not to stumble—though I didn't either, my feet sustaining me on a path whose existence I assumed on trust, like a plane's incredible ability to stay in the air. Then, as happens in a dream of flight, my trust gave way to a nameless anxiety: more than anything else, I wanted to believe that what was happening to me wasn't true, or that suddenly something would happen to render it untrue; and at that moment—possibly the clouds had parted to un-curtain the moon—there appeared, quite plainly before us, the verifiable solidity of a building.

It did seem familiar to me, admitted. But only for a moment. It was one of a million such houses, and merely the surprise of coming upon it like that, isolated, in the darkness, prompted the impression of repetition; and the music, which I now heard, coming from the uppermost floor, where my father had had his 'den', and would for hours on end play his gramophone, and would again when he returned.

A bright flame blinded me. As I threw up my arm in protection, I heard a voice I now knew as well as my own: 'For Christ sake, Mac, you know me. Turn off that buggering glim.'

Two more guardians stood within the front door, hands ominous in their swollen jacket pockets. The music poured down the stairway, so that their mouths opened and closed wordlessly. The wallpaper had bright red flowers on it like mouths. A girl with dark glasses was sitting on a barrel, her legs exposed to the matching pink-petalled crotch . . .

I said, didn't I, there were gaps in my memory. I am in a quiet room; the glass in my hand has dancing elephants painted on it; I think the glass contains brandy. On the periphery of my vision there is a hard white light, beneath which, with breathy grunts, the gamblers slide the cards on the green cloth. A man stands pressed against a whirring machine, stoking it unceasingly. I find it difficult to determine the sex of the person who, now, takes the bottle and refills my glass.

'Where are we?'

'Fancy a hand, Larry?'

'Where are we?'

'Well, you're probably right.'

'What is this place?'

'Don't want you losing all your hard-earned lettuce.'

It was not evasion; it seemed, rather, as if, though I was there and must be visible because I was being addressed, I was unable to *impress* myself. In the glass behind the bar a familiar face, white and glistening, is turned solicitously to a face yet whiter, with livid shadowings, slack lips, thinning hair tousled, my eventual recognition of which, arriving only after point-by-point consideration, fills me with distaste. I order a grimace, and watch it twisting in the mirror.

'You feeling better now then, we'll go upstairs.'

At the card-table, facile fingers dip into a heap of what, considering its dimensions, has to be stage-money. With a prolonged hiccupping, the machine in the corner voids a stream of coins. On all fours the sportsman scrabbles after them, and, 'You lucky black bastard, you,' jests Ossie to Blanco's happy face at our feet.

Then, sailing down the stairs, as we ascend into the beat and roar of noise, sailing down the stairs unstably, her mouth wrenched far off centre, as though that weight of noise had fallen on her like a cerebral stroke, sailing down the stairs like a dismasted schooner, comes Chrissie.

'Here, you got to tuck that in.' Ossie, cupping her exposed breast with one hand, tugs at the corsage of her black dress with the other, and manipulates the monstrosity back into place. 'Gets like this, she does,' still kneading, he explains; then patted her, decent, on her way.

'Funny how it takes some people!' We had come to a long landing, with doors stretching away on both sides, as in multiple-mirror reflections. 'Chrissie, for instance, becomes oblivious. What's more, she can't get a word out, mute as a mole. Yourself now, Larry . . .'—he took my arm—'I'd say you was the type that drink confuses, mixing up what's going on outside of you with the figments of your own perfervid imagination.'

Puffing, we ascended a second flight of stairs. Ossie poked me in the ribs. 'That surprised you, eh Larry—my perception. I told you, me, I'm not just a pretty face.'

When we enter, the furnace sears and consumes. Detail eluded me. I have an impression of a juke-box blaring, but the long table in shirt-sleeves and furs is bawling a separate song. A pack of heated and shuffling dancers; frenzied barmen clashing trays and glasses; everyone else, except for those weeping or sleeping, shout and laugh at once. I have the common sensation of living all this for a second time.

'Never seen anything like this before, Larry boy, I bet you.'

Perversely, I feel disposed to argue. 'As a matter of fact, it reminds me of . . .' Although I had heard my companion's voice quite clearly through the clamour, I can't for some reason hear my own.

Ossie stands like an atoll among the waves of dancers. Two filled glasses appear in his hands. The dancers, even the couple evidently trembling on the brink of undemanding orgasm, fall back unbidden as he leads me to the farthest corner.

The table bristles with bottles, under the shade of a potted palm; Ossie stands and smiles; and smiles. The biggest, most carnivorous, of the youths tilts back his chair, lifts his feet among the bottles, and takes out a clasp-knife, with which in lazy ritual he elegantly trims his nails. His companions lay down their crumpled cigarettes. Ossie sighs, and hands me one of the glasses. The smoke rising from the discarded cigarettes adds a sweet herbal fragrance to the pervasive fetor.

Ossie sighed again. 'Surely you know who I am, sonny,' he barely whispered. 'Your nails look very nice. Very nice, indeed,' he repeated admiringly, flicking the knife to the floor and crushing the manicured hand in one invisible movement; and without spilling a drop.

'You got to have influence, Larry.' He winked as we occupied the hospitably vacated seats. 'Hey, you, rubber-pants,' he called after. 'Take these ash-trays with you, I don't want no-one thinking I smoke that shit.'

Settled comfortably, he drank and belched. 'Now, Larry, you was saying, this place reminds you of . . .'

Was I? I couldn't remember. The tenses were utterly confused.

'When you was in the Army, was it?' he helpfully suggested. 'Some place overseas maybe . . .'

Maybe it was his prompting, maybe it was the potted palm, which did seem to belong to the estate of a genuine remembrance, or the sweetly lingering drug smell, or a combination of all those, and more . . . but, yes, everything started to resemble, in a curiously diffuse and distorted way, a scene and occasion I had experienced before: myself hazed and ectopic with cheap arak, as now with sundry more sophisticated spirits, a room that had contained the same jagged *rhythms* . . . 'How did you know?'

'Know what, Larry?'

'That I remembered . . .'

I remembered . . . from deep within my drunken stupor, the dancers and the drinkers scattered by the shock-wave of blow and stab; I heard again the reckless crash of breaking glass, crack of wood or fractured bone; and the surprised cough of the youth who fell, blood gushing, at my feet, under, yes, a green-leaved potted palm.

I think I remembered. 'But that was years and years ago . . .'

'It's the drink, Larry, plays tricks with time.' Ossie produced his familiar wink and nudged me with his elbow. 'Tell you what, it's when you start remembering the future, that's when you got to worry.' He gave a roar of innocent laughter. 'Also, it stimulates resemblances.'

'What was that?'

'The drink, Larry. And tell you another effect it has . . .' He shifted himself into my vision. 'Makes other people seem, like, less than real. Close your eyes, and they'll disappear.' He bared his teeth. 'Go on, Larry, try it. Close your eyes.'

Finding myself alone, I looked about me. The room bore no resemblance to what I could recall of that Levantine brothel. It was unsurprising that I saw faces I knew: the detective, the noseless syphilitic, Blanco, Chrissie—returned—; the razor-scarred twins were dancing together, and the child prostitute helped a clumsy-fingered sailor to remove her blouse . . . Another item of recollection floated to the scummy surface of my consciousness: 'Jimmy's' reference to the club he had visited, a hell-hole.

Mysteriously, another brimming glass had appeared in my hand. A daisy-chain of dancers had come to a halt before my table, engaging in crude frolics. I closed my eyes again and disposed of the contents of the glass.

Where my view had been obscured by the sportive dancers, there sat a woman aglow. With her gold-flecked eyes, her open nostrils shafts to mossy caverns, the rubbery negroid lips which sucked the juice of pomegranates, she belonged to an earlier time when such statuesque beauty must have been the look of the generality of gentle womanhood.

My legs obeyed my orders. 'Once, centuries past,' I said, 'all women must have looked like you ... like a figure on an Etruscan vase, or one of those wooden idols, pregnant with magic, carved by savages in remote jungles ...' I spread my hands as though moulding her. 'With your placidity, not to mention your superb bust, you remind me also of the proud painted figurehead on an old galleon. But they are all cold and inanimate, while your warm flesh ...' — I reached towards her powdered breasts — '... is live and vibr ...'

An excruciating pain numbs my arm, which, falling, sends a glass spinning into my lap. A wetness spreads over my thighs. A dark-faced man stands over me, chopping hand still levelled.

And then there is Ossie, beaming. 'Can't leave you alone a minute, you get in trouble,' he chides me, though his tone is gentle. 'Close your eyes, I said, and see what happens to you.' He shakes his head reproachfully, though still I feel he isn't really angry with me.

He turns and says something to my assailant who, shortly, resumes his seat. The roar and buffeting of noise, whose volume may only have seemed to have been briefly reduced, is turned on full again.

Nursing my arm, I let him lead me back to our corner table.

'I'd say, you was a man beset by enemies.'

'What? What was that?'

A lithe youth with painted face detaches himself from the pack of dancers and executes a series of graceful high kicks. A wall-eyed woman comprehensively licks a cauliflower ear.

'What do you mean ...' Still, heart, still! '... beset by enemies?'

'Meaning your little fracas, just now. Rough boys those Maltese Crosses.' He seems to search for some consoling distraction, as a mother will try to divert a child from impending tears. 'Still, you didn't really fancy her, did you, Larry – all the booze you've had!' He chuckles, a shade self-consciously. 'Provokes the desire it does, but takes away the performance. As 'amlet said!'

Another drinker falls and doesn't rise. And is that the weeper who, now with jubilant smile, brandishes his proud exposure?

'. . . and with that lovely girl you got, you couldn't truly stomach that old cow. And not especially considering . . .' – roguishly – 'your little private orgy, just concluded.'

But I wasn't going to rise to that one. Had he not already amply demonstrated his omniscience? Beset by enemies, he'd said. I'd have liked to have turned on him, to rip and smash. See if he already knew about that! But I couldn't, I didn't dare. I had troubles enough already.

'So, you got troubles, friend. Know what they say about troubles, don't you – coming not single spies, but in bleeding battalions.' He plucked at my sleeve. 'You like that, Larry, you liked that, eh? Sometimes I surprise myself.'

Madness, now I understand, lies in the angle of one's self-regard. I know too much about myself, like an accomplice in a monstrous crime, whose continued existence is deadly dangerous to my security. Chrissie's strap has slipped again, the buttoned sac joggling to the music's beat. Amid guffaws, an addict sneezed and sneezed and goes on sneezing.

'Know what, Larry, you think too much. Look at you now – stop me if I'm offending you – picking at the sores of your immortal soul.'

But now I believe I have his measure: I can allow his voice to continue, may even hear it, so long as I treat it like just another of my own voices, one of the numerous participants in my interior dialogue. I am seeing and living all this for the second time; now (as I re-create) for the third . . .

'How can I distract you, Larry? I know some conjuring tricks, or would you like to see the pictures I took with my old Auntie on the beach at Brighton? No? Well, maybe you're right, it's scarcely the time and place. Then, how'd you like to hear about my sex-life?'

To be interrogated — any fool would do, psychiatrist or priest or policeman — would be an exquisite variation. To have my most trivial, unconsidered actions given significance, however false, to see the emergence of a pattern, however arbitrary, would be less mortiferous than this incoherent irrelevance that I inhabit. So one tries, in lieu, to become, or to invent, one's own interrogator: creating omens that aren't ominous, correspondences that don't correspond, hallucinations without delusion. A young woman with both eyes bruised purple and a vastly pregnant belly eludes a midget's embrace. I hear a fat woman's vaginal laugh, and an Australian voice discussing the techniques of modern dentistry.

'So, nowadays,' Ossie is concluding, 'I have a predilection for the trappings rather than the orifice itself, you take my meaning. While watching the telly, for instance. Or a good cigar with it. And I've a particular fancy to get them to phone their mothers at the moment critical. But nothing really kinky mind, I draw the line. Talking of which . . .' — he nudges my attention — 'see that brass there . . .'

Yet all the time I feel within me, vibrant as my organs, forces which cogently proclaim I have an I-ness; and sometimes their scream reminds me of what I knew at the moment when, slippery, bloody, naked, with my own first scream, I wriggled out into the world, already then beset by enemies. The mousy young lady to whom my gaze was directed has natural eyes and only the thinnest smudge of salve on her dry lips; she smooths her skirt over her knees with a chaste gesture, difficult to reconcile with the examples related of so extreme a quadrupedantry. One is defined, in both meanings of the word, by one's primordial enemies; that's to say — it makes my head ache and my hands tremble to try to think it through—they simultaneously draw my boundaries and fix my meaning. If I had no enemies, then . . .

Two clasped fists in contention over a knife-blade. Something is thrown and shatters, causing momentary consternation. With no surprise at all, I hear, in the gap between two records, a cracked bog-Irish voice singing a song about dead graveyards.

'Still, *chacun a son gout*, I say . . .'—as though rolling a wine-gum on his tongue. 'Live and let live, or the other way round, what you say, Larry?'

'I . . .'

. . . and then I, then I would re-discover the miracle of my birth, the world's misty beginning in that immeasurable fraction of a second before the sweet turned sour and anguish supplanted innocence. Not only my head aching and my hands trembling . . . but I feel drumbeat pulses in the linings of my intestines, my bowels are loosened—at last—and my sweat's acquired that acrid tang which comes with anger. Only violence purifies. I think I see what I must do . . .

I fell asleep.

When I awoke—tenses tangled—I wondered first whether I had lost anything—wallet, keys . . . myself? My companion's mouth hung slackly open, a yellow dribble bubbling on his lips; his eyes were glazed; and against the oily pallor of his skin the burst veins formed hideous purple blots. My revulsion was indistinguishable from self-disgust.

I could have slept for only a few moments, but in that time, like a drink gone flat—stale, sour-tasting, giving off a smell of corruption—the scene, superficially the same, had changed its character utterly. All the familiar faces—Blanco's bruiser's scowl . . . Chrissie catatonic . . . my odalisque . . . the noseless one . . . even the taxi-driver who had brought us . . . the barmen, singers, dancers—now appeared just ugly, crippled creatures, in their brutishness boring and repellent.

All the significances I had drawn, the mythic sense of fatality, dream's logic, my fantasies of *déjà vu*, seemed totally incomprehensible. I felt ridiculous when I recalled them; I had stepped back over the frontier of reality. All that now remained was to get away as quickly as possible.

I took another glance at Ossie, who gave me an encouraging smile, as though to say: you're back again. Flexing my legs, I tested my capability to walk. 'Ossie, I am going now.' I rose as I spoke . . .

And then the fight broke out. It was confused — of course, confused. The more so for my dazed, numbed condition. It started, I believe, at the bar — where I saw a man in a long overcoat fall backwards, his arms flailing a waiter's tray. I was on my feet. So now was Ossie. The juke-box was still playing and women were screaming. Blanco had come to Ossie's side. It was confused — everything. The dancers and the drinkers were scattered by the shock-wave of blow and stab. Confused. I heard the reckless crash of breaking glass, crack of wood or fractured bone. The carnivorous youth whose knife before had been an implement of manicure lifted a glittering hand. Then fell, with a surprised cough. And lay, blood gushing, at my feet, under the potted palm.

11

There was nothing about it in the papers. The following day I had looked with expectation; then for two or three days half-expecting; and for about a week after that out of habit or superstition.

At the end, all had been confused. I couldn't remember, amnesia abstracting, my exit. I was in a crowded car, squashed between Ossie, Blanco, Chrissie and a bearded giant, who kept muttering to himself in Russian or some such. Next, without transition, time telescoping, I was by myself in a cab, whose driver had a pathological hatred of students and would have them all given military haircuts. I don't remember paying him off, nor entering the block. I am next, tenses still tangled, before the bathroom mirror in my underpants, cradling my Balinese goddess against my naked chest.

The statuette was in the bed beside me when I awoke early the next evening. And the morning afterwards, I returned to the office—with a cold, my rusty voice ironically justifying my absence retrospectively.

I had seen what I had seen: no illusion. Alcohol might have distorted the detail, but it couldn't have painted the canvas. I say, I'd seen what I had seen: with his associates he had loomed menacingly from the mêlée, arm upraised, hand shining; it's not likely that I took my eyes off him, but the next thing he's down under the potted palm, punctured, coughing and surprised; and I hadn't observed what reduced him.

There was of course no certainty that he had been . . . badly hurt. When it wasn't in the papers, I took it that his wound had not been serious—or worse. It did occur to me—friend, you see, I'm not a complete innocent—that the episode might have been staged for my impression; but I dismissed this suspicion on the paradoxical ground that, had it been so, greater verisimilitude would have been achieved.

I found it relatively easy to expunge that evening from my memory; not entirely, of course: images recurred on random occasions; and there was a kind of sticky residue at the base of my skull which sometimes gave off a bad smell and seemed to be disseminating poison. I don't know how else to put it. I felt that, as poison will, it sapped and rotted, but without pain or distress; on the contrary, it provided both comfort and exhilaration. I don't pretend to understand.

Of course, in my regular, or irregular, day-to-day existence all this was buried deep, deeper than one ought to delve. One had problems enough on the surface.

My brief absence from the office seemed to have reduced the place to chaos. Faithful Lydia had, doubtless, done her limited best, and Harvey, to my grateful surprise, had taken over a number of my responsibilities; but the effect of their joint efforts had been sand in the works, broken wires. I kept uncovering fresh disasters, one of which—a matter merely of an o misinterpreted as a 9—obliged me to spend three days at The Fridge in a series of abrasive and sterile conferences. Then, paper and files, like leaves caught by a playful gust, were not where they ought to have been—including one blueprint from another department, which must have been blown right out of the window. As I had abstracted this surreptitiously for use in connection with my 'opus', I couldn't make a fuss about its loss. I couldn't really make a fuss about anything: must be reasonable, everyone had been doing their best.

Possibly my cold dulled me, slowed me up; it proved tediously persistent; without ever incapacitating, it bored and nagged and irritated, like a wife. M.B. was unsympathetic. You don't get colds at this time of the year. He had evidently been reading some trashy popularization: it must be psychosomatic, he asserted, repeating the word several times. I could not have felt more indignant had my sick-leave been genuine. Or an allergy, that's it, an allergy. Know what an allergy is, don't you? Perhaps it's M.C.L. House you're allergic to. He had laughed, but only after a watchful minute's reflection. There comes a time when one feels too old for nursery games!

My troubles were not confined to the office. Waiters had grown still more insolent, it seemed, transistor radios noisier, bills weightier, taxis rarer, the newspaper headlines more affronting—doubtless, all because of my cold. Even though the news appalled, I found myself taking a greater interest in it, the newspapers, the radio and T.V. bulletins—in itself a symptom of ill health, I occasionally couldn't help suspecting. The three or four times daily dose of calamity resembled a mild addiction.

One evening, I had the television on in the living-room while busying myself in the kitchen. The taps were running, the stove roaring, so the volume was a little higher than usual in order that I should hear when the news began. I don't know what was on at the time—some film, I guess, with a score for three symphony orchestras. By the way, I was wearing one of Sarah's flowered aprons knotted round my middle.

I just heard the doorbell above my domestic hubbub. Then the news signature-tune started, so as I shuffled to the door I was at the same time peering over my shoulder at a short-legged politician striding with hilarious grim purpose towards a waiting aeroplane.

In front of me stood my neighbour, my neighbour of the drums, accompanied by the desk-clerk. The matter was a complaint about noise: the noise from *my* flat, the noise from *my* television. I was flustered, what with Sarah's frilly apron, the newsreader's verbless oracularities, my awareness of the bubbling saucepans; so, however justified my indignation, it's possible I went further than I would have done more calm. Ironically, as I was in full flow, an aeroplane passed overhead drowning both the television and my maledications. I took hold of my persecutors by the stuff of whatever they were wearing and threw them back into the corridor. My neighbour fell to his knees, the clerk slid down the wall. I slammed the door, making everything shake seismically.

When I returned to the kitchen my saucepans had boiled over, creating a disgusting mess in the stove.

As I went through the hall the next morning, the clerk was engaged in solemn colloquy with the porter — until they observed me, when they fell abruptly silent, their heads turning with my passage ... All this, of course, was trivial business.

My main concern, naturally, lay with Jackie. A kind of cloud seemed to have condensed between us: it was nothing one could take hold of and examine; misty, diffuse, damp, it cast patchy shadows and deadened our resonance. I was driven frantic.

She refused absolutely to come to the flat again, though without ever explicitly specifying why. 'I don't want to, that's all. I don't feel like it. Must you keep going on and on about it.'

Perhaps, though I found this hard to believe, she was suffering some kind of moral or aesthetic reaction from the excesses of the previous occasion. Certainly I was now restricted to the most orthodox of embraces. Whenever I suggested a variation, or even tentatively adjusted to a more affinitive position, she would, as it were, curl up both physically and emotionally, turning a prudish bony spine. Verbal extravagances were also out.

She created, I thought, an undue fuss about my cold: not sympathy; fear of her own infection. 'You can't keep having a cold at this time of the year, it's unnatural,' she complainingly echoed M.B.

'I suppose,' I retorted with private irony, 'it must be psychosomatic.'

'Or else you're allergic to something. Perhaps you've become allergic to me.' She said it without humour, with a kind of remote un-sad compassion — which made me babble despairing nonsense.

I hadn't wanted her in the flat merely for a repetition, or an extension, of our previous activities. Oh dear me, no. Indeed not. I had constructed tableaux of domestic bliss, warm slippers, cosy breakfasts, hand-holding before the television. Waiting for her ... being waited for ...

'Stop it! Stop it!' she cried in a shrill voice, obliterating my tender fancies. 'That shit! That sentimental shit, all married men try on! I've heard it all before.' She knocked down my restraining hand. 'Yes, I have, I have—dozens of times. You don't like that, do you—middle-aged married lover!'

There were also other things I didn't like. For instance, Adrian, who had acquired the habit of dropping in. Not quite unannounced: he'd knock discreetly on the dividing wall, and if the moment were not entirely unpropitious she'd rap back a welcoming response. I couldn't help but wonder what other secret codes they shared.

Much of their language was like a private code: elliptical and baffling. But about that I was prepared to give them the benefit of the doubt: it simply renewed my sense of exclusion, increased the burden of my years. Adrian irritated me with his whimsical way of reverting to our telephone conversation, slitting his eyes and talking a mock-pidgin English, liberally garnished with obscenities; and sometimes he would pretend to believe that I was in fact The Breather. Incidentally, Jackie assured me, the calls from The Breather had stopped. She assumed that this was because of Sarah's absence, and—for God's sake, don't ask me why!—I chose not to disabuse her.

I suppose, except for his unfunny jokiness, Adrian's attitude towards me was unexceptionable. Sometimes—as he lay sprawled beside her on the bed while I occupied the only reasonable chair—sometimes I even experienced a sense of comradeship, as in one's college days when three seemed a warm and reassuring number.

Nevertheless, it was Adrian, who, however unwittingly, precipitated one of our most devastating passages. He must have heard us enter—I shuddered when I thought of the other sounds he'd heard—for within a moment, even as I undid the first buttons of her blouse, his knock came on the wall, and Jackie slid eel-like from my arms to return it.

He came in dressed to kill, like a peacock—or whatever the

vulgar expression is for the vulgar appearance. His hair sculpted like cake-icing, he wore a scarlet cloak, a frilled shirt of yellow lace, glittering concentration-camp boots. Jackie, her blouse slipping, advanced on him with breathy squeals of delight. Like two greedy housewives they were, just returned from the sales.

I stood back; but my approbation wasn't called for. I stood back. In a few moments Adrian departed for wherever such a harlequinade would not assure his lynching.

Jackie slipped off her blouse. I stood back. She reversed towards me, straightening her shoulders so that I could un-latch her bra. I stepped away. She raised her eyebrows with quizzical innocence.

'That brooch,' I said, 'the brooch he was wearing in that hideous cloak . . . cameo brooch . . .' I loathed the note of whine in my voice. 'The one I gave to you!'

Pointless — even perhaps too painful, still too painful — to reproduce all the obvious exchanges of our quarrel: my whines, her increasingly shrill contempt. I told her it showed she didn't love me, couldn't, that she should casually give away. My tender gift. Chosen with so much. Unless he were her pimp. I got my face slapped then — though I felt it was a ritual response. Selfish little bitch just using me. Who's doing the using, that's rich, rich that is. I didn't own her. She couldn't be bought just like a. What did I think she. Because I'd given her the wretched, just because I, I — that made it fucking sacred, did it? Angry tears. I felt my own eyes pricking in response. We took a few backward steps along the slope to reconciliation.

'What I can't stand,' she said in a quieter, sob-free voice, 'it shows the importance you attach to things, possessions. I suppose that's the difference between us. It's to do with your being so much older, I suppose.'

'I don't think that's fair. Not fair at all. You're the one who . . .' I broke off, not wanting to stir it all up again.

'Yes, go on. Say it. I'm the one who . . .'

'You like . . . you like nice things,' I said weakly. 'You like a good life – wine, food . . . I mean . . . But what does it matter? It's not even what we were having . . .' – I stretched out my arm, just to touch her with my finger-tips – 'this ludicrous, ridiculous row about.'

She didn't answer me straight away, although there were sufficient openings. She looked at me strangely, pathetically. 'How do *you* know what I want, Laurence?' she said at last, but entirely without rancour. 'Do you really, truly care what I am like, what my life is like? Do you know who I really am? You just have your own . . . convenient idea of me, the sort of girl you think you want. Oh, shit!' she cried, 'I'm not like that at all. I'm me. I'm, I'm . . . I want, I want . . .' Sobbing, with a broken, hurt-child's face, she fell into my arms in order to cover her head.

No words to describe my emotion. And before long, of course, my soothing fingers found themselves twiddling with the catch between her downy shoulders . . .

But it was not a good time between us, those weeks of my, relative, freedom. I don't know whose fault it was, if fault there were. I did – honestly, I did – my best unselfishly to please: I was neglectful of my work, laying aside my cherished, and now urgent, 'opus'; I ignored my friends, such few as I had in this bad city for friendship – even including my good friend Ossie, though once, at an improbable art gallery, I thought for an instant that I had seen him, sceptical before a colourless canvas, and on three or four occasions a black man who was Blanco had distantly materialized, and then he'd gone or wasn't.

I took Jackie to places, to bars and restaurants and night-clubs, concerts, cinemas and theatres, which I would never have visited of my own volition. Not bribes. Unselfishly. She was restless and discontented. After her part in the television play, she was eager for other work and thought that opportunities would flow. She attended two auditions without success and, equally fruitlessly, solicited her play's director and 'Jimmy'. I was going to accompany her when she met 'Jimmy', I wished to ask him something, he'd mentioned a certain club . . . But Jackie didn't want me along; I asked her to ask him; but she said afterwards that she had forgotten.

'Jimmy' had been, it seems, her last throw: when nothing developed from their meeting—she was extremely reluctant to talk about it—a wave of despondency rose up and swamped her. She was going to give up the stage. Perhaps she ought to go to evening classes, learn something practical, like shorthand, book-keeping. Otherwise, she'd starve, she'd just grow old and ugly and starve. Or else she'd have to marry a disgusting old man with clammy fingers. Oh, if only . . . if only . . . the cretins hadn't cut her best scene.

In her unhappiness she was—love isn't altogether blind—fractious and trying; disappointment brought out the worst in her: pettiness, pretension, a spoiled child's egotism. I behaved—no matter what my motives!—with forbearance, unselfishness, generosity. Yet I couldn't blame her that it was not a good time, those weeks of my, relative, freedom; I felt the poison was in myself. I didn't know its nature or where it grew from. It was somewhat like my cold, pervasive, demoralizing and sempiternal. And waking each new day I'd hope that it had gone.

Then I had a letter from Sarah announcing her imminent return.

At the restaurant table there is a lover's silence. Anyone at a neighbouring table could sense how ponderous was the space between us, electric the currents of self-consciousness.

'Drink your coffee,' said Jackie at last. 'It'll get cold.'

Our eyes weren't meeting. My blink-rate was excessive. The smoke from her furiously puffed cigarette made a wind-blown curtain.

'I don't want . . .' I said, 'I don't want to hurt her.'

'Drink your coffee,' Jackie repeated. And I obediently drank,

daring a blinking glance above my cup. Through the veil of
smoke she chewed her lower lip; her face seemed bonier and
disdainful. 'Someone's got to be hurt,' she said, still looking into
the distance, above my right ear. 'Someone's always got to be
hurt. You can't live without hurting people.'

There were hushed pauses, as in a game: not a highly skilled or
intellectual game, but one in which the contestants appear
briefly to consider, before making moves which are in reality
conventional, inevitable. 'That may be true but . . .' I let my
words hang.

'What about me? What about hurting me?'

'Oh, my darling!' Even the most banal games have a sort of
minor magic. I leaned intently over my coffee-cup. 'Sweet
Jackie, you know that I would do anything in the world for you.
You're . . . you are the air I breathe, water, salt . . . you are
necessity to me. Why, if I should never come to your room
again, that record, those ridiculous photographs, see you,
touch you, love you, it wouldn't be worth going on living.'

'Well, then?'

'I don't know. I don't know how I. I just don't know.'

'Don't know,' she repeated, with shrewish contempt. 'You
can say all these wonderful things to me, sitting here – but you
don't know. You're so weak – yes, you are, Laurence – weak,
and a hypocrite too, and a coward, because you're not man
enough to do what you really want to do.'

'Perhaps,' I groaned, 'perhaps you're right.' For had another
voice not told me that, with other words, elsewhere?

'You just let it all go on inside you. In your head. It's just
words. You haven't got the strength. You always need . . .' – I
heard what she was going to say before she said it – 'someone
else to do your dirty work for you.'

'There, you agree . . .' – the opening was irresistible – 'it's
dirty work.'

'I agree,' she smoothly countered, 'it won't be pleasant for
you. Or for her, poor thing. But it's what's got to be done,

Laurence, if you want us to be happy. That is, so long as you haven't just been lying to me, if you really want me.'

'Oh, yes, yes—you know!'

'Well, then?'

'You're so young . . .' I began.

'What is that supposed to mean?'

'I mean . . .' I had surprised myself: I didn't know exactly what I had intended. 'I mean, because you're young you believe that life is simpler than it is, you believe in quick, clean solutions. You think people should always . . . act out their desires. But you can't, Jackie, you can't, not always. Sometimes one wants things, sometimes one has thoughts . . . thoughts that are terrible, monstrous . . .'

Somehow, as I spoke, I was addressing not only her, but another persecutor, perhaps within me. Curiously, as though she could sense this, I detected her diminishing reception: her eyes were wandering.

'And then even . . .' I floundered on, 'one feels just as guilty as if there were no difference between the thought and the act. But there is, Jackie, there is, there has to be. Otherwise . . . otherwise, nothing that one does, or avoids doing, has any meaning. After all . . .' I consummated, her attention having clearly left me altogether: 'After all, a thought, a wish—they're really innocent, they can't hurt anybody else, can they? Can they?' I cried. 'Hey! Were you listening to me?'

'Um? Yes, of course.' She gave me a little smile: apologetic merely, but it was a smile. 'Of course, every word. He's gone now, anyway.'

'Who has gone?'

'There was a man behind you.' To my automatic turn: 'No, I told you he's gone.'

'There are several men.'

'He seemed,' she explained, 'to be staring at us all the time. Nobody I recognized, but he looked, somehow, just vaguely familiar—oh, quite ordinary, rather a common little fat man, not fat exactly, square—like, you know, someone you keep on bumping into by accident, so you think they must be following you, though of course they're not really.'

'Was he . . . Had he . . .' I started to seek, doubtless superfluous, amplification, but then thought the situation was sufficiently complex already. I would take advantage of her interruption: 'I expect,' I smiled, eyes twinkling, and risking to lay my hand on hers, 'any forked, red-blooded male, sixteen to sixty, and in his right mind, to stare and stare and go on staring at my lovely, oyster-eyed darling.'

'Just,' she complacently demanded, 'so long as you tell her, that's all. As soon as she arrives. Tonight. You tell Sarah what you're going to do.'

12

I would, as a goodwill gesture, have met her at the airport—just another afternoon of truancy!—but she had written explicitly that I should not.

Why so definite—I was reading at the time a prolix project outline—it occurred to me suddenly to wonder. Could it possibly be because she would be accompanied by a man? A lover. How easy that would make it! I saw him as rather elderly, quiet, distinguished; no Cobber Wal he; a widower would be best—and of substance. I went on reading the closely-typed outline, as he escorted her through Immigration and Customs with courteous efficiency, kissed her chastely or shook hands, before her taxi drew away, leaving him the confidence of her sweet and sacred promises. How easy, how happily fortuitous! 'I agree,' I wrote, and signed without awareness.

Later, I took her letter out of my wallet and read it again. Peer as I might between the lines, I could see no widower in it. Despite a formality of expression and the tone's general tepidity, it seemed, rather, to convey an entirely loathsome willingness to try again.

Loathsome, also, Lydia's deodorant. And Harvey's gin-garrulous telephone calls. I couldn't stand it. Looking at my watch, I let out a cry of annoyance and ran from the room, late for a non-existent appointment. Roving the building and glowing in my skull, I plagued unsuspecting colleagues with redundant consultations.

'Where on earth have you been hiding yourself?' asked Lydia, smiling and reeking. 'We couldn't find you, paged you everywhere . . .' That must have been while I was skulking in the wash-room. 'There was an outside phone call for . . .'

'Was it . . .' I eagerly asked, as if doting, 'was it my wife?'

'Is she home then, Sarah? You never said. I didn't know she . . .'

'Comes back today,'—grudgingly.

'Oh, how nice for you!' Lydia radiated. 'You've been a lonely bachelor so long.'

'Yes,' I agreed. 'The phone call?'

'A man, he wouldn't give a name.' She became business-like. 'He said you'd know who it was, a friend. I asked if there was any message, and he said just to tell you he'd seen you in the restaurant at lunch-time, and . . .'—she looked up from her blank scrap-pad—'he'd be ready when you called him.'

'Have a choccy,' offered Harvey.

'It will be nice for you to have your wife home,' Lydia said again as, resuming my role of eager husband, I excused my early departure. 'You've been,' she also said again, 'a lonely bachelor so long.'

Eager, in fact, I was—eager now to come to the point, to harness all my unresolved conflicts into one tremendous surge of resolution. That thin red wire glowing in my head was burning down to detonate an explosion, as I raced across the hallway, ignoring the salute of the porter—doubtless, wishing also to congratulate me on my wife's return—into the sluggish lift, and at last up to my front door.

Sarah was still unpacking. Hearing my entry, she came out of the bedroom with coats and dresses draped over her arms. These made our home-coming embrace, of necessity, distant and formal. I followed her back into the bedroom, with talk of aeroplanes and souvenirs. How well she looked, I told her.

Her skin was tanned, enhancing the mirage blueness of her eyes, her face appeared fuller, and she moved in a more relaxed way. Despite this evidence of well-being, she still created an impression of a bloodless fragility—at any rate, compared with the plump, smiling demon that sat obscenely exposed on the dressing-table stool. But how had I been managing?

I shrugged uncomplainingly; murmured about a cold, but uncomplainingly. Really, everything had gone quite well. She was grateful to find the flat in so tidy a condition, though what, she wondered, were those stains on the wallpaper over there. A funny place to drink beer, she thought, in bed; I was reverting to my crude bachelor ways.

That might have been an opening; but it seemed too soon. Besides, I was distracted by a sardonic wink from the dressing-table stool. The wire in my skull had cooled to become merely a little nerve, jumping from time to time to remind me of its existence.

Sarah dived into one of her suitcases. 'Look,' she said, 'what I've brought you back.'

She handed me my gifts: an ornate silk scarf, and a bottle of duty-free Green Chartreuse. Having expressed my delight at the former, I then insisted that she should interrupt her unpacking to share the liqueur with me.

We went into the living-room, sat down facing, and smiled at each other. Sarah was wearing a scent that was unfamiliar to me —but, smell as I might, I could detect no whiff of a substantial widower! We raised our glasses, and I said, as I had to: 'Welcome home!'

I sipped, and lowered my glass. Sarah smiled again. I cleared my throat and summoned up my resolution.

We started to speak at the same instant, and I chivalrously acceded.

'I was going to ask,' said Sarah brightly, 'how is our drum-beating neighbour?'

'That bloody lunatic!' Glad to expand, I told her something of my encounters. She laughed and sympathized. We drank again, smiled again. I cleared my throat again. The telephone rang.

I was the quicker off the chair: not in any specific expectation, but merely from a reflex of guilt, though by the time I had reached the phone I was convinced that it must be Jackie or Ossie, more probably Jackie—over-eager, my love, to learn!— and when a feminine voice said, 'Hullo, Laurence', I nearly snapped a monitory 'Wrong number!' It turned out to be, however, a friend of Sarah's, calling to welcome her return; Moira Blenkinsop, her name.

A loquacious friend. I poured and drank another glass of Green Chartreuse, and Sarah, holding the squeaking receiver away from her ear, mimed her helplessness. I poured a third glass and wandered with it back into the bedroom. The liqueur flowered in my chest. I looked at the still gaping suitcases with hatred. 'It's got to be done,' I muttered to myself. But what a homecoming for her, when perhaps she had been pregnant with her own hopeful embryo for the future! When she had just passed over her gifts! When she was yet travel-stained and weary! When ... At the restaurant-table Jackie said: 'Tell her, tell her ... as soon as she arrives ...' And the wraith at the dressing-table, in her bland nudity, confirmed: 'Tonight ... now!'

I heard the tinkle of the replaced receiver. I gulped down the rest of my drink. A glow not only in my chest, but in my skull again! I cleared my throat.

We met in the doorway. 'Laurence, I hope you don't mind ...' Sarah, forgetfully, put a consoling hand to my cheek. 'Moira talked me into it ... I couldn't escape ... and as I've these presents for her and she's going away tomorrow ...'

'What? What?' I was dazed, as one might be — surgeon or patient — turned about at the very door of the operating-theatre.

'And it's no use my saying, I'll just drop in — you know what Moira's like.' Sarah was already again delving into the suitcase. 'It seems terrible my first night back just to. Like this. But it's not as if you and I were ...' She straightened, waving gay packages. 'Ah! — here they are. Well, we're not, are we, you and I?'

'Sarah! I wanted to ...' I broke off. 'Wanted' was most certainly the wrong word; I was aware of a shameful dissolution into relief.

'What?'

Dumbly, I shook my head.

'Laurence.' She turned about. 'You don't really mind, do you? If you do, then I'll call her and cancel.'

'No, no. Of course not.'

She came swiftly towards me. 'Un-zip me, please. I'll have to take a quick shower . . .'

The glow in my skull had gone out, the red wire dimmed; resolution was now superfluous, like a vestigial adornment. I couldn't deny the flood of relief—it was natural—; but now my opportunity had been removed in a way which left me blameless, I could begin to indulge a sense of resentment. It was a bit much, after all, her first night back, too. When I had matters of importance.

Did I say, blameless? I wondered if Jackie would see it so. I turned to the bedroom stool, and met a sneer of shrivelling contempt.

'I'll cook you something, of course, before I go.' Sarah had partially dressed in the bathroom, not in front of me. 'But if you want to go out, I'll quite understand.' She said it in a quick embarrassed way, as though chary of presumption. Ah, yes, I can see these things! One is naturally sensitive to one's own wife's nuances. 'After all,' she went on, 'while I've been away, you must have . . . well, you've had your own routine, I suppose.'

I could stop her now; gently but firmly take from her hands the frock she was carrying like a life-size doll on its hanger; turn her about; lead her by the hand from the three's-a-crowded bedroom; Sarah, I have to talk . . .

'Well, do you want me to or not?'

'What's that?'

'Before I finish dressing.'

'What?'

'Cook you a meal.' She held the dress high, ready to pull over her head.

'I . . . I think I will go out. Yes.' No, it really wouldn't do. Not now. Quite impossible. 'That is, if it's all the same to you,' I added politely.

Sarah squirmed through her frock. 'You do whatever you want to do, of course,' she agreed. 'You must lead your own life.'

'Tell me again,' said Jackie softly, 'what did she say?'

'But I've told you already.'

'No. What did she say—her exact words?'

'She said: "You do whatever you want to do. You must lead your own life."'

'Ah!' She squirmed luxuriously against the pillows, leaving her hand resting on my trousered thigh in ownership. The record-player was on low; blue smoke curled; more rubbish than ever cluttered the bedside-table; and the bed was in its usual post-coital disorder. 'Darling, I'm so happy,' she sighed, squeezing my thigh. 'Aren't you?'

I hadn't for a second planned to deceive her. All the way there I'd been rehearsing various explanations to reduce her disappointment and her wrath, but these had been only mildly tendentious. There had been no intention, I swear it, right up to her door, of pretending that the issue had been resolved. It hadn't entered my head that I might construct a whole pyramid of lies—one false stone after another dropping into place with weighty inevitability.

Even now I couldn't quite understand how it had happened. It had been her fault, Jackie's fault. Before I had spoken at all, she had managed with one smile to express an insulting scepticism, seconds later with another, its non-identical twin, a promise that should I, after all, have bravely triumphed, my reward would be commensurate. One smile I might have resisted . . .

Her first words on my entry, actually, had been: 'Well, did you?'

'I said I would, didn't I?' Playing for time. 'Given any chance,' I hastily added.

'But did you tell her? What happened?'

I sought for a non-provocative truth. 'Everything's going to be all right,' I said, confidently but fatally. She gave me then her second smile.

Certainly, she had not reneged its tacit promise: in her joy, our bed-games had the ardour and intimacy, and in miniature the savagery, of the games we had played in my flat, and never since. In her unbridled joy at the happy, civilized disposition of our future ...

'You must live your own life,' Jackie repeated now, in a tone of wonder, still gently squeezing my trousered thigh. Like a child who's enjoyed an outstanding treat, she wanted to re-capitulate it all. 'Live your own life – that was a very generous thing for her to say.'

'Well, Sarah is civilized.'

'But I wouldn't have expected her to be so understanding, to make it so easy for us.'

'We can only be grateful.'

'Umm – grateful!'

'Actually, I think ...' Forgive me, everyone, for this – God knows why! 'I think she might be glad to be free herself.'

'You mean ...' – with lubricious enthusiasm – 'Sarah's got a man.'

'Well, I don't know for certain ...'

'Who? Who is he?'

'She may have met him on holiday.' At times of such weakness as I was enduring, anyone might be guilty of the most appalling, the most shameful, fatuity. 'I understand he's a widower – rather elderly for her, perhaps, but distinguished. A man of some substance. I'm guessing to a certain extent, mind. She didn't actually tell me.'

'Well, good for Sarah!' Jackie smiled in a dreamy, indulgent way, as though at a romantic story in a women's magazine. 'Good for Sarah,' she repeated. 'But what else did she say, when you two were sitting there swigging all that Cointreau?'

'Green Chartreuse,' I corrected, with pedantic regard for accuracy.

'All right, Chartreuse. But what else? I want to hear it all, every word. Was she upset? Did she cry? Not even just a little?'

'No, she didn't cry.' I suppose, once embroiled in my pitiful fantasy, I had sought to give it conviction by predicting what would indeed be said, I hopefully believed, when the confrontation did in actuality take place. 'She was controlled and reasonable throughout.' Or, by a form of sympathetic magic, I was creating the future: 'She was very reasonable, she couldn't have been more . . . co-operative and understanding.'

'Marvellous, darling!' A more vigorous squeeze. 'Aren't we lucky? Some time I shall have to thank her.'

'Ah well, er . . . yes. Some time.'

She didn't notice my hesitation. She had passed on. 'Just think . . .' A look of horror distorted her bare, love-planed face. 'Just think how awful it would have been, otherwise.'

I shifted my leg away. A discomfort that had fretted me previously had been revived. 'If . . .' I began. She was looking around for somewhere to stub out her cigarette; I passed the brimming ashtray. 'If it had gone . . . otherwise, would it really have been so terrible?'

'What do you mean, darling?'

'I mean, if Sarah hadn't been so civilized . . . co-operative . . . If it had meant a fight.'

'But of course it would, terrible.'

Some of the ash slopped over when I replaced the ashtray — actually, the lid from, I think, a jar of face-cream — but it was unavoidable. 'Why would it?'

'Oh, darling!' She pouted at my tiresome and irrelevant persistence. 'All the squalor of it, the bitchiness. You don't know what they can be like, some wives. No, thank you! Praise God, it's not like that.'

'But . . .'

'All the trouble she could have made. It would have been hell. Impossible!' She reached to comfort to my thigh again. 'You'd have gone through hell, poor man.'

'But, whatever she did, she couldn't stop . . . she couldn't have stopped us . . . having each other.' Her fingers crept upwards distractingly. 'Could she? I mean, whatever happened, we . . . whatever happens, nothing will part us.'

'Licence my roaving hands,' she crooned, probing. 'No, darling, of course not. Whatever had happened, however bitchy she'd been, nothing . . .' A certain conviction seemed lacking; she appeared not to be fully concentrating. 'Before, behind, between . . .'

But, just for an instant, I was tempted. Whatever had happened, she had said; whatever had happened, she had implied, my love would be true to me. Faced by such trusting devotion, why should I, how could I, maintain my cowardly deception?

'. . . above, below . . .'

'Jackie, listen to me,' I began. 'If I told you . . .'

Because of a missing nail, we're informed, the battle was lost. There came a knock on the wall, Adrian's special knock. It froze, as well as her hand, my tongue. Though in life it's nearly always impossible to trace the chain back from the ultimate calamity, I had at that moment, and knowing I was not going on, a vivid premonition of the linking disasters to come.

Jackie, smiling, shook her head in sweet concurrence, rejecting him. Her fingers un-froze. But the moment had passed: the nail had been lost for ever.

'No, Jackie,' she reproved herself before too long, withdrawing her hand. 'And you, Rufus—bad boy—down!' Gentle in her happy innocence, she made huge eyes at me: 'We can be patient, darling, can't we, now we know we have each other always.'

I got off the bed. I stood looking at the wall of pin-ups. Something, I realized, was worrying me: an additional photograph had sprouted, alongside that of myself; it was a glossy, toothy portrait of 'Jimmy'. 'What's this doing?'

'Only a souvenir,' said Jackie. 'It's not a very good one, is it? You know something, sweetheart, I'll tear them all up, or burn them—yes, that's right, I'll burn them, we'll have a ceremonial burning . . . on our wedding day.'

Just a few more moments, having lit another cigarette for her and put it between her tender, smiling lips, and I was on my way slowly to the door.

'You know something, sweetheart,' she said again. 'Tonight—it's funny—I don't mind you going back to her. It's all right tonight, now we know we . . . Be kind to Sarah, sweetheart. She must be upset. Be gentle . . .'

In the street—looking up at her glowing window.

Walking along the tow-path, where, I now recall, two lovers were wriggling and groaning against a tree; and a sleeping swan, disturbed by my steps, menacingly spread its enormous wings.

The porter had a folded newspaper on his knee and a stub of pencil between his fingers. He feigned not to have noticed my approach to the door and ineptly mimed apology upon my unassisted entry.

Surprisingly, for that time of night, the lift was busy, spilling hilarious guests from, I gathered by their chatter, a party at the flat of the petfood manufacturer on the fourth floor.

Surprisingly, after what must have been a wearing day for her, Sarah was still up. Fully dressed, she sat on the couch, a book open in her hands, though I have no evidence that she'd been reading it.

'Hullo,' I greeted, with cheerful, incurious banality. 'Still up, eh? God!—that book must be absorbing. And you haven't even . . .'—I walked across to the television, which was showing an empty, flashing screen – 'turned off the set. Do you know what time it is?'

Sarah laid down her book. Of course – I'm not an insensitive fool – I already had an inkling, but I clung to a soggy straw of optimism, and with yet cheerier fatuity, enquired: 'And how was the garrulous Moira?'

'You know, don't you?' Sarah interrupted.

'Know what?'

'Why I waited up for you, waited for you to come back. Still . . .' – she assumed a wrinkling expression of distaste – 'with her smell on you!'

'Sarah, it's late, and you must be tired, after all you . . .'

'Tired, yes. I am tired.' She spoke with sematic control. 'I am tired to death.'

'All right!' My tone was reasonable. 'You know where I have been. You yourself sent me, with, more or less, your blessing. You must admit. Your first night back, I would have been pleased to stay at home with you, to hear all about your holiday. It was you who. You must admit.'

'Damn you!' she cried. 'Don't pretend. Don't pretend you don't know.'

I assumed, perhaps, a look of denseness. Or, perhaps, I spread my hands. What I did, or said, from this point on is of little matter.

'The only thing I really cared about any more! The one thing I wouldn't, couldn't endure! I told you. And you promised.'

It was the clerk who had informed, of course; I elicited that: in revenge for our little contretemps in the corridor, or simply from the innate malevolence of his mean and twisted soul. 'And now,' Sarah, on the brink of angry tears, lamented, 'even my home, my sheets, my hairbrush – I found her hairs – perhaps even my own clothes have been contaminated by her filthy touch. By her filthy smell.'

She said a good deal more. I found myself comparing this quarrel with that I had had with Jackie at the time of the castaway brooch. There were moments when it seemed the same occasion, or as though I were the victim of a two-headed monster, with identical fangs. Yet, whatever blood had been drawn in that earlier battle, there had always been the assurance of an ultimate tender reconciliation, which gave the blood the innocuity of the tomato-sauce of actors' wounds. Whereas now ...! Whereas now, I bled—though this is all metaphor!—if not from the heart, then from the jugular vein.

And yet, at the end, there came occasion for a marvellous hope: at the end when, somehow, we had changed places, I on the couch, she standing above me. 'This,' she said, at the end, 'is the end. This time we really have finished. She can have you, your nasty little slut, your tart, that's if she wants you—God help her!—she can have you.'

I believe I didn't speak, but she must, even through the deafening howl of her hysteria, have registered the whisper of my unuttered hope.

'No, it's no use your thinking,' She looked down at me silently for a moment, like an executioner measuring the drop. 'Oh, no! Don't you think that. I'm not going to be *civilized*, my sweet. I'm not going to make things easy for you. Not after this! Oh, no! You'll see. It's all going to be nasty and difficult and very, very ... squalid!'

13

In the night, I dreamed of Ossie. He came running to my call, down a stone screw of steps with walls of fur, and into bed beside me. Obviously, I was sleeping alone. His presence created a wonderful sense of reassurance. For a while we conversed: our dialogue was peculiar, in that each in turn would complete the sentences the other began.

Later, I dreamed of the meths drinkers on the razed building-site, and then, because of a missing nail, became one of them, terrorized, abject and abandoned.

Other people's dreams, even if revealing, are not very entertaining, although they may sometimes be funny. It was another night in which Jackie returned to me feverishly gay from a visit to the dentist, and, in an Earl's Court-Australian accent told me: 'It didn't hurt at all. His hands tasted bloody lovely of soap. After he'd filled me, he asked me to call him Wal.'

Enough! Enough! As if my waking hours were not sufficiently ominous—shadowed by dream's inconsequence, coincidence and farce!

'Sarah, your lady wife,' said M.B., more in contempt than in reproof, 'has no relations in the entire dyke-drained Netherlands, let alone tulips or aunts in Amsterdam. We've been making certain enquiries, lad. You told me a taradiddle, lad, a veritable farrago.'

A dead bird, one of millions, had chosen the exact spot where the driver's door of my car opened: a ball of bloody feathers, I had to kick aside.

From the window, powerless, I watched the gratuitous wrecking of the trampolin by a gang of intruding hooligans. When I turned round, the electric clock had stopped.

In an evening paper, casually picked up while waiting in a bar for Jackie, I read that the Coroner had adjourned the inquest on Micky Harris, aged 22, no fixed address, whose body had been found in a North London railway yard the previous Tuesday. He had died as a result of stab wounds and, according to the medical evidence, the corpse had lain undiscovered for some weeks. It was likely that he had been killed elsewhere. The police were continuing their enquiries. The photograph of the youth in life appeared in a column adjoining the report, and it took me a few seconds to marry the two together.

In the bar, when she came, Jackie was more than ever impatient, gobbling crisps and nuts and olives with a tense, neurotic rapacity. All had been agreed, arranged, we were now affianced, yet nothing had changed, and crack went another nut. Sarah and I were still cohabiting. Wasn't it time I moved out? Had I seen a solicitor yet? Down slid an olive. One can't rush these things, not after so many years. But how, with a snap-snap of teeth, did I think she felt? I was being honest with her, wasn't I? Not just playing her along? No, of course not. Of course not, but. Well, I sometimes wonder, Anyway, something had to happen. Soon.

With that, at least, I could honestly assent. But I felt utterly powerless—as powerless as when I witnessed the hooligans from the window: no word or movement of mine, nose to the glass, could halt the onrush to destruction. And the clock had stopped. Since the night of Sarah's return, we had scarcely spoken. We hadn't exchanged a single word concerning our lives together, or apart. Of course, the situation couldn't continue like that, I knew it very well; she knew it, too; I could tell from the feline, *sibilant* way she moved and breathed and occupied space. Perhaps, I allowed myself to hope, she was punishing me temporarily before she would ultimately relent. The best thing was to play for time—with her, with Jackie. So I told myself, knowing that, indolent and will-less, I was incapable for the present of any other course. Decision and action seemed to await the fertilization of hysteria.

That night we met in the bar I stayed with Jackie. The night was not a success. Actually, I was almost impotent, and I prefer not to think about the cumbersome devices to which we resorted. The bed was too small, and I slept fitfully. Moreover, whenever I did fall asleep I began to snore — still sleeping, I could hear myself, like a demoniac hound —; whereupon Jackie, woken, would revengefully wake me again; and so a long martyrdom passed. It was the first time that with her I had been less than sexually competent; I seldom snore: one betrays one's apprehensions in the most shameful forms available.

All the same, in the morning when, haggard, I dressed above her drowsy, wrinkled nudity, I felt a tenderness different in kind from anything in my life I had previously experienced. The fiasco of the night, the room's sunlit sleaziness, her sluttish indifference, like a whore's, combined to produce an overwhelming impression of vulnerability, which brought a, literal, lump to my throat.

As she yawned and stretched and scratched her creases and her orifices — just like an unfastidious whore — I stole furtive glances, delighting in not only her physical blemishes but her *nastiness*, summoning up my recollections of her greed and selfishness and affectation, her moral insensibility — everything ugly I could find, for it seemed far more profoundly appealing than her sweetness.

I had never loved her, so it seemed in my perverse imagination, as deeply, as truly as then. Delighted by my picture of her whorishness, I slipped a five-pound note — evidently, all she was worth! — under a mantelshelf ornament.

My good spirits in spite of everything infuriated her, quite naturally, and she sent me on my way with lovely curses — and a repeated shrill command that I should settle matters with Sarah.

It is, I suppose, likely that I had engineered my overnight absence with the hope that it might precipitate the confrontation with Sarah that I was too feeble to initiate. The morning ran its dreary course, my cheerfulness evaporating as inevitably as dew in the air-conditioned morgue of M.C.L. House. Once, it occurred to me that I should prepare the ground at home: left alone in the office, I asked for an outside line and began to dial my own number, but after four digits got it muddled. When I remembered the right sequence, to phone no longer seemed a good idea. Numbers, those faithful servants, are among the first, sensing dissolution, to betray and revolt. Dialling, I had confused a 6 with a 7; the reverberations of the 0 for a 9 mistake still echoed malevolently, and it was only with difficulty that I was able to defer another visit to The Fridge. Procrastination had become in all things an instinctive defence.

Incomprehensible doodles on my blotter. In my canteen goulash a soggy finger-nail. So I went to the pub: pint-swilling cronies returned me to the office marinated. The long labefaction of the afternoon. Codeine, or some patent menstrual anodyne of Lydia's, with the tea. One incident which seemed curious, but I ignored it: Harvey was summoned to M.B. and returned wrapped in a long cloak of enigma.

Nothing more about — what was his name? — in that evening's paper. I read on my knee in the traffic jams about the unemployment figures: they were considered alarming. I knew a way to solve the unemployment problem: re-instate the law decreeing that each horseless carriage should be preceded by a man carrying a red flag. For that matter, if I were dictator, I'd make everyone over fourteen carry a red flag, or a plague-bell. The plague-bell of an ambulance rang in my ears: you're always within sound of someone's suffering, even when you've trained yourself to close your eyes. And close your eyes, plug your ears, set — as some do — the mind adrift on a glissade of ridiculous, surrealist fancy, and still your own suffering will contrive insistently to stay alive, buzzing in your head like a bee-hive. Or five. Two in the tank, but I might as well fill up. Hasn't that girl got enormous knockers? We give treble stamps: I suppose they must be real. Even these days when, the real and the false, you never can tell. But surely no one would, that size, like balloons. Windscreen, please, just a wipe. I'd like to poke or take a scalpel. Thanks . . . and a hell of a blotchy mess she's made, worse than if she hadn't touched if, can't see a. Of course, all change is for the worse. Until the hearse.

And I was still muttering to myself along such zig-zag lines as I precisely garaged the car, crossed the forecourt, briefcase swinging, and briskly bounded the steps.

Waiting for the lift, I heard the moon-faced porter's penetrating whisper: 'Told you, didn't I,' he demanded of his colleague, 'he's going off his bleeding twist.'

'As if nothing had happened,' said Sarah. 'You just come back from work, after a night with that . . . with your little friend, as if nothing had happened.'

It was as though I had re-entered the scenario of an interrupted dream.

'But we are such civilized people. We know how to control our emotions. We're not . . . peasants, we're not animals.'

'So I should hope,' I said. 'What is there wrong in being civilized?'

'When it's not cowardly and dishonest. When it's not just an excuse for pretending, for evading.' She sat like a governess, knees pressed together, hands clasped in her lap. 'Why don't you say what you want to say? Why don't you tell me — get out, I don't want you any more? I want my little . . .'

'Civilized . . .' I said. 'Civilized.' The word had got stuck on my tongue like a toffee. 'I thought we could discuss it like civ . . .'

'To humiliate me and to shame me, that's what you consider civilized, is it?' Her voice was kept low; except for her fingers, twisting, she sat quite still. 'Then I'd sooner you weren't. I'd sooner you hit me, beat me. I'd sooner you tried to kill me.'

'Oh, Sarah!' I sat down facing her.

'Yes,' she said. 'At least I'd know you meant it. Instead of this horrible, feeble, cold-blooded . . .'

I stood up again. 'Perhaps we had better talk later, when you are less hysterical.'

'Hysterical? I don't think I'm being hysterical.' She looked up at me with a good attempt at amusement. 'Am I? I'm just trying to tell you, in a *civilized* way, that I've finally, definitely and finally, made up my mind. Yes, we are, you and I, finished. Definitely! So you are free, my dear. She can have you. You can go. You can go *now*.'

We stared at each other as though from opposite corners of a vast, empty room. It would be too much to say that my hopes rose, considering the long-drawn distance between us, but I experienced an instant of uncertainty. 'You mean that, do you? You realize what you are saying?'

'Yes, Laurence, I mean it.' But in her evil smile uncertainty and any hope were banished. There was no need for her to say more, though she did, raising her voice only to compete with the drumming, which began at that moment with an occult fidelity. 'But on my terms, Laurence. I haven't weakened. I can hate too. I'm going to have my revenge for all your . . . callousness. I'm going to make you suffer. And her. And her too.'

I swore at her mindlessly. Her smile broadened.

'She might think it's all your fault. Will she forgive you? Do you think she can stand it, when I . . .'

'You vicious, evil . . .' I was holding her by the arms, bruising her. I released one hand to strike.

'Civilized!' Sneering, she shaped the word against the drums' dazzling mosaic.

It was the realization that she wanted me to which paralysed my upraised arm. I pushed her back, knowing that I had failed myself. There was the sense of a circular repetition, of having, this time, not only been here before, but of being here again in a tense-tangled future, with every detail of the scene already graphically inscribed on my memory.

Sarah, still with that mocking smile, vanishes beyond the corner of my vision. Walls of room and then of hallway tilt with the disequilibrium of my paces. My goddess grasped in one white-tendoned hand, the door-lock recalcitrant to the other;

and as I burst through, Blanco's shadow swiftly glides beyond the extremity of the corridor. White naked splinters of wood bristle from the varnished door beneath the detonations of my flailing goddess. I can still hear the drums and am still hearing them when the door falls back and, bobbing like a stringed puppet, my neighbour, all head, chalked gaping face, offers himself as sacrifice to my goddess . . . and I fail myself again, my upraised arm this time slowly folding like an old tower ex-plosively demolished. He falls away from the lurch of my shoulder, bouncing against an oatmeal wall; a ginger-and-white cat scuttles across a yellow carpet . . . But now I have no longer been here before, nor will be again, though the geography is familiar, mirror-image of the map of my own territory, so that I know where to go, even though the circle has been broken, and I could pre-hear the feet that would come running, the shouts of outrage and amazement, while Blanco scuttled to bear witness. Oh yes, I knew what I was doing. Trouble there would most certainly be. I could anticipate the consequences—he's off his bleeding twist, they'd say. But I knew I had re-entered the plane of the explicable and excusable. My sense of having failed myself returned with a sickening deflation—even as, simulating a true passion, I kicked his fucking drums to pieces.

14

From then on — I could say — everything started to go to pieces: I mean, the structure of my existence, with audible cracks and rumblings, began to disintegrate. Yet, in another sense — so I could say — a process of integration was taking place: there seemed no longer to be the same incongruity in the random juxtaposition of the banal and the bizarre, the most trivial episodes and the most momentous — they all held together with the unsurprising coherence of a powerful dream.

So, I kicked my neighbour's drums to pieces ... As I had foreseen, there was a rush of interested spectators to the open door, in the hope of seeing someone make a fool of himself. They stared with eager eyes and uttered cries of simulated shock and delighted malice. Outwardly I remained calm, even as, pushing my way with icy dignity through the gapers, I glimpsed the shadow of Blanco's retreat. Inwardly I was still choking on the sour acidity of my self-deflation.

Sarah had retired — from the conflict, to her room.

In the morning she failed to appear. A petty pride compelled me to prepare the breakfast she would have prepared for me, although I had difficulty in eating it. My constipation having returned, I spent an uncomfortable ten minutes fruitlessly straining.

I crossed the hallway in the protective wake of the petfood manufacturer. The journey was no better and no worse than most mornings. Those thousands of beetles crawling alongside were not deliberately contriving my downfall; they were neutral. Tension is harmless, provided there is an ultimate release. In a holocaust the whole of the victim is consumed. The vagus, or tenth cranial nerve, is known as the wandering nerve, and it is the longest and most widely extended of the nerves of the brain. It has been experimentally demonstrated that if we are deprived of dream we sicken and grow mad.

M.B. awaited me in my own office. The confusion of the o and the 9 was still creating ripples of erosion. I was to go again to The Fridge. Immediately. But he was mild about it, even placatory: the implication was that my competence was required to redeem the incompetence of others. All right, I should, you say, have smelled the rat, but I was unsuspicious, even in my weakened condition childishly grateful.

'Right, sir. Immediately.'

'Wait a moment.' The old man blew a cloud of smoke. 'Just had an idea. Why don't you take Harvey here down with you?'

'Oh, I don't think that will be nec . . .'

'To do the leg work, tidy up the bits and pieces.' He waved his pipe at Harvey, who was already seated at attention. 'Fancy a trip to the country, lad?'

Harvey drove less thrustfully than usual, as though in deference to my susceptibilities. It was, I realized, a beautiful morning, of such a kind as might make you feel it good to be alive. Outside London, the road ran by the broad river, and the barges and the yachts and the bowed fishermen and the twinkling water made a picture of Arcadian innocence which delighted my senses. Then suddenly—no, not suddenly, which implies an awareness of change, nor imperceptibly, but as though it had never been otherwise—the river revealed itself as the open sewer which in reality it was, carrying deadly and irreducible poisons, its glittering surface a sort of garish cosmetic on top of foulness and filth. Fortunately, the road shortly diverted.

The Fridge had its usual depressive effect upon my spirit, but Harvey excelled himself, immediately relieving me of all our mission's most objectionable confrontations. When the Works Director attempted, with no little justification, to place the blame for his troubles upon our heads, Harvey counterattacked with such savage eloquence that in the end it seemed the best to let the two of them go off alone to lunch to make their peace. I didn't feel like eating anyway, and wandered dreamily among the sparrows and the typists in the landscaped gardens, my anxieties subdued, attenuated, as music distant over water.

An odd thing happened in the afternoon. We had a formal meeting to put on record, as they say, the outcome of our deliberations. Little was required of me: it had been a good idea, whosoever's it had been, for Harvey and our major adversary to make their peace together; they had arrived at an accommodation which, allowing for certain face-saving conditions would satisfy the honour of all parties. As I say, little seemed to be required of me. There were eight of us—I think it was eight, it might have been seven or nine—seated around the polished boardroom-table, each with his territory formally demarcated. In the exact centre, a squat water-jug in which the water vibrated to an invisible, inaudible hum. Through the walls of tinted glass the sun was drained as though by a poisoned cloud. Various lunch breath odours persisted. Dehumanized by their ritual roles, the voices had a grinding, gramophonic quality.

Do you remember the Works Director's secretary who'd called me to the telephone, the tall and tubular girl? She sat opposite to me, her notebook on her nyloned knees, blood-nailed, skirt drawn sheathlike to the creases of her thighs. In sleepy reverie I defiled her: rampant prick raging in every dainty orifice, muzzle slavering in the liquids of her lap . . . and such like. The oddness of this poetic ravishment lay in that, so far as I could recall, this was the first time I had so indulged myself with the image of another girl since I had first loved Jackie. I draw no conclusions; I merely report it.

'Well, I think we handled that pretty smoothly, old man. Between us. I reckon it was a pretty crafty sort of job we did. You and I.' Harvey switched on the ignition. 'Care for a choccy? Sure? I think I will, just one. Lush piece that secretary, or didn't you notice? I don't think,' he added, chewing and propelling us in swift reverse from the car-park, 'that M.B. could complain. Not at all. Not on any score. The work I've ... I mean we've, done today.'

My mouth dry, my eyes sandy, I felt tired when we arrived back. Waiting for the lift, I saw the two of us side by side in the mirror: Harvey erect, alert, with a secret smile; myself flaccid and woebegone. I straightened my shoulders.

'I'd like to say, you did an excellent job, Harvey,' I plausibly confided in the lift. 'Be sure I'll see that M.B. learns about it. Might do you a bit of good.'

I stepped out of the lift first and waited for him, but he stood still and smiled at me until the doors had shut. Smiled at me, his secret smile. The lift ascended, and I walked along the corridor alone, vaguely wondering.

Since childhood I have known the sensation of being betrayed. One grows to live with it like a deformity, so that one can ignore its existence for quite long periods, until, without forewarning, the occurrence of some haphazard. Most characteristically the instant of apprehension arises from an innocent gesture against an unemphatic background, but with some shadow or note minimally, but fatally, *out of context*.

Such was the carefree pitch of Lydia's laughter – in response, presumably, to some playful jest uttered by the man negligently perched, his back to the door, on the corner of her desk.

My entry cut her off; a second's silence; and then the laugh she had with physical difficulty suppressed eructated in a high-pitched squeal. Simultaneously her visitor straightened and turned.

He wore a dove-grey suit with a flowered tie. His eyes twinkled. His teeth glittered. A white handkerchief trailed from his hand: perhaps he had been entertaining my poor Lydia with his conjuring tricks. Somehow, it was her laughter rather than his intrusion which constituted the essence of my betrayal, filling me with a sense of primeval anguish and disgust.

'Hullo, Larry,' welcomed Ossie, tucking his handkerchief in his breast pocket with a flourish.

'You! What are you . . .'

'Just a social call, Larry. Nice place you've got here, smart.' He winked with a sickening coyness. 'And very pleasant company too, that I must say. Very pleasant and very fetching.'

Lydia snickered, doubtless from nervousness. I turned on her. 'Are there any messages?' She couldn't speak. 'Then,' I coldly suggested, 'perhaps you will kindly collect those statistics I requested yesterday. Early yesterday.'

'Yes. Of course. Certainly.' She began to rise. 'Actually, I put them in your . . .' She met my gelid stare. 'Yes, Mr Carpenter.'

' 'bye now, dear,' called Ossie, as she scurried to the door. 'Look after yourself, mind, there's a good girl.

'There's a good girl,' he said to me. 'Not, maybe, over-endowed in the places you'd go for a tickle, but a sweet loving girl all the same. And loyal to you, Larry, loyal and true, you don't need me to inform you.'

No, I don't need you to inform me. I put down my briefcase and sat behind my desk. Don't howl, I counselled myself. 'Why have you come here?' was my quiet enquiry.

Ossie smiled, pursed his lips and drew in his breath with a little whistle. Balletically pirouetting, he surveyed the four walls of the room; and while his back was turned I shot him between the shoulders.

'There's no cause, Larry,' he addressed me, 'to show you find my presence so unwelcome. Why have I come here, that your question?' He hesitated only a brief second. 'Because, I reckon, you're just about done for.'

My smoking revolver had fallen from my grasp. My hands, in fact, were pressed flat on the desk-top, stuck by my sweat.

'Done for,' Ossie repeated with a happy grin. 'Least you would be, if you hadn't got me—your old friend Ossie.'

I raised myself inches from the chair, starting to get at him over the desk, with Lydia's disloyal laughter ringing in my ears, and maddened by betrayal.

'Now Larry, I know,' he soothed. 'You've had a hard day, and maybe you're asking yourself why that little aggravation you had next door last night should bring me calling here.' He didn't wait for my confirmation or denial. 'No, it ain't that, Larry. I wouldn't have come here if I didn't have had to. You know I'm not a geezer who likes to intrude.'

As I fell back in the chair, my liquid hands were dragged from the desk-top, leaving their imprints like fatal clues. 'Why?' I whispered hopelessly. 'Why?'

'You wouldn't say that, would you, Larry—that I'm the sort of geezer what likes to intrude. Not when it ain't necessary.' He emphasized his point with a stabbing forefinger. 'Not when it ain't nec-ess-ary.'

Under all my stress, there was still space for frenzy at his repetitions and his rhetorical interrogatives.

'You want to know, why,' he offered. 'See for myself, it's only natural. My information's good, I know that, and I got good boys working for me, boys I can trust. Well, it's got to be like that, ain't it, else, who knows, I might find myself up for the chop, manner of speaking. Only a manner of speaking, of course ...'—he chuckled in self-congratulation—'as they've turned the axe into ploughshares now, as you might say. Not to mention the rope: I wonder what they done with the rope, making productive use of.' His amusement was replaced by a sudden expression of concern. He came closer and addressed me solicitously. 'You thinking about that boy they dug up, Larry, the stiff in the railway yard. You didn't ought to worry about that, not with all your own troubles. Person or persons unknown, wasn't it?'

It no longer surprised me that he should read my thoughts.

'O.K., Larry? You get my meaning.'

But I felt entitled to indignation that he should have them for me before I had conceived them.

'O.K., Larry? You forgotten all about it, ain't you? There's a sensible feller.' Satisfied to have allayed the foolish fears of an excessive sensibility, he clapped his hand down hard on my bowed shoulders. 'Now what was we talking about?' He expected no answer. 'Friends, we was talking about friends. You got people working for you, I was saying, and even if you know they're good you got to watch them, even the best. A trusting 'eart's a noble faculty, but too much trust, Larry, too much trust and you're up to your eye-balls in the proverbial. I'm talking about the proverbial shit-heap, pardon my French. Now you take that geezer . . .' He plucked his example out of the air. 'That geezer you just had your little trip with to the country, now he's a friend of yours you'd say.'

'Harvey,' I said. 'You mean Harvey?'

'That's right, 'arvey he's called. You've got him working for you. He gives you chocolates. You'd certainly designate him a friend.'

I shrugged in acquiescence.

'Larry, he'll have you in the proverbial quicker than you can wipe your arse.'

'Harvey,' I said.

' 'arvey! Lovable Mr 'arvey, creeping, crawling git.' Ossie lowered his voice. 'Didn't come back in here with you, did he? Now why do you suppose that was? What do you think he's been at, with that smarmy smile on his chops? Who's he been rabbiting with? And why's your face not fitting any more? Who do you think's been doing all the stirring for you?'

I was saved from answering any of these pertinent questions: the door opened and Harvey entered, smiling. 'Laurence, M.B. says . . .' He observed my guest. 'Oh, I'm sorry, I didn't know you were engaged.'

I said it was all right, and rose.

Ossie faced Harvey with a look of cordiality and a child's unblinking interest.

'Haven't we,' asked Harvey, appearing a little puzzled, 'met somewhere before?'

Ossie maintained silence and his benign, unembarrassed stare.

I put myself between them. 'He was just going . . .' I apologetically murmured.

'Yes, that's right,' agreed Ossie, unmoving.

'Somewhere,' said Harvey, anxious now, 'I'm sure I've seen you . . . somewhere . . . '

'Maybe you have,' said Ossie, still benign. 'Maybe you have, but maybe on the other hand you haven't.'

He kept his gaze on Harvey, who stood as though hypnotized. We all stood as though hypnotized. Under hypnosis one is unconscious of the passage of time. 'And maybe some day, maybe some day soon, you'll see me again,' said Ossie, breaking the spell. He turned to me. 'Well, I'll be on my way now, Larry. You don't have to bother to see me out.' He paused at the door. 'Renew our discourse some other time then, eh? Don't forget what I was telling you.' He nodded pleasantly to Harvey. 'And don't leave it too long, Larry. You ain't got all that time left, you know.' And he made his exit.

'Extraordinary person!' observed Harvey. 'Laurence, you have the strangest friends.'

I looked at him as though I were seeing him for the first time, but he didn't notice this.

'By the way,' he went on with swift enthusiasm, 'I happened, by sheer chance of course, to bump into M.B. and I told him all about our little trip. He was absolutely del . . .'

But by that time I was no longer there.

Since childhood I have known, besides the sensation of betrayal, the sensation of exclusion. One is alone, outside the structure inhabited by others, with an agonizingly sharp awareness of life going on behind the locked doors, the festive gaiety which animates those silhouttes dancing in a dream across the thinly curtained windows, as though time had stopped for ever.

No timeless silhouettes disturbed the soft pink glow of Jackie's window, but the sensation was the same: I had emphatically been locked out; and, to mock my exclusion, there was music – the adenoidal, harmonica-accompanied voice of our happy beginning, since relegated in favour of a more fashionable sound, and now revived especially, it seemed, for my increased discomfiture.

She had taken my confession badly – very badly. Did I say 'confession'? I had not admitted my 'lost-nail' fabrication. Sarah, I apologetically lamented, had changed her mind, turned nasty, a complete *volte-face*. It was as great a shock to me as it is to you, sweet darling. She didn't believe me. She had thought all the time there was something funny. Or else, before now, why hadn't I. To use her like this. Abuse her. Betray her. And what about your wife's widower, I suppose he never really existed, did he, you just dreamed him up. And the next thing would be a writ or something or whatever they call it, co-respondent or enticement, something horrible like that. Then what about her career, but of course I never really cared about her career, did I, just more of my soft shit.

O, come come really Jackie, this day and age, not living in Victorian, might be rather good you'd find publicity actually, your pictures in the. Oh, you you, kind of girl think I am, and hit me on the face.

All right, yes, I deserve it. I beg, look – on my knees I beg . . . But, Jackie, you said, sweet sweet my darling, you said. Before. You said whatever happened don't you remember you said nothing would really matter. To us. Nothing, you said it, could come between us.

'Did I say that?' she said. 'I must have been fucking mad. I didn't know you then, what you were really like, you dirty hypocrite. Anyway,' – she jabbed her finger against the toothy photograph – 'you can't make love like him, he's twice the man.'

'What? What are you saying?' I looked at 'Jimmy's' picture with disgust. 'But you said he was a . . .'

'You are naive, aren't you? He's versatile,' she said, and, tearing *my* picture from the wall, 'Oh yes, he's very versatile indeed. And you might as well take this, don't want it any more, can't stand the sight.'

I left then, in an agony of sickness. But came back. After a few paces along the musty corridor, I came back. Of course. And suffered it all again, until she ordered me out. I went. And she locked the door.

And now I'm standing in the street outside—the same street that had tolerantly smiled upon my attempts to click my heels in the air. Sweet sour music from her pink window. A man and a woman with a small brown dog emerge from the neighbouring house and look at me with curiosity. I hear laughter: it begins as one person's laughter, a woman's, and then becomes a chorus. The seizure in my thorax arrives so suddenly I have no time to move to the kerb, and vomit where I stand. And the little brown dog scampers back to investigate.

So, in desolation, I move away. A monster, to others insufferable, I have been locked out. Lacking gravity, I feel the world's rotation throwing me off, a speck in space.

But—dear God!—the human spirit is resilient. By the time I had reached the spot of my river dive, my splendid rescue—I make no mention this time of my accompanying shadow, who is by now to be taken for granted—I had persuaded myself that our dispute and my exclusion had been, after all, factitious, a cruel elaboration of the games that lovers play; I would mollify, I would crawl, and then I would be re-admitted. Re-admitted.

Yes, no doubt—but what about 'Jimmy'? Ah, 'Jimmy'—for the moment I'd forgotten! Well, it probably wasn't true at all, just something she'd fantasticated, ingenious words to wound. And even if it were, true I mean, even if they had, well . . . well, youth has a different ethos. Moreover, had I not myself? I'm thinking of the Works Director's tubular secretary. I doubt if 'Jimmy', for all his versatility, had so comprehensively enjoyed.

But that, my friend, *mon pauvre*, was only in your mind, that was not with cock and cunt and tit and tongue, only in fantasy, in dream, imagination's figment. Your Honour, Herr Doktor, dear reader, haven't you understood a word, haven't you got it yet? Haven't you? You mean to say, you're trying to tell us . . . Ah, at last the penny's dropping. You mean to say that everything is only . . . that between the actual and the dream there's no . . . Precisely. Yes, precisely. If I were dead or otherwise non-existent I couldn't either way, could I? Similarly, if you were dead or otherwise non-existent you wouldn't be judging my case, you wouldn't be healing me, you wouldn't be reading this book . . .

But, anyway, back to quotidian reality. I'd walked myself, you comprehend, out of the abyss of despair on to a plateau of relative optimism. Herr Doktor, in your work of healing you must have witnessed miracles of recovery when all's seemed lost, and a very beautiful experience it must be. A very beautiful experience — the patient's joy on recovering from one agony to realize that he is enduring to survive sharper and more protracted agonies. There suddenly had come over me a ghastly foreboding — a presentiment, a premonition, call it what you will — the certain conviction that I would find myself here again, with nothing changed — the sleeping swans, the rustling trees, the poisoned river, the screaming jet — except that then my exclusion would be absolute and irreversible, beyond any possibility of hope.

Did I mention that, again, a riotous wind had been blowing — like that which in legend attends the Devil and his entourage? As I climbed the steps to the road, the wind, with fiendish aptness, ceased abruptly. My tiredness caught up with me like a kidnapper, a smelly imporous blanket dropped over my head. I wobbled and my footsteps slowed and slowed — my shadow's presumably slowing with them. Less than half a mile from home I stopped and leaned against a tree, hoping an available taxi would come by. The moon was ringed by bright clouds, with moonlight falling on my face like an alien dew. The passing cars seemed to be moving along belts of unending light. There were taxis among them, but their drivers either ignored me or swept their hands across their windscreens in rejection. My breathing was so shallow it was a wonder it sustained me.

After a while I mustered the strength to move on. The clouds had covered the moon. I thought I probably wouldn't beat the rain and shrank from the prospect of a drenching, but I was incapable of quickening my stride. As I crossed the deserted courtyard, the first few pregnant drops splashed down—and, even through the mists of my fatigue, I had a vision of a heavy rain descending, in what is known as the future, with myself in the thick of it and oblivious, at the end, or at the beginning of, a new and different despair . . .

In the hallway the porter slept and I didn't wake him. I went up in the lift alone, walked alone—my shadow wouldn't follow this far—along the silent corridor and into the empty flat. Oh yes, I forgot to mention it, Sarah had left.

15

No one laughed at me as I clucked and whistled, clapped my hands, pulled faces. Here, unlike the hostile streets, such behaviour is acceptable. To my sounds and my movements she replied with eager twists and twitches, her sharp yet gentle eyes steady on my face, responsive to every nuance.

And then we played a game: I'd turn about and walk away, and she would scuttle along her branch to her house behind; then together we would turn again and each come back. She enjoyed this game and when I wearied of it, seeking some development of our relationship, she took the lead and made me continue.

Our game ended only when, feigning one of my retreats, I saw an enormous woman whom, without distress, I took for Chrissie, passing behind the distant lion-house. I callously abandoned the quick-stepping marmoset and set off in pursuit; but naturally she wasn't there when I got there.

I had arrived at the Zoo early – on a morning damp and chill, blurred by a thin mist. With the schools re-started and most of the tourists gone home, I expected few other visitors, but even so I was surprised by the almost complete emptiness, so that it was possible to imagine that I was alone with the animals in their cages, the last survivor of my species, walking naked before their bland, unblinking eyes.

To overcome this eerie sensation, seeking forgiveness for my kind, I had attempted to establish communication with some of the creatures. My old friend the gorilla I ignored, for reasons of association, but I flirted with a bright-eyed lynx, a dingo somnolent after feeding, a pair of gentle zebras, even, though mocking myself, the impossible rhino – before I came upon my sympathetic marmoset.

Of course I had come, not in order to make friends with the animals, but out of my old childhood need. You will remember my limp attempt to describe this to Jackie during a previous visit.

Actually, leaving the lion-house, I saw my father walking purposefully across the muddy grass where on more summery days the children queue for their bumpy camel-rides. An elephant distantly trumpeted, to be answered close at hand by the sudden deep-throated roar of a tigress; all the monkeys started chattering at once, and a brilliant red wing fluttered across the boundary of my vision.

He picked up the child who had fallen in the mud and turned with her, squalling, under his arm. Of course it wasn't my father; for one thing, this man was no older than myself.

It occurred to me for the first time: to go quietly insane is one way out.

In the end the Zoo had failed me. I went to all my favourite places: the reptile-house, the walrus's pool, that tucked-away football-pitch where the wolves tamely mope; and I was fortunate to come upon the birds of prey at feeding-time, with the cages full of the flurry of their gigantic wings.

Imperious and reeking of contempt, the magnificent sea-eagle on his uppermost rung spurned the keeper's bloody offering, and I projected him through bars of shadow to an icy North Cape crag, swirled in cloud, above a sea of lead and iron and leaping complaisant fish ... For a moment I shared his inviolable freedom, then the eagle, surrendering, dropped down to the rancid mess on the dusty floor of its cage, clumsily hopping land-bound on one claw, and, my rancour and resentment unabated, I departed more wretched even than on my arrival.

16

After that interlude, get on with my story.

Since childhood I have known the sensation . . .

Since childhood I have known . . .

Since childhood . . . the gap. The gap between life as it is and life as it might be. Unbridgeable abyss.

To go quietly insane is one way out would be to go quietly insane. Get on with my story.

The lawyer. Loose false teeth. Bifocal lenses, behind which his eyes a dead fish's. Bitten finger-nails. 'Repercussions is the word, eh Mr Carpenter?' He observes my non-amusement. 'Repercussions to the destruction of your neighbour's percussion. Haw-haw-haw. That's to say, his percussive instrument. There's also the matter of trespass and assault, so I see.'

He bends his head for closer study of the document. I regard his dandruffed scalp with distaste and . . . No! there is no trace of dandruff. He has a healthy head of hair, dark though faintly specked with grey, giving an air of undeserved distinction. I must not allow my loathing to distort reality.

'Don't see, I'm afraid, we've got a leg to stand on. Sorry to admit.' His smile fails adequately to convey either fear or sorrow. 'That's if the allegations contained herein are substantially accurate, and from what you tell me, Mr Carpenter, I gather that they are. Accurate.' Another cretinous repeater! 'Substantially. Ask my advice: don't go to law.' He has a white flower in his button-hole, curled at the edges like a stale sandwich. 'A pack of thieves all lawyers, keep out of their clutches. Haw-haw-haw.'

I managed to apologize for what it was I said aloud.

'Nerves, just nerves I expect,' he amiably passes it off. 'You're under a strain, Mr Carpenter, I can tell. And very natural too, you don't want to be evicted from your lovely home.'

'Then what do you suggest I should do about that . . .' — giving the document a savage jab — 'garbage?'

'Ah, you're asking my advice.' Hastily, with professional gentleness, he gathers up the paper to protect it from further assault by layman. 'One thing you shouldn't do: put nothing down in writing. Don't admit a thing. On paper.'

'I have no intention.' As if I were not sensitive to all the perils of admissions on paper! No one knows better than I do the possible confusions and ambiguities, how truth may become distorted by emotion, so that, garbled and hallucinatory, truth itself may come to resemble insanity.

'You're a reasonable man, Mr Carpenter — why don't you make your peace with the fellow? If you can.' He rises in dismissal, as though he were paying me for my time. 'Only course. To follow. These things are sent to try us. He's got you, not to put too fine a point, by the short and. Curlies. We all have to do a little crawling sometimes, don't we?' He puts out his hand without halting his speech, and I take it automatically. 'I sometimes think how simple things would be if, instead of hiring a lawyer, one could engage an assassin to eliminate all those who . . .' — our hands part — 'oppose and oppress us. By the way, how's the wife?'

From the solicitor's office I drove to Sarah's new address. *Mrs Sarah Carpenter*, neatly typed beside the bottom bell, her new, white card eye-catching beneath the yellowing, crinkled others. I pressed the bell and nothing happened. Sitting on the wall and regarding me incuriously was a fair-haired girl, four or five years old, her finger in the corner of her mouth. 'Do you know . . .' I began, but didn't finish.

Down the hollowed-out steps I went, by the putrid dustbins.

The curtains were drawn tightly across the windows, totally sealing Sarah's retreat.

Turning about, I stumbled over something soft and giving. The child was startled more than pained, I believe, but I picked her up—as recently, somewhere, I had seen a child plucked up from the muddy grass—saying, 'I didn't mean to hurt you. Don't cry. Please don't cry.'

Snuffling plaintively, she let me carry her up the steps. 'It's all right. Don't cry,' I tried to console, putting her back on the wall. 'I didn't mean to hurt you', and there stood Sarah, wearing a blue head-scarf I hadn't seen before and carrying a shopping-bag with a spiky, and inevitably phallic, French loaf protruding like a divorcee's desire. 'I didn't mean to hurt you,' I repeated, brushing her down; and Sarah said: 'As you're here, you might as well come in.'

In myth and fiction desperate men are, like lunatics, accorded a supernatural strength. I found, to my surprise, I had been invested with a supernatural verbal force. Striding about the L-shaped room—incongruously elegant and *gemütlich* I seem to remember it, as though I had stumbled upon a luxurious apartment in an abandoned castle or at the bottom of a well— I achieved such eloquence as only before in self-indulgent fantasies of political power. First, it melted Sarah's distant stranger's reserve, then kindled a gentle sympathy, faintly tearful, and finally at white heat ignited the cold dead ashes of our sexual passion.

We slid with a bruising bump from the couch to the floor, the French loaf mysteriously fallen from the bag beside us. 'No. No. No, Laurence. I don't want. Oh no, we mustn't. No, indeed not,' she commanded, but her arms around my back kept us rolling together.

My neck was fiercely bitten. 'Put him in me. Put him deep in me. Now,' she counter-commanded. 'Inside me.' Though, as I raised myself to manipulate belt and zip, she wriggled away, straightened her skirt and rose, saying in an even, matter-of-fact voice, 'No, not here, I'd better get undressed.' And she picked up the loaf and put it back in her shopping-bag.

So we made love on the bed, unclothed, with the blankets neatly folded back, like a proper married couple. There were no technical difficulties. Speaking for myself, I found it remarkably refreshing. Afterwards, I soothed her with familiar tendernesses.

What's that you say—was I what? Sincere? That's a strange question. It's the wrong question, damn you. Not only irrelevant, totally meaningless. Was I—you might have asked—was I aware? Was I *literal*? I couldn't have answered, but at least it would have shown you were beginning to comprehend.

Did I mention that the first thing Sarah had done upon our entry, having put down her shopping-bag, removed her scarf and shaken loose her golden hair, had been to open the heavy, sealing curtains? The light—ah yes, I remember—was a typical basement light, shadowy and strained and cool, as at the bottom of a well. Then, before I had found my gift of tongues, she had made coffee, offering me cake, which I had declined, and she told me how she had come to find the flat, through Moira Blenkinsop—the garrulous Moira Blenkinsop—and had gone on to describe, with that cool objectivity which was characteristic of Sarah, those of her new neighbours whom she had so far met ... but that isn't interesting to you, as you won't ever encounter them.

What was I saying? Ah yes, the curtains. She had also opened the window a few inches at the bottom. After our love-making, I got up first and went to wash myself. When I came back, naked, into the room, where Sarah still lay on the bed, her eyes closed, I saw the child, nose pressed against the glass, eyes sharp as a marmoset's, and she was the child we had never had.

'I didn't intend to hurt you,' I said. 'I never meant it,' and our daughter turned without haste from the window, and Sarah, opening her eyes and gathering her limbs together, said: 'Didn't you, Laurence? Do you want me to come back?'

Strangely, it wasn't the thought of her having seen us which came to prey on my mind. I kept remembering the window, the gap at the bottom . . . that she should have *heard* . . .

17

With Sarah's return, you might have thought, my life would have regained a portion of its former measure of order and regularity. On the contrary: I found myself in increasing disarray. Events began to develop a tendency to speed up, like a film run quickly, though – if such were possible – without a distortion of movement, only a distortion, a resemblant mechanical twitchiness, of emotional response. To add to my confusion, with merely minor changes of rhythm and emphasis, situations, visions, encounters, manifested a growing inclination to repeat or parallel themselves, so that I was plagued with the fatality of precognition. And another upsetting development: possibly from some glandular disturbance, I found myself intermittently possessed by a kind of manic sexuality, such as, save in deep faceless night dreams, I hadn't experienced since the burning erections of my adolescence.

Human memory at the best of times – and these most certainly were not those – is capricious. To try to re-create events, however momentous, in an orderly sequence proves impossible. Links fall out of the chain. The dream fades with the morning's first cough. Something heard, seen, smelt, touched, tasted, one will remember in magnified detail, while another sensile message, no less significant one would suppose, has disintegrated, leaving nothing behind but . . . the sound of distant fairground music and a water-stain on the ceiling.

But did even these really exist? The stain did certainly. Lying, supine, on Jackie's bed – as I'd foreseen, I had of course been re-admitted – I stared up at it, tracing its resemblance, according how one turned one's head, to a saxophone, a lobster, to the boot of Italy. It must have been real, for when she came back into the room I recall commenting on it, that I hadn't noticed it before, and she said there'd been a leak, and I told her fancifully what it reminded me of, and she said it reminded her of . . . No, I can't remember exactly: some far-fetched obscenity.

But what about the fairground music? That must have been elsewhere, at another time. When we, that's Jackie and I, stood on the bridge looking down at the lights at the bottom of the water. She wore a new and too sweet scent. Or it might have been that other evening when I drove Sarah into the country, and after dinner we'd walked across the golf-course where, though it was almost pitch-dark, we'd come upon a man chipping golf-balls to an invisible flag.

The fairground music . . . a water stain on the ceiling . . . the button missing from my jacket . . . a child's face above an open window . . . the sudden shower of hail which turned the path into a glittering Christmas decoration . . . all these now, at random, and other such trivia, have a credibility and coherence which are lacking in my desperate affairs.

I can't remember where I lost the button from my jacket, but it was missing during the period of both my 'reconciliations'. You see, I was in no position to ask domestic favours of either. I was on the defensive all round. Sarah, Jackie—not only. At the office. At home—my neighbour, the desk-clerk, and the porter. Each post brought fresh demands. And waiters and garage-hands and taxi-drivers are invariably rude to me now, aggressive. Stray dogs yap at my heels. I don't know what's happening to the traffic, gets more hellish day by day. Eventually, I cut off the loose ends myself with a pair of nail-scissors. A part of the cloth had been torn away with the button, leaving a small, irregular white whole, I mean hole. It was diabolical. You might ask why I didn't put that suit away, after all I had other suits, perfectly good, but for some reason I didn't. Of course, I wasn't wearing it all the time, but still it was diabolical.

I may have performed a number of irrational actions during that period, I may have omitted to have performed some of those mundane tasks which are essential to hold the structure together; but—I should like to stress this—I was doing the best I could, as everyone does, to stave off catastrophe . . .

A CHANGE OF PERSON

And now I am lying on the bed, looking up at the stain on the ceiling which reminds me of a saxophone, a lobster, the boot of Italy. Water-bubbles glistening in her pubic hairs, her head tilted back, Jackie wickedly grins – 'What it reminds *me* of is . . .'

I must concentrate harder, to order the narrative more coherently. Before the morning. Before it fades. Or else I shall never finish.

Why had I taken Sarah back? I will tell you what I told Jackie: I thought there was a chance – the only hope – that I might woo and win her to my way of thinking. In order to do that, I had to have her within my orbit.

It played hell with my nerves, the effort to placate her and to revive an affection which would not be so intense as to encourage her dependence. My inordinate, if spasmodic, sexual urges at this time proved an added complication.

Meanwhile, I was of course striving to increase Jackie's dependence upon me, to win her, notwithstanding.

It's not surprising that night after night I found myself having those bifurcated dreams in which one, while maintaining a small insoluble core of one's identity, melts into a different person, to pass from one situation into another entirely contrary, and back again, repeatedly, with an ever-increasing bewilderment and terror of impotence.

Of course, it all played hell with my nerves. Additionally, the dispute with my neighbour and the management of the flats continued with increasingly acrimony; and at the office there was an atmosphere of dismay.

They must have changed the regulations or amended the flight-paths, because throughout the hours of daylight the planes come over one a minute and at lower altitude, seemingly just above the roof-tops. Over forty cigarettes a day, must cut it down.

I welcomed, though with a suitable show of reluctance, M.B.'s proposal that, instead of myself, Harvey should accompany him to this year's European conference. I thought that their absence might enable me to complete my neglected 'opus', but, what with those minor difficulties I've already mentioned, one thing and another, I let the opportunity slip by.

In accordance with my legal advice, I had disclaimed all liability, but offered, notwithstanding, and as a token of neighbourly goodwill, to recompense for such damage as may inadvertently have been caused, with the hope and expectation that our former amicable relations might be restored. Receiving no answer, I wrote again, more shortly but with equal courtesy. The next day, whether as a consequence or not, I had an absolutely monstrous letter from the Management Committee. It made my blood boil.

It made my blood boil. Naturally, living in such proximity, one occasionally encountered each other. He tried to ignore me, but when I persisted in cheerful greeting, he would nod in an embarrassed way and hasten by with a sickly smile.

In another dream which kept recurring, I was brought low, abysmally low, but then my watery veins became suffused with so powerful a hatred that it resembled genius, and I knew I had the power to dispose of all my enemies, however multiple and powerful. At this point I invariably awoke, before converting my hatred into action; the gun still fully loaded, the knife blood-free, the garrotte loose between my hands; but bathed in a sweet and healing contentment.

One evening, I don't know on what impulse, I challenged the fellow. We had passed in the hallway, one each side of the aquatic sculpture, he simpering to my ringing greeting. I turned about and followed to where he waited for the lift.

'Look here,' I said, 'look here, my good fellow. Don't you think this has gone far enough? Is this not a ridiculous way for two grown men to conduct themselves, and neighbours to boot? Let bygones be bygones, what do you say?'

He said nothing. He blushed like a young girl in days gone by. The lift doors opened, and he tried to push in while the occupants were trying to get out. Not the sort of way to carry on in an establishment of such gentility. So I restrained him, though without using force, mind, merely by obtruding myself. Got a few impatient kicks and elbows in the back for my pains.

'Come, man, no cause to behave like this,' chided I. 'Mistakes on both sides, I dare say. I'm perfectly willing to be the first to express regret. Mark you, without liability. Yet anything I can do to make amends, within reason, I would happily consider. Actually, I'm very fond of music myself.'

He spoke at last. 'My harm,' he squeaked in a curiously emasculated voice. 'Let go of my harm.'

'What harm?' I enquired, a trifle confused. 'I mean you no harm, rest assured. I come in peace.'

In order both to shield him from the impatient persons pushing by us and, as one does, to establish a warmer, closer communication, I had taken a firm grip of his elbow. Firm but not unfriendly. 'Let go my arm, you madman,' I heard him cry. 'Take your hands off me.'

With his importunate wriggling, the intricate joint rippled seductively in my palm. The lift-doors closed and the lift ascended, summoned from above. We are alone together. I don't know what came over me, but suddenly he is lying sprawled on the carpet, and I hear a loud voice which, for the buzzing in my ears, I find difficulty in recognizing as my own.

The clerk is helping him to his feet, brushing him down, and the porter stands in heavy insolence in front of me, his stinking overalls pressed against my jacket. I have a button missing.

The lift comes down again and the doors open, and the petfood manufacturer steps out. 'Good Lord, what's happening here?' he exclaims, speaking for the first and last time. 'Has there been some kind of a fracas?'

Panting, I rushed away, in a hurry to . . .

My accountant returned my tax forms, with a note saying he couldn't make head or tail of the information I had supplied. Bloody fool. Man must be cracking up. Still, one has to be understanding. The professional man, under a lot of strain these days, the middle-classes generally, in a time of tumours and transition. The people one hears about who you'd never have thought, nervous breakdown, complete collapse, they say. I've heard it blamed on over-population; already we drink our own and others' urine. The rivers are full of dead fish.

The motor-car a weapon: more powerful than the gun, the knife, the garrotte; more lethal and more satisfying. If you're looking for symbols. To murder with impunity is godlike.

I have re-read that chapter, and I apologize for its fragmentation. But if you have followed me this far you will understand, perhaps you will even understand better. All I can say is, that I'll try from now on to be more lucid and more systematic.

18

We crunched along a path heaped with glittering hailstones, that on another planet might have been a field of diamonds. In accordance with policy, I made a point of taking Sarah out occasionally. This evening we were on our way to visit friends who properly belonged in an earlier configuration.

Uncertain on her spiky shoes, Sarah skidded, and I grasped her hand. This saved her from falling, but my hand's distant support was insufficient to give her confidence, and she took my arm, linking us in a wedded unity which also properly belonged to a previous sequence. Somewhere, in some distant time, her hair tickling my cheek and smelling smokily of autumn, we had climbed conjoined up some other ice-glazed passageway, and I seemed to remember how our feet kept slipping backwards and that, laughing, I had hurried her on, for we were late for a party, which for all I could say now might never have taken place, or had been, as it were, discarded on memory's cutting-room floor.

As though reading my thoughts: 'We're late,' said Sarah in a low voice against my woolly shoulder.

My watch was on my free arm. 'Not much,' I dismissed. 'Besides, it doesn't matter. You know them, they're always late themselves, so what's sauce for . . .'

'No,' said Sarah. 'I didn't say that.'

'. . . for the gander.'

'I said, *I'm* late.'

'Late,' I repeated. 'Late for what?'

'It could have been that time,' she said, still holding my arm, but getting out of step. 'That time in the other flat. I'd taken no precautions. Of course, it's far too early to be certain.'

Falling out of step drew her away from my side.

'Well,' I said, 'if you're not certain . . .' And that was all I said.

We didn't mention it again. The dinner-party proved im-memorable, and when we left all the hail had melted so that the path was puddled and messy but no longer treacherous.

In the days that followed, the topic was not mentioned; it was not that I consciously evaded it; it simply did not arise.

You will remember, as I remember, although this, too, seems now a long while ago, the day of the recording of Jackie's television play. And what followed. Incidentally, her wanton ghost still occupied the dressing-table stool I knew, and if I didn't always see it that was because of some lack of empathy in myself. For various mysterious and irrelevant reasons, the play had been repeatedly deferred, but now its transmission date was definite.

Naturally, I wanted to see it, and so, despite her feigned contempt, did Jackie; so I had hired a television set for her room. But then the night before the transmission she informed me that the play's director had invited her to a party. I knew what sort of a party that would be—that chain-smoking Lesbian! And 'Jimmy' would be there as well. She indifferently supposed he might be.

Since our reconciliation we had tacitly agreed not to speak of 'Jimmy'. His photograph had been taken off the wall, replaced by an inoffensive magazine picture of fellatio in an underground theatre. I was piqued, and I showed it.

'You don't have to be so stuffy,' Jackie complained.

'I'm not stuffy.'

'Old bear . . . my gorilla!' She had scarcely changed at all, you see, through all these anguished months, and despite the literary convention that a character should reveal development. '*Ticklish* old gorilla!'

Our wrestling bout concluded, she explained, reasonably enough, that she must attend the director's party for the sake of

her career. 'After all . . .' — she gave my parts a warning tweak —
'I've got to have a career, haven't I? So long as your dear wife
hangs on.'

'I've told you, I'm trying to sweeten her.'

'That means,' she riposted with endearing illogic, 'you've got
to sweeten me too. Or . . .' — the party invitation had put her
in a good humour — 'I'll pull him right off.'

We wrestled again. 'A second helping,' she demanded. 'Come
on, you can. I'll help him.'

Curled into a foetus by my sticky side, she murmured: 'So
it's all right then — about the party? You don't mind?'

At that moment of repletion I grunted acquiescence.

'But you'll watch it, darling, even by yourself, won't you?
You've got to — even if they have cut my best scene. Promise.
You promise.'

I gave my promise.

Sarah said: 'I'll know today, they'll have the results.'

I can't remember what I said, or failed to say.

'The test,' she patiently explained. 'I'm going to see the
doctor this afternoon.'

The precise order of events eludes me. Either just before or
just after she had spoken, I was opening the thick legal envelope
which dominated the morning's postal delivery. Notice of
persecution; I mean, prosecution.

'I'll be back by four,' said Sarah. 'Perhaps you'd like to
ring me.'

As I went down the corridor I thought of knocking on my
persecutor's door but prudently decided that the moment was
untimely. In the hall, observing the clerk was disengaged, I had
the notion to enrol him as an intermediary. He agreed to pass on
my polite request.

Although I was a trifle late, the office was empty upon my arrival. Lydia entered a few minutes afterwards and, regarding me with a strange stricken look, burst into tears.

'It's rotten, it's beastly,' she cried through her ugly sobs. 'It's so unfair.'

I tried to comfort her as best I could in ignorance of the disaster that had befallen her.

She lifted her head. 'And you're so calm and . . . and dignified about it,' she stammered. 'You're so brave. If I were you, I'd be . . .' She broke off. A look of horror swept her blotched face. 'Oh!' she cried as if mortally wounded. 'Don't say they haven't told you. Oh! Oh! Oh!' she cried; and she dashed from the office again.

M.B. presently informed me. His assumption of embarrassment quite pitifully failed to conceal a senile, gratuitous malice. My recent lapses . . . that Amsterdam business . . . the directors had lost confidence . . . It would, however, be wrong of me to suppose that my failings alone had been responsible for Harvey's preferment. A very capable young man: moreover, he'd just produced a re-organization scheme of great imagination and ingenuity – quite a little opus, you could say.

I think he was surprised by my restraint. I scarcely spoke. My rage and loathing had been magnetized elsewhere.

'Glad to see you taking it like this, lad,' he finally mumbled, rising creakingly. 'Knew I could rely on your continued loyalty. And Harvey too – eh! Must be disappointed, a set-back to your worthy ambitions – still, face it like a man, your chance may come again.'

He held out his hand, and, although I refrained from crushing its brittle bones, as some might have expected, I had the small mean pleasure of extracting pain and seeing pain, like an intimation of the stroke that would, I trusted, shortly finish him in agony, clouding his seeping eyes.

My own pain I kept to myself. Was I restrained by pride, or temperamental inhibition, or the convention of the good loser? None of these, you won't be surprised to learn. There was a curtain across my mind behind which bubbled all kinds of toxic poisons I knew it was absolutely essential to keep concealed.

It is not as though I lack a sense of history, nor am I unmindful of all the hideous suffering in the world; I despised myself for the trivial, bourgeois nature of my ache. But hell, they say, and nightmares certainly are furnished with the petty and familiar.

Revelation of my chagrin would only have increased his loutish self-satisfaction, so I smiled and smiled and went on smiling, until Harvey, too, offered me his hand.

'I think not,' I said. 'No, I don't feel able. No. A busy fishmonger—perhaps, yes. Or a mortuary attendant at the end of a long day of an ulcerous epidemic. Or a leper. Yes, any of these I could.'

I imagine I didn't exactly say all that, but it's likely that the shudder of revulsion I was unable to contain expressed the gist. Harvey let his hand fall. He bared his teeth, but I could deduce from the frantic tic under his left eye that he was not amused.

'So you don't wish to offer me your congratulations.'

'By all means,' I said, 'if you accept them in the spirit intended.'

'Not if they would be insincere.'

'As to that,' I temporized, 'I'd rather not say.' But leaving him in little doubt. 'All the same, thanks for the sweeties.'

'The right man got the job,' said Harvey, flushing. 'You know that, don't you? Leaving everything else aside, the man who's not afraid to take decisions. The man who wasn't afraid to act.'

'To act,' I said, still looking pleasant, 'like a thief of another's ideas.' And I swore at him.

I was annoyed with myself; it gave away too much of my pique. I had allowed a corner of the curtain to be blown adrift, revealing the earnestness of my hopes and the depths of my insufficiency; and the malignancy that stewed and steamed in boiling cauldrons over leaping flames: the lids were being blown off, and trying to hold them down was like trying to hold back an orgasm after the instant of commitment—with the same sense of profound failure contesting with the sweet surging certainty of relief. The relief was contained in my acknowledgement of my wish for Harvey dead.

'That,' said Harvey, living, and with a look of simulated pity, 'was a silly thing to say, Laurence.' He walked to the door, and turned. 'We shan't in future be able to talk on such intimate terms as these, but I'd like to leave you with a thought: you didn't lose, Laurence, because you were a man of honour too gentlemanly to strike, but because you were too complacent and too timid and too weak. In the deep recesses of your mind you knew exactly what was happening, but you hadn't the will to fight for what you wanted.'

That was his speech. I was beyond speech at that moment, but he was possibly disconcerted by my silence and stood holding the door-handle, seeking for another exit-line. 'If you wanted to get rid of me,' he said finally, 'you had the power, you should have damned well done it. You should have had the guts.'

Not the least trying part of that unsavoury day was Lydia's sympathy. Strong emotion had intensified her wet-fur smell. 'I never liked him, I never trusted him,' I remember she kept repeating. 'Men like that, they ought to be exterminated.'

The latest of my troubles had — reasonably, I claim; not with the sad, sick engrossment of dementia — pushed other matters out of my mind, so that at first I couldn't understand a word he was saying, and demanded repetition.

'Your neighbour,' sighed the clerk. 'Yes, he agrees.' He sighed again, more deeply. 'He says he's prepared to meet you. Not,' he added, 'that he thinks there's any purpose to be gained.'

A time was mentioned, but I forgot it immediately, I'm afraid.

'You didn't phone,' said Sarah, with only the faintest suggestion of reproach. 'Anyway, it didn't matter,' she went on quickly before I could express my regret. 'The results weren't ready. The doctor says he'll ring me when ... What's the matter?'

'Nothing,' I replied. 'Nothing of importance. I've had,' I half-apologized, 'a rather trying day, that's all.'

And it wasn't over yet — oh, by no means! Remember — I've diverted again, but it isn't my fault, it's the pressure of events — remember, that this was the night of Jackie's play. I hadn't forgotten, despite my troubles. Despite the way in which, as from a train departing, everything had suddenly started to slip away at an ever-increasing speed — that's to say, outside the first-class compartment I had to myself — : the grimy platform, the bookstall, M.B. in a cloud of smoke, Harvey's proffered hand, a luggage trolley, relations waving handkerchiefs, Lydia's wet eyes, boys with notebooks spotting numbers, the cool glass in my hand, and then the signal-box with Sarah's face dispassionately watching through the window . . .

'Stop dreaming,' Sarah said. 'You'll see her soon.'

'What's that?' I carefully put down my cold, ice-clinking glass.

'I said, stop dreaming.'

'No,' I pursued, 'after that. You said . . .'

'Her play.' Sarah looked at her watch. 'It will be on in only . . .'

'How did you . . .' I began, but aborted.

It didn't matter, how. She may have been making her own, doubtless discreet, enquiries; or—for I cannot be unique in this—she also could have become infected with the tedious virus of clairvoyance. I jumped up. The prospect of watching the play in Sarah's company, knowing that she knew, made my skin crawl. In some strange way it would be like having her witness our coupling. Embarrassing—no; worse. That sort of perversion disgusts me. Like incest. Incest disgusts me. I am willing to concede that the taboo has only a social provenance, but the thought of my mother, or my father . . . It makes my skin crawl.

'Why did you ask me to come back, Laurence?' Sarah said thoughtfully, as I struggled with my coat-sleeves, which were inevitably inside-out.

'I didn't exactly ask you,' I said. 'Damn this sleeve. Not in so many words.'

'No,' she said, 'I suppose that's true. But, in effect.' She laughed quite pleasantly. 'I think you don't know what you want. I think you don't know what you're doing. I think you're in a dream,' she said, as I closed the door. 'You're living in a dream inside you.'

I did not really expect to find her still at home; and she wasn't. Moreover, she had chosen this of all days to lock her door. I started back down the stairs, and then I remembered Adrian; he'd very likely have her key.

There was no reply to my agitated knocking. I tried the handle, and the door swung open. An Oriental in a string vest, with the profile of a samurai and his trousers gaping, was urinating into a banana-shaped bottle. He regarded me with polite enquiry. I explained myself as best I could, recalling, with an interior giggle, Hoo Flung's Chinese Laundry. He put down the bottle and zipped his fly over what I couldn't help but notice was an outlandishly rustic organ. My friend, he regretted with the faintest suggestion of a transatlantic accent, had buggered off.

Unnerved somewhat, I nevertheless went down to the basement to see if I could obtain entry to Jackie's room and the redundant television set from the manageress; but there was no one at home. In the dank passage a lean, torn-eared kat, I mean cat, was savaging a snake. It was a rubber snake of course. I dashed out to the car, behind which was parked, of course, a battered black . . .

A funny thing, you must have noticed, want a quiet drink, an intimate conversation, and there isn't a single bar which hasn't got the television blazing, blaring. I tried a number—naturally, taking a quick one each time—without success.

Of course, I very much wanted to see the play; but there was, now I have to admit, something factitious in the frenzy of my search—like a hero of myth overcoming self-created hazards in the pursuit of some utterly trivial token. In dreams, also, one may become quite desperate over a dropped pin, a mislaid semi-colon, the absence of a button, while remaining perfectly aware on another level of their meaningless banality.

I came upon this pub at last. I checked that the set, on top of which stood a vase of scarlet blooms from a tropical jungle, was tuned to the right channel. There was ample time. The drinks I'd taken on the way must have been speeded into the blood-stream by my agitation, but I found that I could bring the somewhat fuzzy picture into focus by closing my left eye.

There was ample time, but then suddenly the play had started. I don't know what I expected for all my loyal efforts, but in the event I found it hard to concentrate. Jackie made no appearance in the opening scenes, 'Jimmy' dominating; and instead of following his exploits on the flat, grey, flickering screen, my mind unfeelingly pursued him to the set of the dike-director's party. Party or orgy.

Even when Jackie made her first entry, and I heard again, as it were, my own voice reading the lines from the dog-eared typescript—how many doomed months ago!—I still found myself unable to assimilate the present reality. Drunk or delirious or dreaming, I don't know.

The raucous commercials interrupted. I got myself another drink. She walked to the bedroom door on teetering tiptoe, her shoulders' sudden slump expressive of betrayal and rejection. She threw open the door. This was her big scene; that's discounting the scene that had been so cruelly excised. Her outraged close-up filled the screen, and my perceptions and emotions suddenly unfroze, as though I had recovered sobriety, or as though this was the moment to which all my extravagant exertions had been directed.

Perhaps it was. Tremulously her over-life size lips parted. 'Jimmy—I never thought you could!' That was her poignant line: I knew it from our private rehearsals, and it took me some seconds to apprehend that from the set there came no sound at all.

'That's better,' said a hearty voice beneath the set, and a shiny family-man's face nodded complacently to unseen friends. 'That bleeding rubbish—couldn't hear yourself bleeding think.'

A CHANGE OF PERSON

A hand caressed the blooms above, as I rose from my chair. 'Lovely blossoms, add a touch of bleeding fragrance,' I heard him say, as I plunged forward.

It was a modest, evidently well-conducted house, its patrons a little on the dull side maybe and educationally under-privileged, yet amiable and decent—the sort of pub and clientele which foreign visitors enthuse about, the bars of their own less-favoured lands being brutal and dangerous. You wouldn't think they'd ever have known a rough-house, or how to cope with it.

Yet there I was, after a brief jump in time characteristic of drunkenness, delirium and dream-sequences, flat on my back and tearing in vain at a table-leg, a wetness spreading across my chest, with bony knees and arms pressing me down against the carpet.

As I bit and raved, foam on my mouth, I thought I caught a glimpse of a corpulent family-man tending a bloody nose, but this may have been a wishful illusion, for after another time-lapse I was on my feet with not a damaged face in sight, and the hands which pressed upon me, while still wary, were employed in brushing me down, and I was scattering largesse for any damage inadvertently caused—such as that broken vase and the trodden plastic flowers.

It was only beer that soaked my shirt; I suffered sundry aches but seemed unmarked. The foreigners' cliché must be well-founded: the hands that patted my bruises seemed even commiserative. At the door, my wallet thinner, I shook off their last restraint.

'You shouldn't come drinking, sir, not with that complaint,' the landlord finally, sympathetically and mysteriously, reproached.

I bowed and apologized again, apologized and bowed, cast a parting look at the now blank television screen and went out into the street, still muttering contrition.

To myself, however, I was muttering quite different words: like one of those monsters or robots that the television screen has done so much to popularize—kill, destroy, exterminate.

I had lost my bearings. I turned in what I hoped to be the direction of the familiar river. A number of cars were parked along the kerb, and a familiar voice said, 'Hop in, Larry,' as the nearside door of the first of them, also familiar, was thrown open in my windy path.

There is that in my constitution which abhors violence. If you have followed me this far, you will realize. I despise it: the deliberate infliction of hurt is uncivilized. Even a street-accident, where the violence, the revelation of the hatred, appears impersonal—like everyone else, I might look once, out of what's termed morbid curiosity, but it upsets me, makes me feel physically sick. Even to see a mingled, mangled dog. A dead bird. Laden with shopping-bags, a harassed mother bawls and beats her child in the street—I don't suppose it does any real harm, any physical harm, but it ... makes my skin crawl. Under the crust ... under the bland, twinkling, filtered ripples, lapping gently against the bank, there is an unmentionable foulness, I know.

I can't understand how I got away from him. Forgetting my bruises, I leapt around the swinging door and ran. I heard him shout out something behind me, and then the headlights came on, throwing my spread-eagled shadow along the street and up hard against the walls. I heard the engine start. I bounded a low wall into a churchyard, and lurched between the reaching arms of the gravestones. At the farther end there was a small wicket-gate, such as one comes upon in romantic gardens or set into the crumbling walls of old estates. It opened to my touch with a miraculous ease, and I strolled down a passage into a street which was to all appearances the twin of that I had just escaped from. But I still don't know, in retrospect, exactly how I got away from him: there was nothing, I suppose, to have prevented him from driving round the block to intercept me.

Shortly I came to the river. I decided to leave my car where I had parked it, not all those many hours before, in the neighbourhood of Jackie's room. I walked easily homewards, the twinkling, filtered ripples of the river lapping at my feet.

Sarah was sewing something silky and lifted it to her mouth to bite off a loose thread. 'Did you see the play?' she asked, and she spat out a small end of cotton. 'Do you want anything to eat?'

I replied, 'Yes' to the first question and, 'No, thank you' to the second, and passed through the room.

A close scrutiny revealed no visible damage from the disturbance in the pub; my shirt and jacket were stained and I changed them.

When I went back into the living-room, Sarah said: 'I watched it.' She was still sewing, a shiny flesh-pink slip bunched on her lap. 'I saw her, your little Miss Jackie. I thought she was quite ...' She broke off, her needle poised. 'You'd rather I didn't talk about it?'

I shrugged, indifferent; but she seemed to assume my agreement and dropped the subject. We talked about this and that. I picked up a magazine and riffled its pages. The night for once peaceful ... the soft glow of the table-lamps, her needle flashing with a kind of trance-like rhythm ... there was an atmosphere of domestic tenderness, and my first reaction on feeling the clumsy, lungeing swelling in my groin was to curse its arrogant untimeliness. Perhaps if I ignored it, like an importunate puppy whose demands to be taken out for a walk are unwelcome, it would quietly go away.

It didn't go away, nor subside. The psychology of these uuprovoked urges, was a mystery to me. And a vexation; I lowered the magazine on to my lap.

Sarah chatted on about this and that. She smiled and tossed back her head, her hair catching the light like a blessing, the needle in her hand describing a curious little arabesque . . . and at that moment I had an infallible conviction that this at last was my opportunity to *bend her to my will*. I uncrossed my legs and rose from the chair.

It was extraordinary. I was outside myself, standing, as it were, at the far end of the room, watching my face. Yet at the same time I could clearly see Sarah's face when I ought, to have been consistent, to have been looking at the back of her neck.

I wasn't worried by the anomaly of my two separate viewpoints. I saw myself slowly, humbly approach her, dropping to my knees—despite my bruised legs—at a deferential distance from where she sat, reaching forward to take her hand. The silk garment slid suggestively to the floor.

'If you like,' said Sarah, presumably in answer to a question from the man at her feet. 'If there's any point in further talk.' She stuck the needle in the arm of her chair.

He on his knees suppliant, she stooped in an attitude of attentive consideration: I watched them. His pleas evidently fell on stony ground, as so often before.

But there was a difference, attributable to my detachment. Observing remotely, I was able to introduce a calculated artistry. It was quite horrible but also fascinating. Soft words were reinforced by soft caresses. I lay my hand on the gentle round-nesses of her woolly breasts. Her acquiescence suffuses to response; she has no choice, my ministrations are so coldly skilled. Pornographically, he unfastens clips and buttons.

Dissociation was not complete. Sprawled across her, I find myself, for instance, remembering the similar episode in her basement refuge, and lift my head from her tangled hair expecting to see a child's face against the glass above a window gap. Suppose this is not happening at all, but is only a memory . . . 'Yes! Yes! Yes!' she cried, pledging herself to my demands.

She wanted at the last moment to go into the bedroom, but I wouldn't, fearing, of course, that I should not be able to take with us my position of vantage. Practically naked now, against the wall, I witnessed on the floor — her heaving limbs, her groans and scream, my savage, hammering thrusts — what could have been — the comparison is compulsive — a killing.

She has gone, and I am still lying — unobserved now — on the carpet, a torn magazine under my arm. Overcoming my natural languor, I rise, with fresh bruises, to make myself decent.

Shy is lying on her back, the sheets up to her chin, Her eyes alone acknowledge my entry. I come to the bedside. I look into her eyes; and perceive her answer.

'But you promised,' I said feebly and hopelessly. 'Just now, when we were . . . You promised . . . Yes, yes, you said.' It might, by the look in her eyes, never have happened. 'Sarah, I beg you . . . please . . .'

I cast around for impetus. My gaze fell on the dressing-table stool; I nodded my head in reflective reply. For a long moment, frozen in torpor, I looked down upon my wife. Then, still quietly, 'I loathe you,' I said. 'Sarah, I wish you were dead.'

Evidently, after that I had to get out. Eventful day as it had been, time expanding as it always will to accommodate tribulation, I discovered that the hour was not unduly late; I could make an exit without creating a climax of tawdry melodrama. Besides, tapping my pockets, I was out of cigarettes. And, besides—I didn't think of it until I was descending in the lift— I ought to pick up the car, it would be reasonable and practical to pick up the car, in readiness for the next morning, the day to come, the continuation of my basically unexceptional existence, to which—the lift doors hissing open—at this moment, and despite my acquired precognitive faculty, I could not envisage interruption nor finality.

An opportune taxi discarded two adolescent girls in gauzy dance-dresses. Back early from the ball, I'd never know for certain why, and so subdued, I sympathetically observed, waiting without impatience for them to find the fare, emptying out their two identical gold-dusted reticules. So touchingly subdued, returning without escorts when they must have started out with such high romantic hopes.

Surly the driver: their tip had probably been derisory. I had to shout twice before he would stop at the neon-blinking café, and when I got out, even though I explained my purpose clearly, he emanated silent suspicion, a man too often bilked before.

A black-chinned Levantine sold me the cigarettes, but civil enough. How their ear-drums could stand the juke-box at that level I'd never comprehend. My return, cigarette glowing between my lips, brought no acknowledgement from the driver: he started up with a jerk which sent me tumbling across the seat.

I'd forgotten all about Ossie. For about five-hundred yards along a wide and empty street a car seemed to be trailing us, its high headlights flooding the cab and exploding in my unhappy driver's mirror; but it overtook us at last, a nondescript saloon crammed with an unlikely number of bodies, half-drunk probably.

My car stood where I had left it. The street was deserted. I paid off the cab, tipping no more and no less than my custom. I lit another cigarette.

Two minutes away only, in the direction I was pointed: of course I would drive past. Of course, her window unexpectedly lit, I would stop. Of course. The street-door, not unsurprisingly, gave way to a finger-touch. I climbed the stairs. A welcoming rim of light around the door, which also, and less expectedly, opened with a dream-like ease to my gentle, though eager, hand.

She screamed: she didn't scream: I don't know. Her head, the mouth scream-wide, surfaced indignantly above the naked tangle of their limbs. She pushed at me flat-palmed with her one free hand, like a harassed celebrity blocking a camera lens; and, where I myself had only rarely and on specially favoured occasions been granted oral access, 'Jimmy' reluctantly lifted his glistening, hairy mask . . .

That wasn't quite the end of the affair. I would, I suppose, in good time have come round to forgiving her again, there being, in a sense, nowhere else for me to go. But I was deprived of the opportunity.

Not that night. I'd slammed the door: I'd left it wide: I don't know. I ran. The night must somehow have spent itself.

She called me early, the earliest ever she had done, with a gentle consideration in her voice that was entirely new, although it hardened quickly enough to cut off my cries of woe and outrage, allowing me only to concur. As others have noted before me, the chicken will keep on walking for a while headless; for a while, for a while, we continue with the motions of existence after our hearts have been cut out. So we met for lunch in our usual restaurant.

'I'm sorry, Laurence,' she said. She wore another new scent.

'About last night.' An unfortunate solecism indeed, she implied.
'But perhaps, in a funny sort of way it was all for the best. I
mean, that you should have happened to have come in while we
were . . .' Modesty abridged the sentence. 'Well, it sort of made
the point, didn't it. You see, he's moving in with me, Cornelius.'

'Cornelius?' I queried.

' "Jimmy" ', she translated, with a moue of impatience.
'That's just till we find somewhere better, of course. Will you
pass the menu? Thanks. You saw our play, did you, how did
you like it? The notices aren't too hostile; one paper gave
Cornelius a marvellous write-up. He's going to fix a West End
part for me, he says. I think I'll have the *rognons flambées*. And
whitebait for a starter— aren't I greedy? You know, Laurence,
that wife of yours she'd never have let you go. Women like that,
they ought to be exterminated.'

There was, I suppose, a merciful numbness. I controlled
myself through the meal, though admittedly my appetite was
minimal. I couldn't help noticing how she kept glancing
glitteringly about the room, as a woman will whose companion
is superfluous.

She emptied her coffee-cup and dabbed her lips. She thanked
me prettily, and with a terrible politeness, for the lunch. I
begged; abjectly I begged. My elbow caught the saucer with its
tip—I mean, containing the tip: waiters came scurrying from
all four corners. 'I was afraid you'd make a scene,' she whispered,
as they crawled under our feet for the silver. 'You don't have any
self-respect, do you.'

I followed her out, still raving.

'It's no use,' she said, 'it's absolutely no use. I wouldn't,
Laurence, not even if she dropped down dead tomorrow; I don't
think even then. Get me a taxi, will you?'

Instead, I dragged her round the corner into an alley where
the restaurants' dustbins overflowed and a gay Florentine aria
ascended from the kitchens.

'Cornelius and I,' she said, 'we've got something special

going for us.' Whatever that meant. 'Besides, he's going to help me in my career. I'd be mad,' she said, 'to keep dragging on with you. Even if your dear wife. Because, you must admit,' she said, 'Laurence, you are, you really are, far too old for me. I'd be absolutely mad.'

It was a risky moment to speak of madness: I was pawing at her, pressing her back among the greasy dustbins. If I put my hands round her throat, not knowing what I am doing, without intending it, and squeeze the breath from her lungs, the traffic roar will drown her cries, and not one of the hundreds passing will discommode themselves to intervene: it's for a film they'd think, or tell themselves, it's only for a film, or for the television.

A dustbin lid clattered to the ground. I dropped my hands. She could have run, but, surprisingly, she didn't. Soberly and rationally, for the sake of symmetry and order, I put it to her again in simple, explicit words.

'No, Laurence,' she replied. 'I've told you. I mean it. There's no use going on. It's all over. It's all over between us,' she repeated with uncharacteristic clarity.

After a moment—the operatic aria had changed into a pop ballad I remembered I'd been hearing from every transistor radio for weeks; a limping dog crept in and out again with a discarded chop; I aged a hundred years a second—after a brief moment, 'Come on,' she said impatiently, 'you can't keep standing here for ever.' And she walked away and left me.

She stopped; she turned; she came back. She shook her head with a kind of tolerant impatience. 'Oh, Laurence—look at you,' she said, pointing.

I followed her finger down: a trail of something green, presumably from the dustbins, clung to my trousers.

'Come here,' she said. 'You mustn't walk about like that.' Her trespassing fingers, with a wisp of cloth, dabbed solicitously in the neighbourhood of my groin, whiled I stood like a soldier. 'Licence my . . .'—and she giggled softly over the words— 'roaming hands . . .'

I pushed her away and ran into the shimmering street.

And now I am standing again—again, again, and as I had foreseen—in the dark outside, ultimately excluded. A pink glow at her window, familiar window; a seepage of music—a tune last heard in some remote, disastrous alley—washes around me.

I haven't been up to her room, to their room; I don't think I can have been up, I would remember. I am quite without hope; I am here only because I have nowhere else to be. My bruises ache. Numbness and an acute vibrancy beset me simultaneously. The night is full of baleful noises. Each passer-by convulses me with hatred.

Memories taunt, forming a kind of distant mirage-reflection for ever beyond my attainment. My imagination, entirely out of control, conjures other pictures: grotesque hobgoblin antics, caricature obscenities. I inhabit the vision of a cruel, laughing madman.

After an immeasurable time the music has stopped. The pressure in my abdomen I finally identify, and urinate where I stand. Clumsy with the zip as though my fingers had been cut off at the knuckles. A plane comes low and gaily twinkling, to drop the bomb in a festive spirit. Her light goes out. Their light.

Their light has been out some time, and I still stayed. What moved me at last, to show all reason had not been lost, was a patrolling policeman. A helmet, a cape, a torch at his belt—I didn't know they dressed like that any more; perhaps only in the still small hours. A policeman in the still small hours, dressed as a policeman is in memory dressed, arouses deep residual guilts. Now you listen to me, Constable, there's nothing in the law, Constable, to prohibit a citizen from being abroad in the still small hours. I'll show you my driving licence, Constable. Or my arse. Or my anxiety.

When he came the second time, flashing his torch superfluously into profoundly innocent doorways, I knew that he intended to accost me, so I hitched myself up and made off with the utmost dignity.

My steps took me the way I knew. And when I came to the river-bank I understood that I had had no choice, for this too had been forewritten.

If only this were not my real existence, if only this were a dream from which, in good safe time, I could awake—say, to the happiest day of my life. Or if I were simply a character in a work of fiction whose ordeal had been contrived for obscure artistic purposes alone . . . Such thoughts one has in a fruitless effort to keep at bay the real horrors of one's real world.

The river is real, the sleeping swans, the wind—now suddenly wildly gusting—the leaping shadows, the dank chemical smell of the night . . . and from out of the darkness of the trees there steps a squat, familiar figure.

I forgot to mention there was an almost full moon—along whose shiny path we walked to come together.

19

The moonlight singled him out, creating a man of substance and dark shadow.

'Larry boy, Larry!' He clapped me across the shoulders. Peering into my face, he screwed his own features into a simulation of wry humour. 'Funny time of night for a constitutional!'

I said nothing.

'You want to be careful, Larry—getting out of a warm bed. But I'll bet it was worth it, I'll bet she gave you a . . .' He poked me in the ribs and drew in his breath with a lubricious whistle. 'And now you're back off to your charming home and your lovely wife, you lucky bleeder, you happy old . . .' A look of alarm suddenly replaced his merriment. He stood up on tiptoe to study me more closely still. 'Hey!' he cried. 'What's the matter? You look terrible. Larry, you sick or something?'

I still said nothing.

'Must be the germs,' he theorized, 'or a virus, what they call it. Hey, you should have had them injections, like I told you.' He turned, and turned me with him to face the dark, though moon-glossed, river. He paused—almost, I might have thought had I not known him so well, in romantic nostalgia. 'But that was a long time ago, eh Larry? A long time ago, couldn't have been what happened then, could it? I mean, whatever it is you've got, couldn't be them germs you swallowed saving my life. You remember, eh, dragging me out pewking, and you wondering what the bleeding hell you'd landed with! But that was a long time ago, Larry, must be some other kind of sickness that you got.'

'Please!' I found my voice. 'Please, I'm not in the mood for it.' I turned my back on the water.

He was round in front of me, protective and solicitous. 'But maybe you ain't sick, Larry eh, that it? It ain't the germs. You got troubles, Larry, I should have seen. What sort of lousy friend I am not to have deduced!' Angrily, he punched his chest. 'Ossie, you must be going bleeding silly! I should have known, I should have seen it—specially where you're concerned, Larry, for, I told you . . .'—he whispered it close—'you're like my own bruvver.'

I swore at him, but he took no notice.

'What sort of trouble is it, Larry? Is it love or is it money? Or is it some geezer what's getting at you? Or maybe it's something else, just . . .'

He broke off, and, despite myself, 'What?' I cried. 'What else?'

'Don't want to make you angry, Larry. Some things, I know, they make you kind of touchy, don't they?'

'What else?' I repeated in a loud voice. But I wasn't truly angry; I didn't feel that I was challenging him, my brother, but some less personal adversary for whom he was merely a comic mouthpiece, the ventriloquist's doll.

'You know, don't you?' Like a ventriloquist's doll he wouldn't give a straight answer. 'You don't need me to tell you, Larry. It's all inside of you.'

I turned my back on him.

'Here,' he said, 'don't be like that. Have a choccy, I mean a ciggy.'

I remembered now I had finished my cigarettes while standing outside Jackie's window; I saw the pool of my urine flowing over the approximate hexagon formed by their stamped ends. We lit up together—a comradely gesture.

'That better? Times of stress there's nothing like a ciggy. How did I know you was out of them?' Without expecting an answer, my comrade took my arm. 'Let's walk a bit, shall we?'

I obeyed.

'What we was talking about—your troubles, Larry. Remember, I told you once before, the crux of your dilemma; that time we had our little evening out, our little party—remember that now, don't you, Larry? A night that was!' He chuckled in happy reminiscence. 'The crux of your dilemma . . .' — oh, yes, he liked that phrase! — 'Larry, told you then: how you keep it all bottled up inside of you, scared to admit it. So that there's this other geezer what's inside you — let's see, how did I put it? — kicking and squawking and effing and blinding. Kicking and squawking and effing and blinding, and begging of you for to let him out, Larry.' He, we, paused. 'And remember who that other geezer is, Larry, inside of you.' He paused again, either in modesty or expectation of my answer — which was not forthcoming. 'That geezer's me, Larry,' he finally, unnecessarily, supplemented. 'Your old friend Ossie.'

We had walked through this. We stopped by mutual, unspoken consent; we both recognized the point we had arrived at: the very spot. The lights on the bridge upstream and on the opposite Surrey bank stippled the river's surface. Except for the water's lap and suck there was a timeless stillness. The trees stood as stark as gibbets. 'Bastards', I heard him whisper, and I tasted the river's foulness and stench, as a water-rat slid to its hole in the mud.

'Bastards! They're all hateful bastards, Larry. What chance have you got?' His sibilant urgency penetrated the mists of my remembrance. 'Not unless . . . not until . . . It's the only way out of your troubles, Larry. It's the only way you'll be . . . free.' His face was as close to mine as when I had stooped to kiss life into his open mouth. 'Remember, I told you, Larry — a life for a . . .'

I pushed him away and, caught off balance, he staggered to the very water's edge. I made no move to save him.

'Hey, Larry!' He was laughing. 'Nearly shoved me in then, you did. Into all that shit again. You'd have had to dive in and drag me out, like before, all over again.' He went on laughing.

'Get away from me,' I shouted. 'Get away. I'm sick and tired of you. I don't want you. I don't need you.'

'Sh-sh, Larry! Sh-sh!' He held my arm. 'Take it easy.'

'Sick and tired of you pestering me. So now, if you don't

226

mind . . .' Shaking off his hand, I determined to walk away.
'Hold on.'

'Let go of me.'

'Wait on, Larry.'

'Let go, I tell you. Take your hands off.'

'But I'm not holding you, Larry.' His voice was treacly with
surprised innocence.

It was true: he was not holding me; between us there was a
gap of yards. He was not even looking at me. Standing with a
curiously alert stillness, he stared reflectively into the abject
darkness of the river.

'Just leave me alone,' I said weakly, before walking away
from him for ever. He showed no sign of having heard me. 'Do
what you want,' I said more firmly, 'so long as you leave me
alone. Do what the hell you like—just leave me free.'

20

I must have got away somehow, for now I am standing in an unlit place beneath my father's window. Six dead birds at my feet form an irregular hexagon. In the far dusty distance – but florid and distinct, as though I were seeing visions – appears a column of marching students below an aviary of banners. Everything falls away before them. I raise a rubber telephone to keep them from my father's house, but, pitilessly young and oyster-eyed, they walk right through me, chanting the gatling's jammed and the colonel's, and I pick up myself and a discarded banner in crude black capitals saying dead ...

Unbearably bumpy to my bruises, the mattress tosses and turns me in a sweat of anguish. Once again, I ... look down on the trampolin in the lilac dusk ... humorously pose before the gorilla's cage ... search obsessively for a missing button, a missing connection ... Once again, she fingers herself on the bedroom stool ... a child's face is pressed to the glass ... splinters, like hornets, fly from his door ... The images have the profound and inescapable quality of ante-natal memory. Scientifically speaking, Herr Doktor, is there such a thing as or is it only ante-natal an illusion memory scientifically like the artist's speaking likeness of reality? I mean to say ...

I mean to say: since childhood I have known. I search the human faces at the Zoo for my father's face. And the animals' faces for my own. Mask. A glistening hairy mask. The marmoset scampers back along the branch for ever. The intolerable anguish of a search for ever. Aaahh!

AAAHH! To end the search, there is a way. To pay, today, make hay, and what enormous knockers she gave with her treble stamps. To end the search, to kill. destroy, exterminate, as the television screen has done so much to popularize, along with wars and famines and assassinations. To find at last, the only way, to end the search — AAAHH! If only this were not a dream . . .

Push the stifling pillows to the floor. I dreamed, I dreamed . . . a solution . . . I had it in me like a. Dreamed . . .

Do what the hell you like. He fell spouting under the potted palm. My brooch on the wrong bosom. She tears up my goddess as though paper. Still, heart, still!

I think I am awake. Under my feet a carpet of . . . asphalt . . . wet tracks on the asphalt . . . a milkman's electric float glides silently over a carpet of sand. Down, down, down Rufus, down. I didn't mean to hurt you. To impregnate you. Go quietly. Civilized is one way out. Insane. AAAHH! . . .

'My gorilla, lick me.'
'Where?'
'That little red spot in my armpit.'
'Here?'
'And jump aboard.'
'What?'
'My soapy mauve-nippled Cadillac.'

And we are off, driving towards some bottomless abyss of indignity and abuse, with insolent waiters, contemptuous students, recalcitrant Negroes; the central-heating broken down and the refuse-collectors on strike; and the walls collapsing to the thud of the bongo-drums, and the jet aircraft screaming above the disintegrating roof-tops.

If only this were not a dream, I'd write it all down. I wish I could write it down. To bring it to an end, I have to get *outside* myself—to hand back to an author one hopes to be omniscient, dispassionate, just.

Part Three

CLOSING

21

'Aarragh!' Laurence woke shouting, with the cell-door clang of disaster ringing in his head. He also felt himself to be soaking wet as though he'd been standing unsheltered, fully clothed, in a downpour. He'd had bad dreams, he'd been sweating – his pyjamas were damp, if only slightly. But the disasters were real enough: they took a vivid pictorial form, like masked faces in a carnival crowd, and came pressing in on him mockingly, seeking out his bruises.

In an effort, an only marginally effective effort, to keep them at a less tormenting distance, he propelled himself swiftly into the familiar rhythm of the morning. Nothing very special had happened: a love affair broken, ambition thwarted, a legal contretemps, marital disharmony ... He listened outside Sarah's room, and the sound of her regular breathing was a small reassurance. After all, habit, routine, ritual had kept him going through a lifetime which, considered dispassionately, must be seen as grotesquely *inhuman* – why should they fail him now? A sudden sharper realization of Jackie lost sent him speeding to the bathroom, vomiting his coffee.

His briefcase stood in its habitual place, propped against the, now chipped and dismembered, Balinese goddess. Before leaving, he went again to Sarah's door, and again, for a reason he didn't analyse, knowledge of her presence generated a brief comfort.

Waiting for the lift, he felt dizzy: he had to support himself against the wall until the fit passed. He stopped in the hallway by the aquatic sculpture, the unpleasant thought at that moment dominant in his mind replaced by another only slightly less disagreeable.

With a grimace, whose strangeness he was unaware of, Laurence walked to the desk. 'You gave me a message from my neighbour. Would you mind repeating? I'm afraid I've forgotten it.'

The clerk's sigh was so ostentatiously prolonged it made him choke and cough, and his reply emerged in spray and splutter.

'This evening,' Laurence repeated. 'At six. Six o'clock, is that right?'

He was proud of his calm, but was there some peculiarity in his demeanour that made the porter throw open the door for him and bow him into the courtyard, with a, 'Have a good day, Mr Carpenter, sir.'? Something he hadn't done for weeks.

In the car Laurence found himself testing his control over his thoughts and feelings as though he were constructing a wall to keep out ravaging monsters. Against the depth of his despair he coldly measured his capability to survive.

The traffic had slowed to octogenarian walking-pace and then came to a complete stop. Laurence sat motionless, save for his fingers restlessly tapping the gloved wheel, no more agitated than any of the other drivers, and a good deal less than some—as the deadly fumes silently and invisibly pervaded, and each contraction of his heart pumped the poison more swiftly through his veins. He decided that while it was far too early confidently to assert that the wall would stand, the ravagers be kept at bay, for the moment— as at last the traffic got moving again, past the concertina-ed wrecks, the flashing ambulance, the mutilation on the stretcher—he could allow himself a modicum of hope.

This phase of relative equanimity didn't last long. When he arrived at the office all his spleen and disappointment at Harvey's preferment erupted chokingly, bringing on another dizzy spell and then an outburst of mindless fury. Had Harvey been present there was no telling what Laurence might have said or done; instead, he took it out on Lydia, driving her near tears from the room.

Then his press of troubles momentarily receded—as an importunate queue withdrawing to sort themselves out and decide priorities. When they returned, Jackie was firmly established at their head.

He swore he wouldn't telephone. His resolution lasted only minutes. The first time he replaced the receiver almost immediately after dialling, giving no one time to answer. On subsequent occasions he went on holding it long after it was evident there would be no answer.

His eyes closed in anguish, he laid the malevolent instrument back by touch on its cradle. Opening his eyes he looked straight into the watery gaze of Lydia, who'd at some point returned unnoticed.

'You are unlucky, aren't you?' she said, with a dreadful twinkling attempt at roguishness. 'She must be playing hard to get. Unless she's . . .' Her words fell over themselves in fright, for she saw the blood come into Laurence's eyes, but she couldn't hold them back: 'Unless sh-sh-she's got another lo-lo-lover.' Now quite in tears, she moaned: 'It was just a joke.'

Laurence was required to apologize for his abrasiveness. 'I'm afraid I'm a little edgy this morning.'

Eagerly Lydia seized on this. 'I'm not surprised, so would anyone be—the rotten tricks they've played on you.' She tossed back her head. 'I told him, director or no director, Harvey, and he can sack me if he likes, I told him to his face . . .'

To cut this off, and also because the question had been gently rubbing in a corner of his mind, Laurence interrupted: 'Where is Harvey, anyway? Don't say he's moved himself upstairs already.'

'I don't know. Don't care. Good riddance. Actually a lot of people have been asking for him.'

'Perhaps he's been celebrating.'

'He should be too ashamed.'

'Somehow, I doubt that.'

'So do I. Oh, Laurence!' The tears overflowing, she grabbed handfuls from her box of Kleenex. 'Don't care about Harvey, it's you,' she croaked through her sniffs. 'You shouldn't be here the way you look—terrible, as if . . .'

The telephone rang and Laurence jumped upon it in passionate reflex. But it was only someone else seeking Harvey. He got rid of Lydia, fabricating an errand that despatched her to the deepest, dustiest basement in the building.

He wasn't going to telephone any more. Finding himself with the mouthpiece in his hand, he made a superhuman effort and dialled, instead, his own number. What he would say to Sarah he didn't know, and was relieved that here, too, there was no answer.

He was alone (save, again, for myself). The ceiling and walls closed in. The silence was the silence of a cell—and the sudden jarring intrusions of the telephone, like the gaoler's clanging of the peephole grille, only emphasized his sense of abandonment. Each time the gaoler might be bringing news of his reprieve—but each time it was only an enquiry for the absent Harvey.

As he had sworn to himself not to telephone, so he had sworn he wouldn't go. An overflowing In-tray crashed to the floor in his leap from the desk. No use taking the car: this time of day nowhere to park. For once—let it be Providence, signal of the turn of Fortune's wheel—he got a taxi straight away. Even so, he was half-soaked, the rain streaming down as from an open sluice.

Somehow, as, dripping a trail, he bounded up the mouldering stairs, he felt absolutely certain he would find her and that, whatever had been said and done before and whatever the persistence of 'Jimmy'-Cornelius, a miracle would unfold itself, resurrecting the glory of the past from the ignominious abjection of the present.

The door remained closed to his hand; his knocking and his cries collapsed in a grave of silence. A miracle would not take place—today or any day. Though as Laurence turned slowly away from her door he felt obscurely that his aching desire had receded, to become merely emblematic—like a drowning man's last memory in the darkness of wave and choking and panic.

It was still raining with the same ferocity, but it was not the rain which halted him at the street-door; for the third time in the morning he was afflicted by giddiness. This was the worst attack: he shivered and he staggered and he had to hold on to the rusty railings to keep from lurching down the steps. At the same time, dissociated from his faintness, he felt a cold tremor of fear, springing from a source unknown.

'Hey, you!' A woman's face peered up at him from a thin opening at the door in the basement. 'Was you shouting for Jackie?' Only a segment of her face was visible; the toes of one bare foot poked out into the rain. 'You that chap of hers, ain't you?' At another time, the description might have afforded Laurence gratification, but now he couldn't bring himself to answer. 'So you don't know where she's gone to neither.'

To confront her he had moved out of the shelter of the doorway; the rain streamed down his face. The thirsty toes curled and then, refreshed, withdrew. 'I thought you might have known then. There was another fellow here looking for her.' Even this cruel reminder of her new lover couldn't at that moment arouse the fire of his jealousy. 'I didn't like the look of him at all,' she said. 'A coloured chap he was, I caught him skulking, creeping down.'

There was a long and substantial pause. 'Just gone it seems she has,' said the landlady at last. 'Just disappeared, I mean she always lets me know, she's good that way at least, I'll give her credit. But now she's gone, I don't know where she can have gone,' she finished, grumbling to herself, 'she's simply gone and . . .' Her face followed her toes inside.

The door was closed. For a moment Laurence's fear, which had never left him, had seemed to have been—again—precognitive, its murky obscurity, like a photographic-plate in a developing bath, taking on recognizable and familiar features. It was all over in a second, dismissed as an absurdity, fearful phantasm of fear itself. He took a deep breath, pushed his neck into the inadequate shelter of his shoulders and plunged down into the street. This time he was less fortunate with a taxi.

Soaked to the skin when he arrived back, he dried out quickly in the aridity of the office, although a coldness seemed to have settled permanently in the area of his chest, extending into his bowels and shrivelling his genital organs.

'Can't understand it, can't understand it at all,' grumbled M.B. petulantly, drawing noisily on his pipe. 'An hour late now —to meet his fellow-directors for the first time. Not like Harvey at all. You sure you don't know where he's got to, Laurence, not covering up?'

Sullen, Laurence shook his head.

'We haven't seen him all day, sir,' ventured Lydia. 'Everyone's been looking for him.'

'Over an hour.' M.B. blinked at his watch. 'Been on to his wife, and she can't understand it—left home this morning just as usual. Seems he's absolutely vanished.' He shook the watch as though reproaching it. 'Now, how can a man just vanish off the face of the earth—you tell me that? Here, where are you . . .' he began, getting no further as, in his surprise, his pipe fell from his mouth to the carpet in a shower of sparks—by which time Laurence was already out of the door.

The recognizable and familiar features had a familiar name and voice. The voice echoed in his head, as distinct and familiar as his own. Descending in the lift and then—coatless, hatless— racing into the rain again, Laurence wrestled with his reason. Ossie wasn't real, he was only a projection of his own deranged imagination. Ossie, real enough, was a macabre joker; or a glib braggart. Fear disintegrates reality's adhesion. Jangled nerves, as is well known, reach out for coincidence.

To have acknowledged the previously suppressed shape of his fear brought a limited relief: there was no longer the same frozen obstruction around his heart; he felt the reassertion of his sexual parts. That isn't to say his anguish was any the less acute: from a numbed and northern inertia it had swung to the pole of an equatorial fever.

Burning, he speeded the car along the cluttered commercial

roads, successfully challenging adversaries several times his size. Sneaking inside a looming bus, he felt the scrape, and something tinny fell and rolled. Much, much more would have been required to halt him. He became ensnared in a tangle of new one-way systems and when he broke loose lost again in a reticulation of narrow and hostile streets identically recurring.

But suddenly, surely, this was the street! There was no name-plate, but then there never had been. These hoardings, the shattered street-lamps, the abandoned shells of cars ... He thudded his foot on the brake and was thrown hard against the wheel.

Yes, it was the same street, but ... different. It had changed into a film-set: the mean terraced buildings presented the dream-like insubstantiality of two-dimensional façades; and at the upper levels, beyond the cameras' requirements, the walls termi-nated in emptiness, defined by jagged and precarious masonry.

When Laurence stepped out of the car he could hear dis-tantly under the spindrift of the rain the rolling growl of bull-dozers and, like an underwater bell, the clanging of some gigantic invisible hammer.

All the windows had gone, and the door; heaps of rubble stood in the place of the ordered piles of fruit. Incredulous, and ignoring the rain, Laurence stood for quite some time, his head thrown back, staring up to where the sky shafted through the holes and cracks in the upper floors. What did he do now? Where did he go? It was difficult to reason when he felt himself im-prisoned in a dark and relentless nightmare. He turned away from the shell of the shop, making a great effort to repudiate the nightmare's logic. Command reality ... think objectively ... weigh the evidence—and the outcome was that he was beset by a fresh and more terrible fear ...

In this district, he might have known, none of the public telephones was working; mostly the fittings hung adrift above conglomerations of human or animal excrement. Quite forget-ting the time, he tried the door of a shuttered pub. He asked a shopkeeper but, startled by his appearance or antagonized by his peremptory rudeness, she sent him packing. He must have wasted twenty minutes.

He raced along the by-pass, the windscreen wipers pumping as frantically and as ineffectually as his pulses. However swiftly they cleared the glass, instantly the mist returned. The car rocked and juddered. He splashed through oily pools, leaving a ship's wake behind, along with the outraged hootings of the motorists he'd all but wrecked.

A foot-stool lay on its side. But it was a light piece easily, and frequently being, overturned. That heavy earthenware jug—out of place on the table? Rack his brain as he might, he couldn't remember. Wouldn't she have thrown out that torn magazine?

Both the beds had been made. Her clothes—so far as he could tell, they were all there. So far as he could tell. And the suitcases.

The windows were all shut tight—naturally: the rain. Not a sound within, without. The runways must be flooded. He put his hands to his head. Something in the stillness impressed his senses with the ponderosity of an irreversible emptiness.

For one or two minutes, as a shocked survivor on the periphery of the blast, stunned, he couldn't think of anything at all. He had to do something, do something—tear at the mountain of rubble with his bare hands.

What was the wretched woman's name? Blenkinsop—that was it. He threw the telephone pad across the room. What was the matter with her, couldn't she understand a perfectly simple enquiry? He shouted his question again; and, recording her negative, slammed down the receiver.

Then he dialled a second number, imprinted on his memory—and listened intently to the brrpp-brrpp, brrpp-brrpp repeating itself endlessly, as though it might convey some desperate coded message from the locked, pink-curtained room.

And he dialled a third time. 'For God's sake, Lydia' —
interrupting her shrill cries — 'just answer me: they haven't
found him yet?'

He was standing with his hand still resting on the cradled
telephone when, all of its own accord, it sprang clamorously
to life. Instinctively though he had grasped and lifted the receiver, he brought it to his ear with a dazed and trembling
reluctance; and couldn't, failing to recognize the voice — which
was none of the voices for which his apprehensions had prepared
him — himself get out a word.

'No,' said Laurence at last, in response to the increasingly
gruff demands at the other end, 'Mrs Carpenter isn't at home.'

'Is that Mr Carpenter?' Possibly Laurence's agreement
lacked conviction, for the voice persisted: 'That *is* Mr Carpenter?
Well, this is Doctor . . .'

He lost the name, lost what came next, the word 'doctor', in
the context of his dread, temporarily numbing. 'What? I didn't
quite . . .'

'I said . . .' — the voice, in conflict with his message, irritable
at the demands for repetition — 'my congratulations to you
both: the tests were positive.'

With a small cry, Laurence let the receiver fall and threw
himself down on his knees, pressing his face into the carpet.
Finding they were odourless, the fresh dark stains like a spoor,
he'd noticed while holding the telephone, he dabbed at them
with his fingers, then licked, but tasted nothing, and spat the
carpet-fluff out of his mouth. Still, baffled, on his knees, he
followed the tracks across the room and back again. Where he
himself had walked: he looked down at his shoes. He looked
at his shoes for a long while — funny how the leather whitens
in the folds as they dry!

Suddenly he couldn't, if his life depended on it, stay in the
flat a minute longer. Moving is delay: activity, evasion.

Shouldn't go out my shoes like this. 'Have you seen . . .' Why
was the fellow looking at him like that? '. . . my wife?' The

answer, like the other answers, fell on the bare nerve of his foreknowledge.

Some water must have got into a vulnerable component of the mechanism. He clicked the switches, pumped the pedals, and the engine expired with ominous hiccups. 'My congratulations,' repeated the doctor, and Laurence cradled his head in his arms over the wheel, but couldn't cry.

The rain rattled on the roof like small stones. Laurence lifted his head, unthinkingly reached to the ignition, and the engine started.

The traffic much heavier now, he couldn't have driven at the same reckless speed as before, even if the heat of his urgency had not burned out. He had travelled some distance before acknowledging his destination, and even then the journey seemed merely a gratuitous and ill-timed gesture. The rain stopped, but without suggesting it had cleared for long.

Knowing what he knew, it was scarcely worth getting out of the car. He turned off the engine and lit a cigarette. Then, going to the other extreme, he admitted a fantastic prospectus of hope, and, throwing away the half-smoked cigarette, he bounded down the hollowed-out steps to the basement, clattering drunkenly against the dustbins.

The curtains were open; a single low-powered lamp on a table at the junction of the L illuminated the room with a soft and flickering glow, more candle than electric. It was the rain running down the glass which produced the flickering-candle effect. Laurence pressed his nose to the window.

At first he could see no one. Then, undulating through the watery glass, a woman appeared in the dim distance, leaning forward to straighten the cushions on a chair, or some such familiar gesture, her fair hair falling over her face; and Laurence, at the window, gave a little cry of recognition—and more.

Before he could make his presence known, smiling the woman straightened and turned, tossing back her hair, and nodded with a kind of mocking affection towards someone—a man, quite certainly—who remained invisible in the L's other leg. Comprehending that, despite his cry, he had never really believed it, Laurence backed away.

Getting out of the car he hadn't noticed the child sitting on the low wall. She seemed immune to and oblivious of the evening's damp discomfort; dressed, with a ghostly incongruity, as he had seen her previously, in something skimpy and transparent, she might have been sitting there for ever. Her finger in her mouth, she looked at Laurence as though she had never seen him before, nor *heard* him; or as though one or the other of them had no actual corporeal being but existed only in some state of timeless feasibility. Laurence made to address her— but what would be the use.?

The rain resumed as soon as he had re-entered the car. He drove in a kind of slow dark tunnel, illuminated only by the glaring red eyes of the cars which passed him. The device was to keep going regardless of where one would find oneself on emerging.

Laurence stood leaning against the car, allowing the rain to lash his face and soak through his clothes to his skin. This rain, his wetness had, he remembered, also been presaged. If his lungs filled with water, or pneumonia raised a sudden raging fever, it would be one way of subverting fate—the fate which had still a final grotesque trick to play.

With puzzled face, the clerk lowered the receiver at last, murmuring, 'How very odd! How very odd, indeed!'

Laurence stood dripping before his remotely reflective gaze. No one spoke. The clerk beckoned with a broken wrist, and as they waited for the moon-faced porter to slouch up, appeared to notice for the first time Laurence's bedraggled condition, his eyes narrowing and his pouting lips contracting in an expression of cautious distrust.

The clerk and the porter conferred. 'Well,' said the clerk, eyeing reproachfully a small puddle deposited by Laurence on the polished desk, 'it seems he most certainly hasn't gone out.'

'Perhaps he's just having a good long . . .' the porter began, but the clerk shushed him with one of his looks.

'I know he was expecting you,' the clerk admonished. And as Laurence slowly and dully started to come to awareness he saw that the two faces of his interlocutors had taken on a look of open accusation. 'But he appears to have vanished completely. It's just as if . . .' – his voice rose in epicene flutiness – 'he'd been *spirited* away.'

Crossing the hallway, Laurence gave a short laugh at the inclusion of even his trivial neighbour. It was too much like one of those old interminable jokes based on incongruous accumulation. The laugh emerged as a choking groan.

As the lift haltingly ascended, his fear, his tension and his frenzy, waking from their unfeeling hibernation, rose with it. He exploded out like a cork from an effervescent bottle, and ran lop-sided along the corridor, scrambling his key-ring from his pocket.

He turned the lock and pushed open the door but, the water dripping off him, stood for a moment numbed and stupid, an indefinable reluctance preventing him from taking the next and most relaxing step.

There wasn't a sound from within the flat; behind him the lift squeaked descending again; there was the hum of the central-heating and a rattle from the plumbing. Distantly someone slammed a door, sending a tinny vibration under the soles of his feet, and releasing his frozen muscles. A dark shadow with the casual elegance of a dancer flitted past the end of the corridor as Laurence crossed the threshold.

22

'Sarah?' Laurence called tentatively. 'Sarah?' he called again, walking through, 'are you there?'

Too quickly, too predictably for it to arouse either alarm or hope, the bedroom-door opened on his approach. Smiling, Ossie stepped forth; he made to offer his hand but let his arm fall as though deciding that such a gesture between old friends would seem extravagant.

'Sarah—where's Sarah?' Laurence said in a low voice but perfectly distinctly; then, less clearly: 'What are you doing here?'

Ossie passed by him, close enough for Laurence to identify the lavender-lemon smell of his aftershave. As Laurence followed, a rustling tearing noise mounting to a roar—just as though he'd been caught up in a gale—filled his head and brought about a recurrence of his dizziness. When all was once more quiet and the floor and walls and curtains had stilled after their wind-blown agitation, Laurence whispered again: 'Sarah?'

'What's that, Larry?' His visitor turned away from his casual inspection of a, resurrected, wedding-photograph. 'I didn't quite catch. There's no one here but me, Larry,' he went on, nevertheless, 'and barring yourself of course, barring your own personal presence.'

No, said Laurence to himself, oh no.

'Just the two of us, face to face, like . . .' He broke off, a look of alarm clouding his expression. 'Hey!' he cried. 'What you been doing, Larry? You're soaked right to the skin, you ought to get them wet clothes off of you.' Advancing, he punched Laurence painfully in the chest as he himself bent in a great roar of laughter. 'Like the very first time, eh Larry, you remember,' he continued through his mirthful coughs. 'Like two bleeding drowned rats, wasn't we, you remember. The wheel's, like, turned full circle now.'

Making an enormous effort, 'What have you done?' Laurence started to say, but even as he shaped the first word, a plane— the runways presumably having been cleared—passed low overhead, obliterating everything.

'Well,' said Ossie, when the scream and the vibrations had ceased, and as though answering a spoken question: 'Well, I couldn't go hanging on for ever, could I, looking after you for ever. I mean, just waiting till you called the day and hour, until you said the name.' He winked in his old familiar and warm-hearted way. 'I had to, like, exercise my own discretion.'

Such a tremendous effort it had been, so sapping and self-mortifying to have once formulated the question, Laurence for the moment lacked the capability of speech.

'Been neglecting my own concerns for you, I have,' without reproach, Ossie continued. 'Not that I'm complaining, mind. By the way, there's something you can do for me—you still got that old suit of mine, I gave you that first night?' His eyes flickered downwards in the direction of his lapels. 'This one seems to have acquired some rather nasty sort of stains. Might be best, it might be pol-i-tic, to do a swap and dump it quick, you comprehend.'

Following instinctively where Ossie had indicated, Laurence could faintly observe a cluster of small dark spots on the bright blue cloth; to the naked eye they were unidentifiable, arousing no special repugnance.

'Course I'd take this one away with me. I wouldn't want to leave behind anything that might incriminate.' He walked forward with confidence. 'Keep it in the wardrobe, don't you?'

Laurence came to life only after the other had passed him. Ossie allowed himself to be held, bending to the arm around his chest. 'There's nothing in there, Larry,' he pacified, indicating with a nod of his head the open bedroom door. 'Nothing un-toward, I promise you. I wouldn't be so maladroit.' With a twisting movement he released himself, simultaneously pro-pelling Laurence forward. 'Go on, see for yourself.'

A curious effect: he saw the room just as a blind man, reliant on memory alone, might see it, memory so well-established he has no need of sight: the beds, wardrobes, dressing-table, the dressing-table stool ... 'See, Larry,' said a laughing voice behind him, 'no ghosts, is there?'

Like a blind man, bumping against unseen obstacles Laurence backed out. 'Nor nothing,' the cheerful voice pursued him, 'what could agitate a squeamish stomach.'

'What have you done?' said Laurence, as to himself.

'What have I done?' Ossie had followed him from the bedroom. 'You ask me what I done, Larry.' He thrust himself forward so that they were pressed together, twin-headed. 'What I done you don't know, see, it's best like that. It's pol-i-tic. Best not to spell it out.' He reproduced his familiar wink. 'Remember what I said about that geezer kicking and squawking inside of you? I done what he'd have done, Larry, what you wanted me to, what you'd have done yourself you had the guts.'

'What ... I ...' Laurence hoarsely croaked.

'Leave it there then, shall we.' He made as if to return to the bedroom but, his better nature taking over, halted tolerantly to make it clear. 'Do what you want, you said, Larry. Do what the hell you like, that's what you said to me — remember? Well, I don't need telling twice, Larry, not your old friend Ossie.' He laughed lightly, bashfully. 'I read a bit of history once. Some king, like you, said that or words to that effect — talking about some turbulent priest, as I recall. I mean to say, Larry, I know you better than you know yourself.'

'Tell me!' As a psychotic's cry of anguish may indicate a return to rationality, so Laurence's despairing howl. 'Tell me! Tell me! Tell me — who?'

'Shush! Shush, Larry.' Ossie sighed earnestly, his chest visibly expanding. 'Remember what I promised you all that time ago? I promised you then, I said: a life for a life.' For the first time there was something in his manner that was not entirely convincing: he was beginning to prevaricate, or trying to assume the harmlessness of an hallucination. 'A life for a life.' He went glibly on: 'But I didn't ought to mention no names, Larry, for then, see, you can, like, act innocent, they start asking questions. After all, that's what you are, Larry, ain't that so—innocent! It was just that geezer what's inside of you. So better leave it, Larry,' he concluded, 'leave it where it is.'

Far from his subterfuge working as he intended, he seemed to be taking on a new definition: the figure assumed to be a nightmare apparition seen on one's slow awakening to be looming over the bed in solid menace. Laurence nodded thoughtfully. 'A life for a life,' he belatedly repeated.

'In a manner of speaking, to coin a . . . Hey—watch it, Larry!'

The events of the day, of his life, dancing a kaleidoscopic jig behind his eyes, Laurence grabbed him again, more forcefully. 'What do you mean? What have you done?' His voice rose shrilly: 'What have you done? All of my . . .'

'All!' Ossie dragged himself free, so that Laurence, caught off balance, fell to his knees. 'All, Larry—that's a very funny way to talk. Very funny I don't think. What you take me for— a bleeding butcher!'

Laurence's damp clothes stuck to the surface of the wall as he levered himself up against it, not trusting his unsupported legs. The faces in the kaleidoscope shimmered and sparkled in patternless confusion.

'That's silly, Larry,' Ossie said mildly, as though his anger may have been assumed. He peered into his face. 'I know what you're thinking, but that's silly. It's just in your own mind, Larry, like your own secret thoughts.' He seemed to find in Laurence's inward-staring eyes evidence that he had failed to reassure. 'Oh, come on Larry,' he gently chided. 'They're just coincidence, the other cases you're considering. Know what that is, don't you—conicidence? It's just another way of saying, it's only your imagination.'

Coincidence . . . imagination—Laurence repeated to himself softly, as though he were alone. I must not make another mistake, he thought as he crossed the room. Make . . . mistake—he said aloud, turning with the statuette of the goddess in his hand. Congratulations—he heard another voice entirely—to you both. He was aware that he was walking strangely, lifting his knees high as if picking his way through an extremely squelchy marsh.

'So all right, Larry?' Ossie appeared oblivious to anything untoward. 'Let's leave it that way, shall we. We're wasting too long talking, we ought to . . . Here, that's nice,' he interrupted himself, taking the statuette from Laurence's unresisting grasp. 'And I very much appreciate the gesture, Larry, but no, no thanks, I really couldn't accept. 'sides I don't want no souvenir now, do I. Don't want no one knowing I've been here, after they've found . . . Like that way's . . .'—he continued without pause, tapping his nose with a conspiratorial forefinger—'more salubrious, I'm certain you'll agree.' Courteously he passed the goddess back to Laurence. 'But the thought I very much appreciate, you know that, Larry, don't you.'

Something in Laurence's gravity and steadfast doggy look, the complement to his own vivacity, seemed to touch him more deeply still. He laid his hand on Laurence's shoulder. 'Larry boy,' he cried with a throb, 'we've been like two bruvvers you and me, sharing our deepest, darkest secrets, but now we've got to part for ever, just like we'd never known each other . . .' He wiped the back of his hand across his eyes.

Laurence still said nothing. The pieces of the kaleidoscope had settled, leaving no colour, no pattern, no movement—only a black nothingness, which cast, however, an adumbration of serenity.

'But you, Larry, you're free at last. It's what you wanted most, you know. Now—you'll excuse me hurrying you—I'll just change the suit . . .' He made a brisk move forward. 'If you'd kindly step aside, Larry, so I can . . .'

The impact to his arm descending was unexpectedly resilient so that the statuette flew from his hand and bounced across the carpet, even as a long, and reminiscent, stripe of molten red emerged in the scanty scalp. The upturned eyes regarded Laurence with morose surprise; three or four times in a moment of suspension the mouth opened and closed silently, seeming to shape the words: your friend ... your friend ... yourself ...

As Laurence took him by the throat another screaming plane flew over. In the rending windstorm of its onslaught they bucked and plunged, gripped together; and finally fell together. Laurence maintained his hold with remarkable ease, regardless of the nails clawing at his hooked hands.

His body pressed the other's down as in the conjunction of love, and he could distinctly smell the lavender-lemon sweetness in the process of turning sour. The dentures popped out of the gaping jaws to fall against the goddess lying by their side. Laurence was entirely deafened by the howling jet above and the blood beating drum-like in his head.

Only when at last he became slowly aware of the long silence, and the long stillness in his hands did Laurence relax his hold. The red-gashed head, its lashless eyes extraordinary, lolled in his bleeding fingers, and out of the black mouth escaped a bubbling 'Aarragh'—like a gurgled cry for help from the dark river.